Colonel Brandon

...in his own words

—————

SHANNON WINSLOW

~~*~~

Colonel Brandon... was silent and grave. His appearance however was not unpleasing, in spite of his being in the opinion of Marianne and Margaret an absolute old bachelor, for he was on the wrong side of five and thirty; but though his face was not handsome, his countenance was sensible, and his address was particularly gentlemanlike.
~Sense and Sensibility~

~~*~~

In the evening, as Marianne was discovered to be musical, she was invited to play... Colonel Brandon alone, of all the party, heard her without being in raptures. He paid her only the compliment of attention; and she felt a respect for him on the occasion, which the others had reasonably forfeited by their shameless want of taste. His pleasure in music, though it amounted not to that ecstatic delight which alone could sympathize with her own, was estimable...
~Sense and Sensibility~

~~*~~

Poor Colonel Brandon has the misfortune to share the same haunted expression of having witnessed firsthand too much of the cruelty of which men are capable.
~The Persuasion of Miss Jane Austen~

~~*~~

Author's Preface

This work should be considered a supplement to *Sense and Sensibility*, not a variation from it, because none of the essential facts presented in Jane Austen's original story have been changed. I've only added, filling in some rather large blanks on Colonel Brandon's side – before, during, and after the events of Austen's novel.

I want to explain a little about the use of personal names in this book before you start reading.

We are used to thinking of the well-known and well-loved characters of *Sense and Sensibility* in informal terms, because that's how Jane Austen writes about them. In her narrative, she doesn't treat us like strangers who must continually hear Elinor called "Miss Dashwood" and Edward "Mr. Ferrars." She treats us as close friends of these people, entitled to think of them by their Christian names.

Colonel Brandon and I do much the same in this book.

Although in dialogue he addresses each person very properly – with whatever level of formality the situation requires – in his thoughts as well as in his storytelling, he often employs their first names instead. This is justified because he knows these people so well, if not from the beginning, then by the point in time when he is telling his retrospective story.

Someone known from childhood might still be addressed by their first name into adulthood (e.g., Eliza Brandon, John Middleton). The same is true of close family members (e.g., Marianne, now Colonel Brandon's wife; Elinor, now his "sister"). In other words, he has earned the right to use their Christian names, and he treats us as if we have too. I hope you will agree that to have done otherwise would have been extremely cumbersome and made the story unnecessarily stilted.

One more thing. You will notice that I have taken the liberty of adopting a couple of names from a movie source. Jane Austen never gave Colonel Brandon a first name. She didn't need one for her story, but I did for mine. And since we have grown accustomed (from the 1995 film adaptation) to hearing that his name is "Christopher," I thought anything else would sound wrong to the reader's ear. From the same source, I have chosen to sometimes refer to Miss Williams (the younger Eliza) as "Beth" – another derivative of the name Elizabeth – instead of "Eliza," in order to spare the reader the need to constantly sort out which Eliza is meant. If not for this expedient, confusion over these two ladies with the same name would have been more of an issue in this book than in the original.

Thank you for your understanding, and happy reading!

Shannon Winslow

Prologue

I t is happening again, and I suddenly feel very old. Although I survived it once before – just – I have the gravest doubts that I can do so again. Some days, I do not even wish to.

The current circumstances are quite different, it is true. But the pain is the same – the sudden wrenching in my gut each time I think of it, which I do nearly every minute of every day; the repeated jolt of panic in my brain, which tells me that I must do something to stop it; the hollow ache in my heart and the certain knowledge of my own pathetic powerlessness. It is all too familiar, for once again the hand of the woman I love more than life itself is being given irrevocably to another, and there is absolutely nothing I can do about it.

It is no doubt weak and self-indulgent, as I have repeatedly told myself, but my mind *will* persist in entertaining questions of morbid curiosity. I cannot seem to help asking if, overall, it is better or worse this time. Is my disappointment more or less profound, the circumstances more or less regrettable? Will the resulting pain last as long as before and leave scars as deep?

Perhaps it is only the proximity, but the current event appears worse – at least for myself personally – for I shall not only have the pain that she is lost to me forever, but the additional mortification of knowing she does not care for me. In truth, she thinks nothing of me at all. So, God willing, I shall be the only one to suffer, which was not the case before.

Poor Eliza.

I would not wish her fate on Marianne Dashwood, not for the world. In fact, that must be my chief consolation: knowing that

Marianne is happy, even if it must be in the arms of another man. I would willingly sacrifice my own happiness and more if it would secure a lasting one for her. And yet who can say that her present bliss will endure, dependent as it is upon a man of whom I have every reason to think ill? And so my mind can by no means be easy.

I have been to her sister in Berkeley Street to have my worst fears confirmed, and now I know I should put Marianne from my mind and retire to Delaford to lick my wounds. And so I have made ready to do more than once. Still, as long as she is in London, I feel compelled to stand by – for what purpose, I cannot even conceive – at least until she is well and truly married. After that, it will be nobody's right except her husband's to be concerned for her welfare.

Until then, however, I will wait. Perhaps there may yet be some small service I can render. If I am needed, I swear I will not fail her. Whatever the cost, I must do better by Marianne than I did by Eliza… or by Rashmi.

Meanwhile, I have nothing to do but think of the past. Although there have been enough joys and compensations over the years, the regrets and failures continue to haunt me. I am in a dangerous state of mind.

~1~

I shall never forget the day I met Marianne Dashwood.

It was at Barton Park, the seat of my old friend Sir John Middleton. By his invitation, I had come to stay, whereupon my first arriving, I was met with the immediate intelligence that he had succeeded in procuring a fine family for Barton Cottage.

"Some cousins of mine," he continued with great animation after I was barely inside the door. "A widow and her three grown daughters. Well, two are grown and the other nearly so. You have never met with a more delightful lady in the whole course of your life than Mrs. Dashwood, I would wager! See if it is not so. And her daughters are just as pretty as can be. I defy anybody to say otherwise!"

"I will not dare to dispute the fact, especially before I have seen them for myself," I said.

"That will not long be an impediment! You will meet them tomorrow, for they are invited to dine here. And your coming to us just now, Brandon, could not be better timed, for you know it is my solemn duty – they being new to the neighborhood and all – to provide them some amusing entertainment."

I had to laugh aloud at the absurdity of this statement. "I am glad to do what I can, of course, John," I said, "but I am amazed that you should think of me and 'amusing entertainment' in the same breath."

"Well… perhaps 'amusing' is the wrong word, but you should not think of yourself so meanly, old friend. A sensible man, like you, with a well-informed mind will always be considered good company. Besides, it shall not all be on your shoulders, you know.

I will ride about the countryside in the morning with invitations, and no doubt the house shall be full in the end."

Since a large, noisy gathering was never my preference, I was not sorry that Sir John's efforts on this score met with frustration. It seems that, owing to the full moon expected, everybody else had prior engagements. So our party that night would consist only of the Middletons, the Dashwoods, myself, and Mrs. Jennings – Lady Middleton's mother, who was also staying at Barton Park. Such an evening I could well imagine and abide.

I knew Lady Middleton's table would be elegant as always. Mrs. Jennings would be jolly and full of commonplace raillery. Sir John would join wholeheartedly in her jokes and laughter, while his wife sat passively by. Very likely *she* would treat us to at least a brief visit by her boisterous children, which while it lasted, would remove all power to think of anything else. Although I liked children in general, the Middleton offspring were too numerous and too unruly – especially when they came tumbling into the room all together – for me to take much pleasure in them.

But what of these new neighbors? As yet, I knew so little of them, and *that* only by Sir John's unreliable report. He was a dear friend – our bonds founded not only on history and similarity of station, but through the fiery forge of shared military service – and yet I had learnt not to allow his opinions to form my own unquestioned, especially when it came to people. Although I sometimes envied Sir John his open, good-humored approach to life, when coupled with his insatiable appetite for company, it had often led him astray.

Delightful and *pretty as can be*, he had said.

That would be agreeable, of course, but *I* only hoped they would be pleasant, sensible, well-mannered women with no propensity for silliness and flirtation. There, my age had become my best protection; no doubt it would be the same in this case. At five and thirty, I must have been too old to be of any interest to the girls and too young for the mother. That was as it should be, for I was comfortably resigned to my bachelor status, having long since relinquished any idea of wanting a wife of my own and content for my nephew to be my heir.

Then I walked into the room that night, took one look at Marianne Dashwood, and everything changed. A part of me that I had

given up as dead, flared to new life. Miss Marianne was very fair...
and very young. She was exactly of an age and of a remarkable
likeness to my Eliza before I lost her. For a long moment, I was
struck dumb and stone still; I could do no more than stare. Then I
gave myself an inward shake and dragged my eyes away before I
could be thought too boorish. Still, I am afraid I was quite stupid
when introduced to the ladies, for I could not quickly shake off the
startling impression that some measure of the sweet friend of my
youth had been miraculously resurrected before my eyes.

~~*~~

Just as Eliza had been, Marianne Dashwood was excessively
charming to look at, with her pretty features, dark and sparkling
eyes, glossy light brown hair, and a smooth, glowing complexion.
To all this was added the appeal of a striking figure and a sweet
smile.

That immediate impression – my finding in the person of this
new acquaintance an uncanny reflection of one long lost to me –
persisted throughout the entire evening, reinforced by more and
various aspects of Marianne's mind and manners as they revealed
themselves. It was a bittersweet discovery for me, a mingling of
pain and pleasure. Here were Eliza's warmth of heart, her passion,
and her eagerness of feeling, reincarnated. I saw them all reborn in
Marianne – in her obvious affection for her mother, her professions
of rapture over music and poetry, and her zealous stand for Cowper
over Pope, part of which I overheard.

"...How can you say such a thing, Elinor? There can be no
comparison at all between the two! Pope is of the old school, and
he quite tries my patience with his sharp tongue. No, it will not do!
I will not allow him a share of *my* heart..."

At dinner, I had no opportunity of speaking directly to Miss
Marianne, who sat on the far side of her elder sister. This was just
as well, since I was still too overcome by the shock of meeting her
for any hope of fluency in her nearer presence. Instead, I did what I
could by way of conversation with those closest to me: Lady
Middleton, Mrs. Jennings, and Miss Elinor Dashwood. To these
three, I deemed my time and attention particularly due.

My obligation to Lady Middleton was quickly discharged by praising her table and expressing my wish that all her children were well.

"Oh, yes, Colonel," she responded mildly, "except Tommy, who has a little cold. On his account, I have ordered them all kept in the nursery tonight. I hope you will not be too much disappointed at not seeing them. I know how you dote upon them."

"It will be a loss to us all, certainly," I said, "but I think you are wise. One can never be too careful where the health of children is involved."

Mrs. Jennings presently joined her daughter in a discussion of this concern, followed by their general canvassing together of other domestic matters, large and small, which carried them right through the fish and game courses.

Consequently, I was left to Miss Dashwood's agreeable company. Turning to her, I said, "I hope you are finding Devonshire to your liking, Miss Dashwood. You have come a long way to be here, I believe."

"Yes, Colonel Brandon, from our former home in Sussex, but I think we shall learn to love Devonshire just as well. There is beauty of a different kind here, which I long to capture on paper."

"You draw, then? How delightful. And I agree; you will find no shortage of inspiration for your pictures in this neighborhood."

"In addition to that, we must love Devonshire for the warm welcome we have received. Sir John, and Lady Middleton too, of course – they have been so generous and obliging. Have you long been acquainted with them, Colonel?"

"With Lady Middleton only since their marriage. But I have known Sir John from boyhood, since our families were on friendly terms. And then we served together in the East Indies. You could rightfully call him 'Colonel' as well, Miss Dashwood, although he prefers his civilian title."

"Really? That is unexpected. Although we are not yet thoroughly acquainted, I never would have pictured Sir John as a soldier. I can hardly tell you why, however. I suppose he does not seem serious enough somehow."

I smiled weakly. "You are perceptive, Miss Dashwood. I can tell you that he made the most of it, but he was not really best suited to a military life," I said, with an unavoidable recollection of the past. "It did not suit either of us in the end."

"Oh? I am sorry to hear it. I have always considered the army a worthy profession."

"Yes... Yes, it is, of course – a worthy profession and an unquestionably necessary one. I can only testify to my own experience, which was not particularly gratifying." Realizing I had strayed too far into the darkness, I tried to end the topic on a lighter note. "Common wisdom, however, says we learn valuable lessons from difficult times, so I trust it was all of some use."

"One day, I should like to hear more, Colonel, about what your military years taught you."

They taught me that I should never have gone to India in the first place. That is what I was thinking but did not say – that, along with another melancholy recollection about Eliza. How had I been brought round to her again? First through the sight of Marianne herself and now by this conversation with her sister. I could not get away from Eliza that night, it seemed.

The brief silence that followed was soon filled by Mrs. Jennings. "What have you been telling Miss Dashwood, my dear Colonel Brandon? She is quite entranced, if I am any judge, hanging on your ever word, I daresay. Well, this is very promising indeed! I always say that one need do no more than bring young people together and let nature take its course. Although sometimes even nature needs a *little* help." She winked and laughed lustily. "That is where I am happy to step in and do my part!"

This was the first, but not the last, of the evening's unwelcome jibes from Mrs. Jennings. Like Sir John, she delighted in fresh company, especially young, unmarried people she could make the targets of her good-natured but often rather vulgar teasing. I was accustomed to it, however I felt much discomfort on behalf of the two eldest Miss Dashwoods, who were repeatedly subjected to her witticisms on the subject of romance. *Could not their mother find them husbands? Or perhaps they had left all their lovers behind them in Sussex. In either case, something must be done about it,* and so forth.

It was a relief, therefore, when we left the table for the drawing room, where a more welcome entertainment awaited, something we could *all* enjoy. Happily, Miss Marianne was discovered to be musical, and she willingly went to the instrument to play and sing for us, which she did for more than half an hour. Most of what she played was familiar to me, and yet her interpretation, her style of performing, was quite fresh.

It was all very well done, and yet some of the others would not properly attend. Sir John was loud in his admiration at the end of every song, and just as loud in his conversation while every song lasted. Lady Middleton frequently called him to order, scolding him for his inattention to the music. Then she showed herself no better by asking for a particular song which Marianne had already played.

For me, however, there could be nothing more worthwhile listening to than Miss Marianne's performance. I soon moved to a place where I could both see and hear her without distraction.

When she had finished, received her final applause, and risen from the instrument, I felt I really must act. I would speak to her at last, before she could return to her seat between her sisters. So I also stood and moved to intercept her. Meeting in the middle of the room, I blocked her way enough to detain her. "Miss Marianne," I began. She looked up at me with those dark, luminous eyes, and I nearly forgot what I had meant to say.

"Yes, Colonel?" she prompted.

"Miss Marianne, I merely wished to express my appreciation, to tell you that it is a long while since I heard anything I enjoyed half as much. You play and sing very well."

"Thank you," she said with an air of mild pleasure and surprise. "Do you appreciate music, then?"

Sir John, who was sitting near enough to hear our conversation, answered for me, turning to talk loudly over his shoulder. "Colonel Brandon has a very good ear, Miss Marianne. I know not one song from another, but *his* approbation means something and is well worth having."

I acknowledged his compliment with a slight bow and then resumed with Marianne. "I am a great appreciator of music, yes. I particularly enjoyed the Mozart *andante...*"

"And he plays the pianoforte himself, you know," Sir John added as an afterthought before his interest was reclaimed by Mrs. Dashwood.

"Do you?" asked Marianne. "You are a fellow musician, then. So much the better. The instrument is now free, sir." She motioned in that direction.

I smiled. "Another time, perhaps. My skill cannot compare to yours. I hope, though, that I shall have the pleasure of hearing you play my Broadwood Grand one day."

"A Broadwood Grand! I would like that, Colonel. Now, if you will excuse me..." She returned my smile and then walked away.

That was all the first conversation between us entailed. No looks of instant recognition or words with meaningful overtones, at least not on her side. And I took care not to embarrass myself by looking or saying all I felt on the occasion. It was enough, however, to guarantee that I would never forget the encounter.

I thought about Marianne that night before bed, her own charms but also all the ways she resembled my long-lost friend, cousin, and sweetheart Eliza. Marianne's hair was just the same color, I was sure, the shape of her face so similar. And when I catalogued all those other little traits and mannerisms the two had in common, the likeness was truly astonishing.

Or did I deceive myself? Was it possible that these impressions of a strong resemblance were merely a product of my own fancy or wishful thinking, working on my old, tender, cherished recollections? After all, I had no portrait of Eliza to consult – not anymore – and nearly twenty years had elapsed since our days together at Delaford. How could I be sure of anything after so long?

The more I reviewed the evidence, the more I wrestled with the question. The more I wrestled with the question, the less certain I became. Like rubbing a pencil drawing, the longer I worked over it, the more hopelessly blurred the lines between the two ladies became, so that by the time I gave up the exercise altogether, I could no longer distinguish between their images. They had merged. No doubt that is why I fell asleep thinking of Marianne, but I dreamt of Eliza.

What can I say about Eliza that would do her justice? She was the sun, moon, and stars to me.

In every other way, my childhood was quite unremarkable. My father ruled our household unchallenged, and his seeming need to prove that point only increased when he came into his property. Delaford and its occupants became his kingdom to do with as he saw fit. This I accepted as a matter of course; I was a mere boy and knew nothing different.

My mother, from what I was old enough to apprehend, diligently worked to avoid drawing my father's ire. Her efficiency, competency, and her unfailing conciliatory manner towards him left little room for criticism. By the same practiced arts, I believe she did her best to shield her children as well. Now, however, I can understand what a drain the continual effort of maintaining peace in our home must have been on her youth and vitality, and I cannot help wondering if the strain became too much for her, if it in fact hastened her to an early grave. Thus, when I was twelve years of age, her ultimate escape from my father was made.

My sisters, Evelyn and Clarissa, both several years my senior, likewise made their flights from Delaford shortly thereafter. In their cases, it was through the means of eligible marriages. They did well, choosing to plant their affections where my father could not reasonably object.

My elder brother could not avoid my father's constant attention, however. As the heir, much was made of Maximus, whose very name declared his place in my father's interest. Max was of supreme importance, perpetually being trained to step into my father's shoes when the time came. So his every word and deed were scrutinized, judged, and corrected. It was my father's intention, I believe, to eventually conform him into an exact copy of himself, something he very nearly achieved.

I did not envy my brother or the officious attention he received from my father, considering what that entailed. And I was as yet too innocent of the ways of the world to resent the fact that he and not I would inherit everything. At the time, I was simply glad to be the youngest, and therefore of too little importance for my father to take any notice. While my mother lived, and with Eliza as my constant companion and playfellow, I was content. No, more than content. Those years were truly the happiest of my life.

I cannot imagine what my childhood would have been like without Eliza. My mother was dear to me as well, of course, but her time was much in demand elsewhere. A series of nursery maids and private tutors hovered nearby, to none of whom I ever developed a tender attachment. Too many years separated my siblings from myself for any true camaraderie between us. But Eliza and I were of an age, of compatible temperaments, and in a common state of need. She had nobody else and neither did I. In many ways, we lived in a world of our own, especially in the early years, taking all of our meals and lessons together sitting opposite each other in the school room, where a kick under the table or a conspiratorial look between us served as secret communication.

I recall one occasion – we must have been ten or eleven at the time – when Mr. Loshbough was our intrepid tutor. He strolled about the schoolroom while trying to drum the order of kings and queens into our heads in a dry monotone. "…Then we come to the Norman kings: William the Conqueror, William II, who was followed by his brother Henry I, and then King Stephen…"

But I could not attend.

"…Henry II, Richard the Lionheart, and bad King John…"

A tap on my shin had caused me to look up and see Eliza grinning at me. When our instructor, who happened to be behind her back at that moment, mentioned the Lionheart, she silently opened her mouth wide and made an exaggerated face as if roaring like a lion, sending me into helpless peals of laughter. I *was* an adolescent boy, after all. Eliza, who pled innocence – and looked the part – was entirely spared. But I was required to write the long list of British monarchs ten times over as a punishment for my outburst. It was worth every bit of it to share that joke with Eliza, though. In my mind, I can still see the comical face she made that day.

Eliza had come to us in her infancy, the orphaned offspring of a distant Brandon cousin, now become my father's ward. So we were raised together like brother and sister. And yet I always knew she was *not* my sister in reality. I believe I would have known it even without being informed of the fact. From my earliest recollections, my young heart told me that Eliza was something more, something special, something unique – not a sister but a friend of the bosom, my sweet partner and confidante, the perfectly designed counterpart to my own soul.

In short, I cannot remember a time when I did not love her. Who could have helped it in my place – so tender and affectionate as she was, so giving and vulnerable?

I was drawn to Eliza, not because she was exactly like myself, but because she was different, irresistibly so. Whereas I was naturally shy and reserved, she was open, artless, eager, and warm. While I lived confined by what my mind told me was true and logical, Eliza knew no such bounds. She was light and air – a free spirit – and she frequently took me along on her flights of fancy. In exchange, I balanced and steadied her, I believe, keeping her feet planted on solid ground... but only when absolutely necessary.

As long as we stayed clear of my father – something we became very skilled at doing – Delaford was our own private playground, indoors but especially out. The great but forbidden garden wall would have been an irresistible temptation to nearly any child of a certain age. My brother walked it first, of course, and then he dared me to do likewise. I was too young at the time and shortly tumbled off – fortunately, into the brambles on one side and not the rocky drop-off on the other. I came away bruised and scratched to pieces but otherwise unharmed. A few years later, though, both Eliza and I had mastered the feat.

There were lovely fruit trees to climb and to stuff ourselves from in season; stew-ponds and a lazy canal to float ourselves and our toy boats upon; and a place in the old yew arbor – we called it our fort – where we could spy on horsemen and carriages passing on the nearby turnpike road, imagining them enemy troops. Between the two of us, Eliza and I never lacked for ideas of games to occupy our leisure hours.

I cannot say what age we were when we first agreed we would marry. It seemed like a foregone conclusion from the start, something kept secreted between ourselves but never questioned. As we matured in years, our feelings did as well. My love for Eliza – now that of a young man for a young woman – knew no bounds, and she gave every proof of her equally fervent attachment to me. It would be only a matter of time; we would marry as soon as we were old enough to do so.

Then one sunny day when she was sixteen and I had recently had my seventeenth birthday, I found her weeping in the garden.

"What is it, Eliza?" I asked, sitting down beside her on the sparse grass beneath the mulberry tree.

At first she could say nothing; she only shook her head and cried all the more.

"Indeed, you must tell me, friend, or you will make me sick with worry. Say what the matter is so I may help you."

Although professing to be worried, at first I was not. I had known Eliza, who was prone to bouts of excess sensibility, to occasionally suffer a fit of weeping over nothing more than seeing some small rodent taken to its demise by a hawk, or having an anticipated pleasure outing ruined by foul weather.

"Come now," I continued in a teasing manor. "Tell me the truth; you are making all this fuss about nothing at all, only to get me to put my arm about your shoulders. Is not that so? There, I have done as you wished, so smile at your success, why don't you?"

Instead, she turned to cry into my shoulder, blubbering, "Oh, Christopher, it is the worst thing imaginable!"

"No, I cannot believe it is so," I said, petting her hair, but less confident now. "Dry your eyes, and start at the beginning. Together we will see what can be done about it, whatever it is."

A few minutes more and she was recovered enough to speak. "My uncle…" she began in faltering words. "Your father, that is… He has said that I must – Oh! How shall I tell you?"

I was genuinely troubled now. If my father was concerned in the business, it could not be good. "Steady, now. You know you can tell me anything, my dear Eliza."

"He has told me that I must marry Max as soon as I am seventeen!" And she dissolved into wretched tears again.

I felt as if I had been kicked in the chest by a mule. I could not speak; I could barely breathe.

"I explained to him," Eliza continued a minute later, "that I could not, that I was promised to marry you instead. But it made no difference to him, though I reasoned and cried and pleaded for mercy. He is determined that I will marry your brother and not you! He says it is my duty and what my father intended all along. Now you see why I am so distressed."

I did indeed.

~~*~~

Leaving Eliza with the audacious promise that I would soon set matters right, I sought out my father at once to confront him. For the moment, my rage overpowered the fear that would otherwise have held me back from so bold a move. I found him in the billiard room at last. He briefly looked up from his play upon my entrance.

"Ah, there you are," he said with bored sarcasm before I could even open my mouth. "I thought I should be hearing from you before long." With a sharp crack, he took his shot, missed, and swore under his breath. "I suppose you have come to plead Eliza's case, but it will do no good, I assure you. My mind is made up to this course, as it has been for years. The indignant protests of a young whelp like yourself will make no difference."

I drew myself up to my full height and, standing ramrod straight in the doorway, I barked out my words with as much command as I could muster. "Sir, you cannot be serious about forcing Eliza into marriage against her will. You have no right to do so."

"No right, you say? Oh, that *is* rich." He chuckled sardonically. "Have I not fed and sheltered the girl all these years? – a child who is not my own? Have I not at great expense educated her and seen her groomed to be a fine lady? I have not done all this, believe me, to now be told I have no rights! No, it is time my generosity was repaid in full. It was always intended that she and her fortune should prop up this old estate by marrying the heir. Now is the time, and there's an end to it." So saying, he turned his attention back to his game.

I had known nothing of this plan, nor, I was sure, had Eliza. I was not even aware that Eliza was supposed to be rich. Astonished by this information, I could only stare at my father in disbelief. At least now I comprehended his motivation, though it disgusted me.

"Why do you stand there gaping, boy," he asked presently, "as if you had never heard of such an arrangement before? Are you still such a child, Christopher? Well, it is high time you became a little better acquainted with the ways of the world. Eliza too."

An obvious question was before me, and I had to know the answer. Through clenched teeth, I forced myself to speak. "Does... Does Max know? Does he want to marry Eliza?"

"What is that to do with it? He will do as I say, just as she will."

"He does not love her, then?"

"No, I should imagine not, but that hardly signifies. He needs to marry a fortune, and here is a generous one easily within his reach. He will take it and be grateful for it."

"*It*? He is not marrying a fortune. Eliza is a young woman, Father, the dearest creature who ever drew breath! You speak of her – your blood relation, your own ward, whom you are bound by honor to protect! – as if she were nothing more than an object, a thing to be bartered, bought, and sold for pecuniary advantage."

He leveled a glare at me. "I am not displeased to see you have the pluck to take a stand for something; good to know that a son of mine possesses a backbone after all. But you have pushed me as far as I am willing to allow. Now drop the matter and go. Or will you join me in a game, like a gentleman?" He held out the other cue to me.

"No, sir, I will not," I spat out.

"Suit yourself."

I left him at once, and Eliza and I began to plot our elopement that very day.

~3~

I returned to the garden to find Eliza. She was waiting not far from where I had left her, sitting on the edge of the fountain, employed in making a daisy chain. She looked so beautiful there in the sunshine, her hair glistening – like something out of a painting. Her cherubic face turned up to me as I approached, her dark eyes brimming with hope as well as tears. I hated to spoil that poignant picture, and her faith in me, with the news that I had failed to achieve any amelioration to our odious situation.

Instead of speaking at once, I reached down to pull her to her feet.

"What has happened?" she asked tremulously. "Christopher, tell me what my uncle said to you."

I led her to the bench within the fragrant lilac grove for what I knew would be a long and very important conversation. There, I related to her the substance of my contentious exchange with my father. "…We shall not simply bow to his decision, however," I said in conclusion.

"Oh," she cried, "but what choice have we? My uncle is in control; everything gives way to him, and he will certainly force me to do as he pleases."

I put a reassuring arm about her shoulders, looked down into her elfin face, and said cryptically, "He cannot make you do anything if he cannot find you."

"What do you mean?"

"We shall elope," I said decisively.

"Elope!" she repeated in disbelief, pulling away to look me in the face. Then confusion turned to eagerness. I saw brightness dawn in her countenance as her mind examined the idea, which to one of her heightened sensibilities no doubt carried an air of romance.

"Yes, before your birthday," I continued. "It is the only way forward that I can see. We will marry in Scotland. Then perhaps, once the thing is done and cannot be undone, my father may relent and have the grace to accept it." I hoped, rather than believed, this to be probable.

"Yes, perhaps he will," Eliza agreed, leaning into my side again. "After all, if it is my money he cares for, it will still be in the family. We could use some of it to relieve Delaford of its encumbrances. I would be glad to do so. My uncle is correct that I owe him something, and I am ready to pay my debt when I come into my money." She paused, and I felt her tense. "I *will* still come into my money if we elope, will not I?" She looked up at me, apparently expecting me to have all the answers.

"I honestly do not know," I admitted. "I would not put it past my father to try to prevent it, but it does not seem right that he could succeed. Do you have the name of your lawyer?"

"Oh, let me think," she said, her brow wrinkling deeply. "I believe his name is Scabbard... or Scarborough, something like that. I heard my uncle mention him once or twice. He is in London; of that much I am certain."

"Of course. Then we will go there after finishing our business in Scotland – find the man, tell him what has happened, and determine your rights. He is *your* lawyer, after all, not my father's."

"But I have never met the man in my life!"

"That should make no difference. My father may be your legal guardian, but the money belongs to you, and it is your lawyer's responsibility to see that your rights are protected. The will probably stipulated that your inheritance be held in trust until you come of age or marry. I believe that is usual. Then the fortune comes to you... or rather your husband, if you have one. That is why my father is so determined to see you married to Max as soon as possible."

"Yes, I see. And if *you* are my husband instead, then *you* would be in control of my fortune, and we will have nothing to worry about!"

"I pray that will indeed be so." One thing more needed to be said on that subject, however. Holding her by the shoulders, I turned her to face me. Then, looking straight into her eyes, I went on. "My dearest Eliza, be entirely serious for a moment. I have told you my plan and what I think we may expect, but you must understand that I cannot know any of it for certain. What I mean is that we must be prepared for the possibility that things may go against us – as to the disposal of your fortune specifically. Now consider carefully. You have been raised in affluence and comfort. Could you bear to be poor, do you think, if it should come to that? Could you give up the wealth that is rightfully yours, only to marry me?"

"Of course I could!" she cried without hesitation. "You *know* that I could. I can bear anything so long as we are together."

I relaxed, returned her smile, and took her hands. "Very well. Then this is what we shall do. I have a little money of my own put by – enough for the journey, at least – and I am quite certain I can take out the phaeton and the bays without raising suspicion, since I am in the habit of doing so. Not an ideal equipage for such an extended journey, but perhaps we can trade it along the way for something more suitable. Most importantly, though, it is light and fast. With a head start and a little luck, no one will catch us. In just a few days, we will be across the border and married."

By this time, Eliza's eyes glowed with excitement. "When shall we go? Tomorrow? At midnight?" she asked eagerly.

I laughed. "No, not tomorrow, midnight or otherwise. We need more time to plan. Every detail is crucial to our success. We will have only one chance to get it right, and we dare not fail. Too much depends on it – the rest of our lives, really." That sobered us both. "Calm. For now we must remain calm," I counselled. "We can give my father and brother no reason to think there is anything in the wind. We must go in to dinner tonight as always."

"Oh, but how?" she cried, springing to her feet and throwing her arms out wildly. "I cannot pretend all is well when I have a sentence worse than death hanging over my head! And only a few weeks away too!"

"Come," I said. Rising and retrieving one of her hands, I drew her deeper into the shrubbery, where we could not be seen from the house. There we clasped each other in a desperate embrace, exchanging kisses and clinging tightly for several long minutes without speaking.

"Well, well," a voice interrupted, making us break apart in alarm. Max approached and continued. "What have we here? Why, I do believe it is my lovely bride-to-be. In my little brother's arms, no less. Tsk, tsk. This will never do."

"Max!" I said. "We were just…"

Feet wide apart, his hands went to his hips. "Oh, yes, I believe I can see for myself just what you were doing. But it must stop at once."

"You cannot be jealous, Max," I said. "You care nothing for Eliza yourself. Admit it."

"That may well be, but I will marry her all the same."

"No, surely not. You must see that it is madness! Join us in opposing this match and find somebody else to marry – a girl you could love and who would love you in return."

"Ah, well I might do just that…"

My hopes rose for an instant.

"…except for one thing. As the old pater has recently made known to me, I will be ruined and the estate almost certainly lost if I marry a girl who has not a great deal of money. And heiresses are rather thin on the ground at the moment, it seems. So Eliza, my dear, I fear we must both resign ourselves to our fate."

Max took her arm from me, tucking it firmly inside his own instead. As he escorted her away, Eliza turned pleading eyes over her shoulder at me.

Raw anger smoldered in my belly. To see him touching her, taking possession of her, as if she were already his wife… I held my brother in no particular esteem, but until that moment, I had harbored no ill will against him either. Now, so violent an antipathy was kindled in my heart, such a loathing as I had never experienced, exceeded only by what I felt for my father. The day before, I should not have considered myself capable of such violent feelings, and towards my own blood too!

Had my long-held but chiefly untested Christian principles deserted me so swiftly? What of *honor thy father* and so many other tenets? Or if I held to *love your enemies* and *turn the other cheek*, here was my chance to prove it. But no, I could not give Eliza up in order to demonstrate my selflessness; she was not mine to surrender. The biblical principle truly at stake in this situation was the directive to care for *the fatherless and widows in their affliction.*

Eliza was indeed fatherless, especially now that her appointed guardian had abdicated his sacred responsibility to defend her welfare, and she was certainly in dire affliction.

My higher calling, therefore, was to come to her aid. My love and service to my father and brother must take the form of preventing them from dishonoring themselves by doing the evil they intended. As for me, I could only pray that the anger burning inside my soul was of the righteous sort, that which our Lord himself experienced without sinning. But I doubted it.

~~*~~

On the surface, Eliza and I kept to life as usual at Delaford. We went about the routine of eating regular meals, attending to our lessons, and taking some outdoor exercise, always careful to appear appropriately melancholy and dejected before the family. Under the circumstances, an artificial show of cheerfulness would not be believed; it would in fact arouse unwanted suspicion. No, it was far better and more reasonable that my father and brother should see us both in a state of sad resignation.

The long evenings in the drawing room were the most difficult, for then we were constantly under my father's sharp eye with no opportunity for private conversation. I felt as if he were indeed watching us, and probably the servants were as well, although that may have been a product of my paranoia.

As for Max, he wore his own gloomy cloud about himself, from which he occasionally emerged to torment me or Eliza – or us both together – thereby making certain that others suffered more than himself.

And yet, all the while we wore our sad faces, Eliza and I were supported by a great undercurrent of nervous excitement over our secret plans. Indeed, Eliza often behaved to me as if her uncle had done us a tremendous favor by hastening an event that otherwise could not have been reasonably looked for until at least a few years hence. I was by no means unhappy at the prospect of my sweet friend becoming my wife sooner than expected. However, although I had all the confidence and optimism of untried youth, I was at times beset by misgivings – questioning first whether the elopement would come off at all, and if it did, what unforeseen consequences would result. And so I daily analyzed the plan, looking for possible pitfalls and ways to improve upon it.

"I have been thinking, Eliza," I told her when we finally had a few minutes alone. "It will be quite impossible to make our escape in the dead of night, as you suggested. The cover of darkness would be beneficial, I agree, so long as we had a tolerable moon for travelling. But I cannot hire an equipage in the village without my father hearing of it. And to take a horse from our own stables, let alone a carriage, without rousing somebody would be out of the question. The coachman's apartment is attached, and the stable boy sleeps in the hayloft. If they should come to investigate the noise, what possible excuse could I give for wanting to go out at that time of night?"

"You could say that somebody is ill and you go for the doctor."

"True. That is a good thought," I said considering. "Oh, but I could hardly take you and any baggage at all with me on such an errand."

"Will not you have the same difficulty during the day?"

"By day, any excuse for my taking out the phaeton will be believed. And you and our bags can be waiting for me where the path meets the road. We will have to travel extremely lightly as it is, taking only one handbag with the bare essentials apiece."

"Oh, but to leave everything else behind – my books, my precious keepsakes, the portrait of my mother and father? Dear Christopher, you cannot be serious."

"Perfectly so, I'm afraid, pet. You must remember this; all that matters is getting safely away. Besides, you need not think of giving up these things forever. One day, after we are securely married, we will be able to come home to Delaford again."

I hoped by saying this to not only comfort Eliza but convince myself as well. Although my logical mind told me it was entirely possible something would go awry, I could not dwell on such a calamity. We simply *must* be successful, I reasoned – because we had right on our side, and also because the alternative was un-thinkable.

~4~

I have since canvassed the events of that day again and again, second guessing every part of our elopement scheme, and wondering where we could have done better. I remain convinced that, though far from perfect, the plan was a viable one. It certainly could have succeeded. Indeed, it most probably would have except for one unlucky accident.

With Eliza's birthday coming soon, time was running short. And so, after a couple of other intended dates had been aborted, I chose this particular Tuesday because there was nothing scheduled requiring our specific attendance. That, plus the fact that my father meant to be shut up all day with his land steward, would, I hoped, ensure that we were not missed until many hours after we had gone, when we would be miles and miles ahead of any pursuit.

I had slipped out the night beforehand to take my bag and Eliza's to the rendezvous point, where I hid them in the overgrown hedgerow to be retrieved the next day.

In the morning, Eliza and I were to dress in ordinary clothing – nothing that bespoke the idea of travelling costumes. Then we would present ourselves in the breakfast room as usual to eat a leisurely meal, just as if it were any other day.

We began well, I think. Eliza came in to breakfast shortly after I did. A long, speaking look passed between us. My father, who was there as well, was too absorbed in his newspaper to take any notice of us, and Max had yet to put in an appearance that morning.

We were all quiet for so long that it began to make me uncomfortable, lest it should strike my father as highly unusual, which it was. "How did you sleep, Cousin?" I asked at last, for something to say.

"Tolerably well, I thank you," Eliza answered.

"I am glad to hear it."

Another long silence ensued, broken finally by my father. "You will both remember that I am meeting with Mr. Jeffries today and not to be disturbed."

We both acknowledged the fact.

"I have a small task for you to accomplish while I am occupied," he said, looking at me for the first time. "I would see you begin directly after you finish your meal."

My heart sank. This would undoubtedly mean a postponed departure for Eliza and myself. I must be seen as submitting to my father's authority, though, and to abandon the job he gave me before its completion, even after he was closeted with Mr. Jeffries, would be sure to sound an alarm as soon as it was discovered.

"I want you to make a courtesy call to each of the tenant farms. You know, do a bit of the civil in my place. Keeps them from complaining so much if they receive a little notice from the family now and again. And you are old enough that it is time the tenants learnt to see you about the business of the estate, as one of my representatives."

My first dismal thought was that completing the task would take hours, meaning the possible putting off of our escape until another day altogether. My second, however, following immediately upon its heels, was that it would consequently be hours before I was expected back at the house. This would in fact be the perfect opportunity to be away as planned, with no delay at all.

"Well?" said my father when I did not answer quickly enough. "I trust you have no objection, Christopher. Nothing more important to do today, have you?"

"No, sir, certainly not. I will go directly," I promised. That much was true, for I could not wait to be gone.

"Begin with the Jones's place," he added.

"Very well."

When my father had returned to his paper, I gave Eliza a significant look. We shortly finished our meal and left the breakfast room together. Once I was sure that nobody was about who could observe us, I took her arm and hurried her down the passageway to a small sitting room, rarely used by anybody but ourselves. I could see concern in Eliza's countenance.

"Oh, why should my uncle have chosen this of all days to give you such an assignment?" she said in a plaintive voice, just above a whisper. "When he asked if you had anything better to do today, I wanted to shout that yes, you did! Such a piece of bad luck."

I pulled her close and kissed her forehead. "Do not be alarmed, my dear. This may work to our material advantage."

"How can it do so?"

"Do not you see? I now have the perfect excuse for taking out the phaeton. No one will question it. I will set off as if to do my father's bidding, but drive off to meet you instead." I frowned. "I think I must indeed go to the Jones's farm first, however, since it is within view of the house. From there, though, it will be no difficult matter to turn back along the road to collect you, just as we planned. If you tell your maid you have the headache and want to be left alone, hopefully nobody will miss you for hours either."

"Oh, Christopher, how wise you are. I have never been so thrilled in all my life! To think we will be off together this very morning and married within the week!"

"Yes, the time has come. Take courage and play your part well, my love. Now kiss me and let me go, for the sooner I am off, the sooner I will be with you again and forever."

It was a bittersweet parting, as well may be imagined… and it would have been far more so if we had known then the issue of those next few hours.

I affected nonchalance as I strode to the stables to take out the phaeton and bays. In reality, however, my heart was nearly beating out of my chest at what I was about to do, at the outrageous fact that I was soon to be in full rebellion against my father and in absolute disobedience to his direct orders. There could be no coming back from it. Once I stole Eliza out from under his nose, no retreat was possible, no pardon for me, no making amends. Despite the words with which I had encouraged Eliza, I thought it unlikely my father would ever speak to me again, and a return to Delaford while he lived seemed highly unlikely.

"I could drive you, young sir," the old coachman offered when the equipage was ready. "I've nothing else pressing to do."

"Thank you, Winston," I answered, momentarily alarmed in case he should insist, saying that my father had ordered him to accompany me. "But you know I like the ribbons in my own hands best."

He smiled, saying with what I understood to be genuine affection, "I do know it. And a fine driver you are too, Master Christopher. You always did have a way with the 'orses."

Realizing I might never again see this faithful servant, whom I had known all my life, I had to fight the urge to tender him a heartfelt final farewell. Instead, I briefly laid a hand on his shoulder and thanked him again. That would have to suffice. Then I climbed aboard the phaeton, slapped the reins, and drove off.

Everything was going according to plan. With the perfectly matched bays responding to my light touch, a blue sky and an open road before me, I already felt freer. There was only the stop to make at the Jones's place first, and I expected no difficulty there. I prayed that Eliza was doing as well on her side.

No doubt Mrs. Jones was surprised to find me at her door. Her husband was in the field, she reported, sending a boy of about ten off to fetch him home at once.

The minutes ticked by ever so slowly as I sat waiting for the farmer to come in. To fill the time until then, I did a lot of listening to his wife, nodding, smiling, and admiring whatever fell within my scope of observation: the heavenly aroma of bread baking in the oven, the neatness of Mrs. Jones's housekeeping, and the obvious health of her children and poultry, all of which ran freely in and out of the house.

Finally Mr. Jones appeared, dirty from working the fields. He snatched the cap from his head at the last moment and, making a small, nervous bow, said, "Sorry to keep you waitin', governor."

I rose to face him. "Not at all, Mr. Jones. It is I who should apologize for interrupting your work, but I will not keep you long. My father only desired that I should greet you and find out how you do."

He paused, exchanging a look with his wife before answering. "That be very civil, sir. Me and the missus scrape along pretty well. We 'ave a lot of mouths to feed, but we're none of us afraid of 'ard work."

"Very commendable, I'm sure, Mr. Jones. I am glad to hear you are comfortable."

"Well... I would 'ardly call it *that*, and you might remind the master that he was goin' to send somebody by to fix the leak in our roof." He inclined his head in the direction of a bucket in a corner, where I had not noticed it. "I hate to complain, but it's been nigh on six months and we still be waitin'."

"I am sorry for that, Mr. Jones." I hardly knew what else I could say, except, "I will be sure to mention it when I next see him." Then I moved as if to leave.

"Won't you take some tea with us before you go, sir?" volunteered Mrs. Jones.

"Thank you, madam. That is very kind, but I've kept you both from your work too long already, and I must be getting on."

My hosts made no further protests, and I was quickly out of the door. Giving a coin to the lad who had been holding my horses, I reclaimed the phaeton and drove away.

Before I reached the point where I knew it would disappear from view, I spared one more glance back at the manor house that had been my home for so long – had been, but possibly never would be again. It was a grand old place; too grand for our means, apparently, although I was not privy to what had created the current insolvency. My father, whatever his faults, was never a gambler as far as I knew, so perhaps general mismanagement over the years or bad luck of some kind was to blame. In any case, though it would be a misfortune to lose the estate, one thing was certain; the accounts must not be balanced at the cost of Eliza's liberty and happiness. No house, no plot of earth was worth that, and I would gladly part with Delaford to save her.

I resolutely turned away from my home and set my eyes on the road ahead. It was time to leave my old life behind, to cut loose the chains that had kept me enslaved to my father's tyranny, to escape to freedom with Eliza! The idea sent a surge of pure joy right through me, and I was impatient to begin. As soon as I joined the main road, I urged the horses to a faster pace. With a rising tide of anticipation, the beat of my heart quickened likewise.

"I am coming, Eliza!" I proclaimed aloud, as the fleet-footed bays flew down the road. I did not wish to lose any time. She should already be at our meeting point, waiting for me, and I would see her in only a minute more.

Then I rounded the bend and began to slow the horses. There she was! My dear Eliza… but she was not alone.

When I saw my father standing there at the rendezvous, holding Eliza's arm tightly against her struggles, his face like thunder, my blood ran cold. Utter shock and disbelief, morbid dread, a frantic grasping at straws: all these clawed at my chest in the seconds between recognizing the situation and bringing the phaeton to a halt before my father. I might have cracked the whip and driven on, of course, getting beyond his reach myself. But without Eliza, there would have been no point.

Once stopped, I could spare no glance for my father; Eliza was my only concern. Her cheeks were flushed and tear stained, I saw at once, and in her eyes I observed the very reflection of my own love and violent distress. Then she silently mouthed the words, "I am so sorry."

Whatever had gone wrong, she apparently blamed herself.

"Get down from there!" my father shouted. "At once!"

I made the reins secure and climbed down. Eliza broke free and flew into my arms. We clung together, both sobbing now.

"Enough!" came the order from my father only moments later. "You, sir," he continued to me, "collect those bags and take them back to the house. The young lady is coming with me in the phaeton. Then, you will both have a great deal to answer for."

There was nothing else to be done. Somehow we had been found out, and now there would be the devil to pay.

5

There are moments that change the course of a man's life: turning points, the places where what *is* departs irrevocably from what might have been. Although we do not always recognize them at the time, when we look back, we see that, *yes, I was at a crossroads then. If only I had been able to turn right instead of being carried left, what a difference that would have made.*

This was such a moment. Before it, all possibilities were yet open, I was free, and a life with Eliza stretched into the future before my eyes. Afterward, everything had changed. I knew at once that the door to the sweet life I had imagined with my beloved friend and cousin had slammed closed forever.

By contrast, the moment, years later, that divided me from any chance with Marianne Dashwood, slipped by entirely without my knowledge. My fate was sealed the instant she set eyes on Mr. Willoughby, an event for which I was not even present. Therefore I was at first perfectly unconscious that anything of significance had occurred.

Despite the immediate and vivid impression Marianne Dashwood had made on me at our initial meeting, I will not call it love at first sight. I have heard of such cases, of course, but if they exist, this was not one of them. How could it be love at first sight when my own eyes deceived me? In the beginning, I looked at Marianne and saw only Eliza. I could not properly know or appreciate the lady before me as long as I only valued her for her resemblance to my long-lost friend, her ability to rekindle the sensations of my youth and allow me to relive the old, happy memories.

No, real love took just a bit longer to settle upon my heart. A light snow falling will amount to nothing at all at first – it weighs nothing, changes nothing – and yet by morning it may have transformed the landscape into something else entirely. So the gently collecting impressions of the true Marianne began to obscure my original false view of her. She was no duplicate of Eliza, no resurrection of my former friend. There were indeed marked similarities, but there were just as many differences. Meeting nearly every day as we did that first fortnight – at Barton Cottage or at the Park – the balance soon began to shift in my mind. Marianne herself moved to the forefront while Eliza receded into the past again. That was as it should be, for Marianne deserved to be loved for herself alone.

And love her I did. I felt reborn, young once more and light as air. As in those early days with Eliza, everything seemed possible again.

After that first meeting at Barton Park, we were all invited in turn to the cottage, where the same pleasures were repeated on a more modest scale. Mrs. Dashwood had arranged for a very good dinner – spending more than she could comfortably afford, I fear. The conversation ran along similar lines as before, and Marianne played and sang for us again. This time, however, at her own insistence, I did as well.

She sat attentively by, saying afterward, "Your playing is quite accomplished, Colonel."

I bowed my thanks.

"But it is your singing voice that I particularly like. It has an interesting quality that I cannot quite describe. A deep, mellow timbre, I shall call it. Quite unusual."

This was an unexpected compliment. "I am pleased you found some merit in my performance," I said.

"Oh, yes. Your talents are well suited to the ballad you played, too, but I cannot help wishing I could hear you sing something with more spirit next time. You know, something with a more animated tempo."

"Animated tempo?"

"Yes, most assuredly so. That would be just the thing."

"Very well, Miss Marianne, I will attend to your advice. Next time, you shall have something livelier from me, I promise."

She smiled. "I shall look forward to it, Colonel," she said before moving away.

Again, it was a brief exchange, and yet I could not help but be encouraged by her interest. It was something to build on, and I started rummaging through my brain at once for what lively piece I should play and sing for her next time.

I had not thought to have so obviously singled out Marianne for my regard, for I had been careful to speak to Elinor, Mrs. Dashwood, and even Margaret just as much. And yet, someone had noticed.

Wasting no time, Mrs. Jennings started in on me as soon as we – Sir John, Lady Middleton, Mrs. Jennings, and myself – returned to the Park and settled ourselves in the drawing room. "We-e-e-l-l, Colonel Brandon," she said with exaltation, "I have found you out!"

"Madam?" I returned, refusing to rise to her bait.

"It is exactly as I perceived t'other day. Miss Marianne is to be the one!"

"What can you mean, dear lady?"

"Just this. It is she and not her sister who has quite captured your fancy! I daresay it is love, too, for you could not take your eyes from her for a minute when she was at the piano-forte – not Tuesday night and not this. Why," she added, laughing, "I spoke to you once and so did Sir John. Is not that so, John?"

"Yes, you are correct, Mother. I perfectly remember it."

"Well there you are, Colonel. As I said, we both spoke but you were quite deaf to us. All the world knows that inattentiveness to others and general incivility are sure signs of love, so you may as well admit it!"

I had weathered many similar assaults by Mrs. Jennings before, who was forever seeing symptoms of love in every unattached person she met with. And so I endeavored to deny her the satisfaction of a violent response to her accusations. "If paying a performer the compliment of my full attention is proof of love, then I have been in love with dozens of musicians of every description before. And yet you notice that I have married none of them."

"Deny it if you wish, but I will not be talked out of my convictions. Besides, I daresay none of the others you mean were as charming as Miss Marianne. An excellent match it will be too, for she is handsome and young – young enough to bear you many fine sons!" Here, she bubbled over with wicked glee.

"Mrs. Jennings, I beg you…"

"Oh, very well, Colonel. I know you are not squeamish yourself, so I suppose it is on the lady's behalf that you exercise such scruples. We shall put talk of such indelicate matters aside for the time being, if you like, at least until the young lady admits to being in love herself. But I daresay it will not hurt if I were to drop a little hint in her ear now and then, just to get her thinking."

"Now, mum," said Sir John, taking up the objection in my place. "It is all well and good to practice your teasing on Brandon, here. He is a grown man and knows how to defend himself. But take a little more care with the young ladies. Indeed, you must."

"Nay, nay, this is fine talk from you, John, for you know you enjoy a good joke as much as I do. And what does a young lady like more than an excuse to blush, for she knows it is then that she looks her best. No, Miss Marianne will thank me one day, I am sure, if I help her to know her own good and catch our dear Colonel Brandon. Any girl would be lucky to get him."

"Well, of course she would, Mother. You know I should never disagree with you there. It is only a question of the best way to help the lovers along…"

The debate continued between these two with no further comment required from me; I had become completely superfluous. It is doubtful they even noticed when I excused myself and quit the room.

~~*~~

I judged Mrs. Jennings the biggest threat to my burgeoning hopes, for contrary to what she had boasted, I expected her teasing would be highly unlikely to drive Marianne into my arms. And so it proved to be in the days that followed. I observed Mrs. Jennings making repeated, jocular intimations to the young lady, presumably about me. I also observed with consternation the unfortunate result. Far from promoting the match as intended, the exercise of Mrs. Jennings's wit seemed to drive a wedge firmly between us. Our friendly exchanges about music were at an end. In fact Miss Marianne seemed discomfited whenever she was required to be in the same room with me. Still, I thought If I were patient and did not alarm her by being too bold, she might in time be brought within my reach. A skittish filly may learn to find a friend in a man who shows her unfailing kindness.

And yet, it was not Mrs. Jennings's teasing that ultimately doomed whatever chance I might have otherwise stood with Marianne, whatever influence patience and kindness might have worked in my favor. As it happened, there was no time at all for patience, for a mere two weeks and a day after my introduction to the lady, my rival appeared on the scene, one against whose irresistible appeal I was ill equipped to compete: Mr. Willoughby.

Sir John came home from having visited at the cottage on his own that morning, and upon seeing me, his face fell, looking as if somebody had died. "My poor fellow," he said somberly, placing a hand on my shoulder and shaking his head. "I'm afraid it is all over for you."

None the wiser, I waited to be enlightened.

"You might well look concerned, and with good reason. You see, I cannot now think much of your chances with Miss Marianne, Brandon, for a new contender has taken the field. I am sorry to tell you that he's a handsome young fellow, and a bolder rider you will never meet. He is to inherit Allenham Court and comes down every year to visit the old lady there. Name is Willoughby. Do you know him?"

"We have met," I said cautiously.

"Oh, yes, of course, last Christmas, here at the Park. Well, then you remember how he carried on that night!"

"I do, indeed."

"Danced till dawn and was up again not four hours later to ride to covert. In any case, today, like a storybook hero, he came to the rescue of your young lady in her moment of distress. And who can be expected to compete with that?"

"What are you speaking of, John? Was Miss Marianne truly in some kind of distress?"

"To be sure! Slipped and tumbled down the hill in the rain this morning, spraining her ankle. You needn't fear, though. Nothing that a little time will not mend. But it placed her in need of assistance, and there was Willoughby, you see. Carried her home, so I am told. I cannot help but wish you had taken the notion into your head to walk out that way yourself this morning. Then perhaps she would now be swooning over you instead. I have just come from the ladies, and they can speak of nothing but Willoughby."

"Is that so?"

"Oh, yes, more's the pity. Wanted to know my opinion of the man, and I had to admit the truth. 'As good a kind of fellow who ever lived,' I said. That commendation did not satisfy, however. No, to be sure, it did not. They must know every last jot and tittle: talents, pursuits, and I know not what. I certainly could not judge as to all that, and so I told them plainly. But it is clear that Mr. Willoughby – or 'Marianne's preserver,' as Miss Margaret has styled him – is become their new darling."

What could I say? This was bad news indeed.

"I did try to do you a good turn, though, old friend," John continued, "by suggesting that Miss Dashwood should set her cap at Willoughby herself, instead of leaving the fellow to her younger sister. So we shall see."

I had no ready reply to Sir John's lament or to his vain wish that things had occurred differently. I, too, would have preferred that the office of saving Marianne had fallen to me. Although I should have been glad some gentleman – any gentleman – was in a position to help, rather than that she should have been left alone in pain in the wet and the cold. And I was, of course. But I could not help thinking that if Marianne needed a "preserver," why did it have to be Willoughby?

I had no very high opinion of the man after having met him on the occasion to which Sir John had referred. A coxcomb. A strutting peacock. A careless philanderer. He spent the entire night dancing, it was true, and I do not fault him for that; I danced a great deal that night myself. No, it was his swaggering air and his conduct towards the ladies that marked him out as a man not to be trusted.

At the beginning of the night, he selected one young lady – really no more than a girl – for his special attentions, persuading her to dance with him three dances in a row, although two should have been the maximum allowed. Then he left her flat and turned to another with gestures of just as particular a regard. And so on. It appeared to me that he meant to make every female in the room, under the age of forty, violently in love with him by the end of the evening, just to flatter his own vanity.

Willoughby's liveliness and easy manners were enough to convince Sir John, right from the start, of his being *as good a sort of fellow who ever lived.* But I saw something very different, especially since the first girl Willoughby had toyed with and left that night was my own young ward, poor Eliza's daughter, Beth Williams, whom I had brought to the event as a special treat.

Having observed all this for myself, one may imagine how I felt at hearing that Miss Marianne had fallen within the sphere of Mr. Willoughby's influence. Still, one encounter could hardly put her in serious danger. I had also observed how quickly the man lost interest and moved on. Despite Marianne's considerable charms, I thought it likely that her lack of fortune would prevent an ambitious young man like Willoughby from forming any serious designs on her. He would soon be gone again with no harm done, I hoped. And I would still be here.

This was my expectation at the time, Sir John's proclamations of doom notwithstanding.

When I went to the cottage the next morning to enquire after Marianne's health, however, I could immediately distinguish that a great alteration had taken place. Mrs. Dashwood and Miss Dashwood welcomed me as warmly as before, and even Marianne civilly acknowledged my presence. But there was such a general air of distraction about them all as I had difficulty explaining at first. Then Willoughby came to remove the mystery. They had been anticipating his arrival, every one of them. Of course they had. With that event, my comparative importance faded into insignificance.

Marianne's preference was instantly clear; she had eyes for nobody but Willoughby. And who could fault her for it? Willoughby was handsome and charming. He was much nearer her own age and decidedly more animated. I had experience on my side and perhaps a better informed mind, but these count for very little in the estimation of the young. Even the question of music – the one point upon which I had been able to establish a promising connection with Marianne – could not be clearly decided in my favor, because I learnt that Willoughby's own musical talents were considerable. I was entirely eclipsed.

So it was from then on. Despite my friend's initial sympathy for my faded chances with Marianne, Sir John's love of lively company and his desire to accommodate everybody else's wishes quickly made him forget. Mr. Willoughby was now included in every engagement. Sir John soon set about gratifying the imaginations of the juvenile portion of the neighborhood, as well as his own, with a succession of schemes for enjoyment: dinners and private balls at the Park, and as many outdoor entertainments as the October weather would permit. Even Mrs. Jennings transferred her attentions without any seeming effort. Her raillery about love and forthcoming engagements now found a new, more prosperous target in the apparent match between Marianne and Willoughby.

I admit, I felt very much like the forgotten man. My chief concern, however, was for Marianne, not myself. What would become of her if she fell wholly under the power of a man like Willoughby? It must not happen, I vowed, while at the same time having no idea how to prevent it. Although I had formed an unfavorable opinion of the man, it was founded only on my own observations and intuition. I knew no actual harm of him as of yet, nothing that could justify an interfering word of warning to her mother or to Marianne herself. It seemed all I could do was wait and watch as the disturbing tableau unfolded before me.

6

It was not only Miss Marianne's situation that weighed heavily on my mind. I had other worries as well, primarily the unexplained absence of my young ward Miss Williams. She had been missing without a trace for eight months now, and all of my many enquiries had met with frustration. And so it was difficult to be cheerful while I remained in doubt of Beth's safety and well-being.

Had it not been for Miss Elinor Dashwood's kindness, I might have entirely despaired. But in her friendship and conversation, I found the best antidote for my cares. Her attentiveness to me was the greatest consolation for the total indifference of her sister.

Hers was a fine mind and a truly sympathetic heart, I discovered. She always made the effort to speak to me, and we soon developed an unguarded ease in each other's company. Although as yet I knew none of her personal history, I had the distinct impression that she too understood something about disappointed love, as well as perceiving the gist of my own situation. If a person of Mrs. Jennings's limited powers had correctly guessed the leaning of my affection, I could not doubt that Elinor, with her superior intellect, would have divined it as well. Therefore, since our hearts, however fruitlessly, were both engaged by others, there could be no misunderstanding between us.

My idea that Miss Dashwood's heart was engaged elsewhere was shortly confirmed in a most unfortunate way. We were all dining together at the Park again – in a party which included Willoughby, of course – when Mrs. Jennings's wit turned in a new direction. Having made the most of Marianne and her amorous suitor for a considerable length of time, she looked for a fresh source of sport in Elinor. Perhaps she had already tried and failed with a direct approach, for she now attempted a roundabout way, attacking the youngest Miss Dashwood for the information she craved.

"My dear Miss Margaret," she began slyly. "You have not yet told us your secrets, and high time it is you did so, too! Have you some fine beau in the corner? Any young man you particularly fancy?"

Wide-eyed, Margaret looked from Mrs. Jennings to her mother for help.

"Mrs. Jennings is merely teasing you, Margaret," said Mrs. Dashwood. "She well knows you are far too young for such things."

"I suppose that is true," admitted Mrs. Jennings. "Another year or two will soon change that. In the meantime, then, Miss Margaret, you have two older sisters to study, have you not? We know all about Miss Marianne's romantic adventures, but we have as yet heard very little of your other sister's. Surely Miss Elinor Dashwood, pretty as she is, must have a particular favorite. Perhaps a handsome young man left behind in Sussex? Now, do tell us his name."

This time, Margaret looked to her sister and asked, "I must not tell, may I, Elinor?"

This of course made everybody laugh. Elinor herself tried to join in, but it looked to me as if the effort greatly pained her. My empathy was immediately aroused on her behalf, for Mrs. Jennings was now on the scent and none of Marianne's efforts to silence Margaret on the subject could call her off. She did not relent until she had got the girl to give up the enticing information that there was indeed such a gentleman and that his name began with an F.

Even when the subject finally dropped, Elinor's look of alarm remained. She no doubt understood that she had not heard the last of it. She had nothing to fear from me on that score, however; I would never mention it.

A different evening, Elinor and I sat together at the Park, while some of the others were dancing. My eyes involuntarily followed Marianne as she moved gracefully about the floor with her now nearly constant partner, her eyes sparkling and her countenance merry. I spoke my thoughts aloud to my companion.

"Your sister seems very happy," I said.

"There can be no doubt of it," Elinor responded with a sigh.

Her tone made me redirect my eyes to her. "Are you not glad of it, Miss Dashwood?"

"Oh, yes, certainly I am! After seeing how Marianne suffered at the death of our father and then being torn away from our home at Norland, I am grateful to anybody who can make her forget her troubles and be happy again."

"And what of you, Miss Dashwood? Do you still miss Norland terribly?"

"I must say that I do," she said thoughtfully. "Not Norland itself so much as the friends I left behind. Good friends, most of whom I have probably seen for the last time."

Again that tone of slight melancholy.

"And now you must share the best of the friends you brought with you from Sussex with another," I suggested, nodding to the pair of dancers just swishing past us: Marianne and Willoughby.

She looked at me in some surprise. "That is very astute, Colonel. Truly, I have never put the feeling into words before, but that is exactly the case."

"You should not credit me with any greatness of mind, Miss Dashwood. It is just that I too know something about loss."

We were silent for a time while the dance finished and another was called. When the music commenced anew, Elinor resumed where we had left off.

"Other than yourself – and I hope I may count you my friend, Colonel – I have no new acquaintances here to replace those I am missing. And although I sincerely wish my sister happy, I can hardly bear to think of losing her entirely."

I proceeded tentatively. "Do you think…? I mean, surely there can be no immediate danger of that kind. Your sister is quite young, and this apparent attachment between her and Mr. Willoughby is still very new. Your mother will be wise enough to discourage anything hasty."

"What you say is altogether reasonable, Colonel, but I dare not depend on it." Then she hurried on. "Oh, do not misunderstand me. I like Willoughby. Very much, in fact. We all do, and he has done wonders for my sister's spirits. It is just that as yet we know so little about him. I could wish Marianne would proceed more cautiously, but she does not approve of hiding her feelings. Her ideas are all romantic, I'm afraid, and a heart such as hers cannot love by halves."

Oh, what I would give to have Marianne's liberal, whole-hearted devotion directed my way! The thought left me speechless for a moment. But, no, for more than one reason, that would never be. "I understand that she does not approve of second attachments either. I wonder if she makes any allowances for those who, through no fault of their own, have been disappointed in their first."

"I cannot tell you. I only know that I never yet heard her admit any instance of a second attachment's being pardonable! But I dare-say a few more years' experience will settle her opinions along more reasonable lines."

I paused before answering. "While you are probably correct, Miss Dashwood, I cannot bring myself to desire it, not entirely. There is something so amiable in the innocent prejudices of a young mind that one is sorry to see them give way. The world will soon enough supply cause for disenchantment. If that process is unfairly hastened, the result can be disastrous." She looked at me askance. "I speak from experience, I assure you, for I once knew a lady who in temper and mind greatly resembled your sister, who thought and judged like her, but who, by a series of unfortunate circumstances was broken..." I stopped myself. "Forgive me. I should not have burdened you."

"Not at all, Colonel. It is no imposition between friends to speak freely."

"You are kind, Miss Dashwood, and I am very glad indeed of your friendship."

~~*~~

Before the party broke up that evening, I made a rather bold suggestion for the following day. I had been thinking about the possibility for some time, trying to decide if it were advisable to propose it. I finally decided I had nothing to lose. Sir John should not carry the burden for our entertainment alone, and perhaps it would give an opportunity for Marianne to see me in a different light. I was not completely devoid of resources and ingenuity.

"If the weather is favorable tomorrow," I began when I was sure I had everybody's attention, "perhaps you would all care to join me on a little expedition. I have the care of a place called Whitwell, about twelve miles from here, whilst its owner, my brother-in-law is abroad. In discharge of my duties as temporary overseer, I must travel there tomorrow myself, and I thought perhaps we might make a party of it. The grounds are quite beautiful, as Sir John can attest, and there is a fine lake for sailing."

This was all that was necessary to create an instant flurry of excitement.

"Sailing!" cried Marianne. "I am quite wild for the idea of sailing!"

"You may depend on what Brandon says, too, Miss Marianne," Sir John confirmed, "as to the beauty of the place and as to sailing. Why, I have sailed there myself many times, and a more ideal setting for the sport and a more noble piece of water you will never find!"

"Open carriages," Willoughby declared decisively. "For a complete party of pleasure, nothing other than open carriages will do. One must carry these things off with a bit of style, you know."

"Willoughby!" Mrs. Dashwood exclaimed. "It is nearly November, and I have a cold besides."

This could not dissuade him. "We must not be timid, Mrs. Dashwood. *Audentes fortuna adiuvat.* Fortune favors the bold!"

"We will be wanting cold provisions along," suggested Mrs. Jennings, "for we will be all day, there and back."

Lady Middleton had no objection to the proposed outing, "As long as everything can be done properly."

The idea had swiftly taken on a life of its own, and animated discussion of the particulars extended several minutes more. In the end, only Mrs. Dashwood declined the invitation in consideration of her cold, while encouraging the others to, "Go, by all means!"

I was heartened by the universal enthusiasm for my proposal, and when the clouds broke the next morning, a successful outing seemed assured.

The whole party met at the Park at ten o'clock, where we were to breakfast before our departure. As usual, Lady Middleton had seen to it that no ordinary meal was served. Delectable sights and smells met us as we assembled and filled our plates: ham, kippers, some kind of potato dish I could not name, as well as a variety of fruits and freshly baked breads.

Everybody was full of high spirits and good humor, eager to be happy and determined to submit to the greatest inconveniences and hardships rather than be otherwise. It surely would not rain. The few clouds that remained would prove of no consequence, and what were twelve miles to travel when such pleasures awaited us?

For once, I was not the forgotten man; I was at the center of all this affability for providing the anticipated delights. Miss Marianne had smiled and thanked me when she arrived, and even Willoughby had shaken my hand.

Then it was all over in the blink of an eye. While we were at breakfast, the letters were brought, including one for me, which had been forwarded from Delaford. Upon seeing the direction, I left the room at once, not stopping to explain or turning when Sir John called after me. The letter was from my solicitor, and I knew it could contain intelligence on only one topic, and that of the utmost importance: the fate and whereabouts of my missing ward, Miss Williams.

It was one note contained within another. I read the outer one first.

To Christopher Brandon
Delaford

Dear Sir,

At last I have had some news about your ward. She is alive and in good health; I can at least assure you of that much. You may have already guessed the reason for her leaving all her friends in Bath. My man traced her to a mother and child home near Oxford, to which I immediately went. It is a dreadful place, however, under the supervision of the most tyrannical example of womanhood I have ever come across.

I therefore took the liberty of removing Miss Williams to London, where I have placed her in much more respectable care. The girl, who is now nearing her confinement, is understandably distraught, sick with guilt and worry that you will despise her and cast her off, as you will see from her enclosed note. Do come at once.

Your Servant,
A. Hemlock, esq.

I opened the other note.

Dear Uncle,

I write to beg your help and forgiveness. Oh, how shall I tell you? I have been very foolish and I daresay very wicked as well. I trusted in a man who professed to love me. He promised to return and marry me, but he never did. I am now preparing to bear his child. Nobody could blame you for casting me off, but if you will not help me, Uncle, I do not know what shall become of me. I suppose I shall end in a work house or starve. Take pity on me, I beseech you.

Your own Beth

The news was no worse than I had expected and yet still a blow. How could I have allowed this to happen? My sweet Eliza had entrusted this girl, her illegitimate but beloved daughter, into my care before she died, and now history had repeated itself. Thanks to my inattentiveness, the daughter had met a similar fate as her mama years before, and there was no one to blame but myself. No, that was not quite true; I would gladly share the blame with the libertine who had seduced and left her. But as yet, I knew not who he was.

Of course I would leave for town at once. There was clearly nothing else to be done. I could not let the girl suffer such anxiety a moment longer than necessary. She was my responsibility, and a mere pleasure party did not compare in importance.

Before rejoining the others, I sent a servant to collect my things and another to order my horses. Then, I took a minute to compose myself so as not to give away the true extent of my distress. My rude manner of abandoning them all at the breakfast table would already have raised lively speculation, I knew – questions I was by no means prepared to answer. And my cancelling of our excursion would be unpopular as well. Still, it could not be helped.

"No bad news, Colonel, I hope," said Mrs. Jennings, pointedly, the instant I returned.

"None at all, ma'am, I thank you," I answered with unfelt tranquility.

She would not leave it at that, however. "Something from your sister in Avignon, then? Or perhaps news from your cousin, or Miss Williams? Come now, it must be something out of the ordinary to have discomposed you to such an extent. So let us hear it."

"My dear Madam," said Lady Middleton with uncharacteristic warmth, "recollect what you are saying!"

I was grateful for Lady Middleton's timely intervention, which allowed me to address my answer to her. "I am particularly sorry, ma'am," I said, "that I should receive this letter today, for it is on business which requires my immediate attendance in town. I am therefore obliged to give up your generous hospitality at once, and this agreeable party."

Lady Middleton received the news calmly enough, but the same could not be said for her mother.

"Going to town!" cried Mrs. Jennings. "What can you have to do there this time of year?"

Turning to the others, I went on. "Although my own loss is great, I am even more grieved that the rest of you should suffer by it, for you cannot gain admittance to Whitwell without me. I urge you to choose a different destination, therefore, and continue on with your party as planned. We will go to Whitwell some other time."

More protests and questions followed. Could I not put off my journey until after our return, or until tomorrow? It would be too cruel to disappoint the ladies. Perhaps if I would tell them all my business, they could help to find a solution. If not, then, when would I be back?

No doubt the debate over the nature of my troubles carried on long after I was gone, for I answered none of their questions to their satisfaction. When my horses were announced, my last sight of Marianne as I left the room was to see a sneering Willoughby whispering something in her ear, and her responding in kind.

7

So it was that I was taken away from Marianne while she was still vulnerable, forced to leave her protection in other, possibly less vigilant hands. She would not miss me, I knew, but I would regret my inability to keep faithful watch over her. One clear duty now prevented the exercise of another self-assigned obligation – an obligation of the heart.

When I reached London, I went to Mr. Hemlock's offices first so that he might direct me to where Beth was being cared for. It was a house for young mothers in like circumstance to hers, just as the place where she had first been discovered. This establishment, however, sponsored by a Christian charitable organization, was clean, orderly, and operated by a compassionate woman named Mrs. Hastings. After speaking to her at length and being satisfied that the arrangement was safe and suitable, I was taken to a sitting room where I could meet privately with my ward.

Although I had been prepared to see Beth heavy with child, as she entered it was still an effort to keep my face from betraying what I felt when confronted with the undeniable fact of it. She came towards me, eyes downcast and still looking like a girl, despite the womanly shape of her body. My mind could not make it fit.

I met her halfway and immediately took her into my arms.

She rested there for a minute, crying quietly before asking, "Are you very angry with me?"

"No… I am not angry with you," I said, stroking her hair. It was accurate, but more than that I could not say. In truth, I was crushed and deeply disappointed, but not angry. Not with *her*, at least. "Do not fear; I will take care of you – you and the child. You shall, neither of you, want for anything."

When I judged that she was sufficiently calm and reassured, I led her to the sofa and we seated ourselves. Then I set about making the necessary inquiries, beginning with the easier questions. How was she feeling? Had she experienced much sickness during the course of her pregnancy? When did she expect to be confined? Was she hoping for a boy or a girl? But eventually the more difficult questions needed to be asked. What was the name of the villain who had done this to her, and where would I find him?

Beth did not willingly give me these answers. I could perceive that she, even then, wanted to believe there was some reasonable excuse for the man. "Perhaps he was unavoidably detained on business," she said. "That kind of thing can happen, I believe. Or perhaps there was a terrible accident or illness that prevented him from returning. And now, of course, he will not know where to look for me."

I nodded and went along with the idea. "It is possible," I agreed, "which is all the more reason for you to tell me the young man's name. I shall discover what has become of him and urge him to do the honorable thing by you, whatever may have prevented him before."

"Do you promise, Uncle?"

"I promise."

She did tell me then, and my blood boiled. It was Willoughby.

Horrified, I remembered the night the two had met at the Christmas party at Barton Park. I should never have brought her; she was too young. I could see that now. I should *never* have allowed her to dance, especially with Willoughby. Clearly he had made a lasting impression on her mind. And *this* was the ultimate result.

Well, I would keep my promise; I would find him and compel him, by every means at my disposal, to marry Beth. It was his duty to do so, and I must make him see that.

Then I thought of Marianne. If I succeeded, how grave would be *her* disappointment. And yet I doubted not that, were she fully acquainted with the facts, she would herself agree that Willoughby's greater obligation was to Beth.

~~*~~

51

Locating my quarry was my first task. I did not care to challenge him in the presence of my friends at Barton, even if he were still there, for I could hardly do so without explaining the reason and involving my ward in the disgrace. No, for the time being, this was a private matter between myself and Willoughby. Although one other person arguably had the right to know – a person who would, I hoped, support my cause: Mrs. Smith, Willoughby's elderly relation at Allenham. She could likely inform me of his whereabouts, at the very least. And if she were a principled woman, she might bring pressure to bear to see her heir do the honorable thing. So I wrote to her, explaining the deplorable situation.

A week later I received Mrs. Smith's prompt reply, which was not very encouraging. She had confronted Mr. Willoughby, representing to him that her pardon and continued patronage depended entirely on his doing what he ought: marrying Beth, as he should have done in the first place. Good woman! Unfortunately, Willoughby had refused, and their conference ended in a total breach. He had left Allenham at once, thence to London, or so she supposed.

Although Willoughby had not capitulated to Mrs. Smith's demands at the time, it seemed reasonable that he might reconsider. Perhaps the thought of losing his legacy, when added to my own urging and that of his conscience, which must tell him what was right, would ultimately cause him to relent. I could only hope so.

Once I ascertained that Mr. Willoughby was indeed in town, I sent him a message demanding that he meet me on the field of honor. There I intended, as dueling conventions and my promise to my ward required, to make every attempt to persuade him to do the right thing instead of facing the sword. Much as I believed it would gratify my righteous indignation to spill some of his blood in the sand, I knew I must think of what was best for Beth.

And so we met early one morning in a secluded spot, where we could depend on not being interrupted. It was a level, grassy area surrounded by a thick wood – ideal for the purpose. The sun was no more than a bright blotch rending the clouds just above the treetops, and a thick mist swirled about our feet. With the physician and our seconds cooling their heels at a distance, Willoughby and I faced each other unarmed, and the negotiations began.

"Colonel Brandon, how tiresome you are become," said Willoughby, affecting boredom. "I am here as honor demanded, but I cannot imagine how I have offended you."

"I find that difficult to believe, sir, unless your memory is even more faulty than your principles. But allow me to state the case plainly. You wantonly despoiled and abandoned my ward, Miss Williams, leaving her to bear your child alone. You will agree to do your duty by them both or answer to me today at the point of a sword. Which shall it be?"

"Ah, then you come on business. Very well. But why these threats? Why this belligerent tone? I suppose I should not be surprised, for you have always disliked me."

"My personal opinion of you is immaterial."

"At last, something upon which we can agree! Now, cannot we discuss this other matter like gentlemen?"

Clearly, he intended to try my patience. His cavalier attitude toward a most serious offence outraged me. And yet, if there were even one chance in a hundred of gaining justice for Beth... For her and for her mother's sake, I was willing to bear with his nonsense, at least to a point.

"Your behavior towards Miss Williams has hardly been that of a gentleman," I said. He had the decency to look at least a little uncomfortable, and so I pressed my advantage. "Do you dispute the facts as I have named them?"

He raised his chin and said, "I do not, not in essentials, that is, only that you have put the worst possible construction on my motives and intentions."

"Can you give any explanation where you are not very much at fault? Here is your chance."

"I am not as heartless as you seem to think. I did in fact care something for Beth, at least at the time, and I had every intention of looking after her. When I went away, you understand, I had no idea of her being with child."

"Well now you *do* know it, and still you tarry in doing what honor clearly requires. Get a license, man, and get yourselves to church!"

He sighed wearily. "You cannot be serious, Colonel. A gentleman of my consequence saddled with such a common little wife? A nobody with uncertain parentage? No, it is quite out of the question, as she knew from the beginning... or at least she should have, for I never promised her marriage."

"She told me otherwise, and I assure you I am quite serious about it. You may go to the devil once you have married Miss Williams. All I require is that you give her and the child the respectability of your name, such as it is. I will grant them *my* protection after that. You need concern yourself no longer."

He laughed derisively. "*Your* protection? Perhaps if you had done a better job of protecting your ward in the first place, none of this would have happened."

It was absurd of him to excuse himself by blaming me, but at the same time it was the very accusation I had hurled at my own head over and again. Still, I could not allow my guilty conscience to show. I could not allow Willoughby to know that his arrow, shot so carelessly, had hit a mark most painful – the place where I was most vulnerable, my consistent inability to protect those I cared about. So I leant close and snarled, "You disgust me."

Willoughby, enlightenment dawning on his face, jabbed an accusing finger into my chest. "You!" he shouted. "Of course! I might have known it would be you who spoilt everything, telling tales, trying to ruin my chances with Marianne!"

Clearly he had correctly guessed that I was the source of Mrs. Smith's information. But I said, "I have not the pleasure of understanding you, sir. I have told no tales. And do refrain from touching me without leave." I pinched the cuff of his sleeve and pushed it far from me, wiping my fingers afterward to show that even this minor contact had been extremely distasteful.

"By God, you have a real nerve – pretending to be so superior when all the time you have done the very same thing. You call her your ward, but everybody knows she is your 'natural daughter.' I notice you did not marry Beth's mother, whoever she was, and yet you expect me to marry her."

I admit that I was taken aback by this. Had the accusation been true, Willoughby would have a fair point. But of course it was not. "Not that it is any of your business, but you have been misinformed. Miss Williams is *not* my daughter, 'natural' or otherwise."

He continued as if he had not heard me. "...and now you have carried rumors to my relation behind my back. Do you have no sense of honor, sir?"

"I have spoken only the truth; there is no dishonor in that, certainly nothing compared to what you have done. Besides, it was done for the best."

"Ha! For *whose* best? For Marianne's? I think not. It was for your own! It was done out of spite. You could not have her, and so you intended that I should not either. I have never heard of anything so selfish in my life! If you truly cared for her, which I doubt, you would not seek to ruin her one chance of happiness. I *do* love her, and she might be content as my wife all her days, if you would leave off your interference."

"Such a superior woman content with a liar and a blackguard for a husband? Impossible!" I could bear the sight of him no longer.

"Do not you turn your back on *me*, sir!" he remonstrated. "I will *not* be disrespected."

I flexed my fingers, suddenly feeling an itch for the weight of a sharp sword in my hand. With difficulty, I maintained control and looked him directly in the eye. "Disrespected? On the contrary, Mr. Willoughby. I am diligently trying to restore you to respectability, while at the same time saving your blood from being spilt. Now, for the last time, sir, will you do the honorable thing and marry Miss Williams?"

"I most certainly will not!"

"Then there is but one way this can end."

Bloodshed was inevitable now. I strode back to the others with Willoughby on my heels.

Mr. Willoughby's second opened a long case to reveal a matched pair of dueling small-swords and offered me my choice. I carefully inspected the weapon I selected. The blade was sound and sharp. It felt balanced and sure in my hand as I gave it a test slash and thrust. I was satisfied.

Willoughby grasped the other weapon, and we moved away a short distance again, where we should have room enough to maneuver. Then we faced off in our stances and prepared to set to.

This was hardly the first time I had found myself standing opposite an armed man intent on doing me harm, and yet it never became so routine as to be a matter of perfect indifference. Even if one could manage to subdue one's mind into calmness, the body will react in a primitive way regardless. *There is danger here*, it declares, demanding that the heart will race, the limbs will tense, and the senses will heighten to readiness. This occasion was no exception.

We circled warily to start, taking each other's measure. Then we began trading turns at launching simple exploratory attacks, easily parried by the other. When I tired of these preliminaries, I pressed my opponent more aggressively, and the battle commenced in earnest.

The ring of steel against steel shattered the quiet of the sleepy morning as I charged him suddenly. Quick to respond, Willoughby ably defended himself, giving as good as he got from me. He would not go quietly, then. Undeterred, I redirected and attacked again. It would have been easy to imagine myself back on the battlefield, facing some nameless foe, but this fight was much more personal.

Swords clattered, clashed, and clanged, again and again. These sounds were joined by our grunts of exertion as the struggle wore on. Then all at once a yell, an oath, and finally a cry of pain.

Willoughby dropped his weapon and went down, and I saw red on my blade. I raised my sword again to finish him, as my military training had taught me to do. Before I regained control and lowered my arm, I had the satisfaction of seeing him cringe in fear.

The contest had lasted only a matter of a few minutes. Willoughby was a competent swordsman, but I was better, and first blood ended it. When I examined my opponent, still cowering there on the ground, I saw with some disappointment that his wound was little more than a three-inch scratch below his left ear, bleeding but hardly a threat to life and health. He would recover. I hoped he would also wear the scar until the end of his days, along with the knowledge that I could just as easily have slashed his throat.

Instead, I walked away. I had already seen enough bloodshed in my life to thoroughly sicken me at its wastefulness. More would accomplish nothing it all.

I left the field the victor, and according to the tenets of dueling, I had received my necessary redress. Why, then, did I feel so little gratified? Doubtless it was because Beth was no better off than before. In spite of my exertions, *her* honor had not been restored.

There was Marianne to think of as well, with Willoughby's words on that subject still ringing in my ears. Since he refused to wed Beth, he would be free to continue his pursuit of Marianne. He had declared he loved her and desired to marry her, an assertion which I could not disbelieve, despite his history. Neither did I doubt her being in love with him. If they did marry, there was at least some possibility he might be reclaimed by her virtuous influence; I had seen it happen before.

His reclamation did not concern me, however, except for how it might affect her. If Willoughby was indeed Marianne's one chance for happiness, which seemed a distinct possibility, what right did I have to spoil it?

8

In the wake of the duel, I had the unpleasant duty of informing Beth that all hope of Willoughby's marrying her was at an end. She must deliver her child knowing that its father meant to have nothing to do with them, and make plans for the future accordingly.

I shall not attempt to depict the extent of her grief at the news, for that is something she alone can know. Nor shall I describe my clumsy efforts to comfort her in the hours and days that followed. I can only say that each fresh wail that escaped her lips was a knife to my own heart and conscience. At last, however, she grew calm enough to decide she would prefer to retire with her child to the country as soon as she recovered from her lying-in.

While awaiting this event, I had time to think about how imperfectly I had discharged my responsibility to my ward. Not only that, but to reflect with sad irony on the resemblance between the destiny of mother and daughter. I had equally failed them both. I had failed to protect Beth from an unscrupulous man, just as I had failed her mother Eliza those years before.

There seem to be two opposing schools of thought amongst Englishmen when it comes to children and the fairer sex. The first says that, due to his perceived superiority, a man rules by God-given right; the rest are merely chattel. The other says that strength is not given as an invitation to dominate the weak but with a profound obligation to protect those who cannot protect themselves. Unfortunately, my father had been of the first order. I profess to be of the second but have very little to show for it.

When our elopement plans were found out by my father, Eliza had been at a natural disadvantage, as a woman not yet fully grown.

And I, at seventeen, had been little more than a child myself, much as I would have quarreled with that characterization at the time. As such, we, neither of us had any power over what would happen next.

My father ordered us both to his study and shut us up there with himself. He sat behind his desk and left us to stand before him, as he had always done whenever one of us was in trouble before, although the gravity of those earlier occasions now paled by comparison. Just as in any court of law, the accused stands in the dock; the judge sits and pronounces sentence.

Leaning back with his hands folded together on his chest, Father barked out, "Well, what have you to say for yourselves?"

I looked briefly at Eliza and then back to my father. "It was my fault, sir, my doing. I talked Eliza into it. If punishment is due, it is due to me alone."

Laughing incredulously, he shot to his feet. "*If?*" he cried. He leant forward across his desk to glare at me. "Can there be any doubt of it? You have disobeyed me in the extreme, boy. You have attempted to deceive me and plotted such treachery against me and against this entire family as can never be forgiven. Had not the wicked scheme been discovered in time, the damage done would have been incalculable. Yes, by God, there is punishment due, and to you *both*!"

After a long, indignant exposition on these themes, he finally dismissed us under the escort of a footman. We were each to go to our separate bedchambers, there to contemplate our sins until he had decided what to do with us. We were not to leave our rooms for any reason in the meantime. And to assure our obedience to this decree, a footman would stand guard in the passageway round the clock. We were, in effect, to be prisoners under house arrest.

We left my father's study with leaden hearts. My feet dragged as we walked together towards our mutual but separate captivities, daring to hold hands along the way. Why not? What more could my father do to us than what he already contemplated?

Just as we reached the stairs, Eliza leant her head close to mine. "It was my maid who betrayed us, Christopher," she told me in low tones. "Although I do not believe she meant to. Still, it is my fault. I should not have trusted her to keep our secret."

I squeezed her hand. "Do not reproach yourself, my dear Eliza. You could not have known."

A bit further on, she whispered, "I have never seen my uncle so angry. What do you think he means to do to us?"

"I can hardly imagine," I answered honestly, matching her hushed voice. Then I added, "And it hardly matters either, for one thing is sure; we will never be given another opportunity to escape together." I immediately wished I had kept this last to myself, however, for I perceived that Eliza was weeping again. "Never mind, dearest. Between us we will think of something. Do not lose heart."

Despite our sluggish pace and many little procrastinations along the way, we soon reached the point of ultimate separation. My room came first. I kissed Eliza's hand and regretfully let her go. There I lingered in the doorway, not willing to part with the sight of my sweet friend any sooner than absolutely necessary. At her door, she turned for one last look back at me before slipping inside and out of view. I then likewise closed my door, wondering when – or if? – I would ever see Eliza again.

Alone in my room, it did not take me long to divine what my father's course of action would likely be. To be certain of no further attempts at elopement, Eliza and I must be separated by more than two doors, a footman, and a short length of corridor. My father was not so foolish as to believe that such unsubstantial obstacles would keep us apart for long. No, he would perceive that we were not to be left in the same house together. One of us would be sent away; that much was clear. But which one?

The answer to that question was not difficult to develop either. My father needed Eliza at Delaford so that he could be sure of her marrying my brother as soon as possible. He had no use for me, however. I was unnecessary, dispensable, entirely in the way. No, worse than that; I was nothing to him but a dangerous liability, and therefore *I* would be the one to go. Where, was the only question that remained.

In view of all these things, and of the likelihood of our being denied a farewell suitable to lifelong companions forced to separate, I set to work at once writing a parting letter that must perform the office as well as possible. I wrote first and foremost of my steadfast love and faithfulness to Eliza, of the fact that I would never give her up as long as I had life and breath left in my body. And I pleaded with her to do the same for me.

...Remember, my darling, no matter what occurs or what he may say, your uncle cannot legally force you to comply with his wishes as to marriage. No doubt he will bring uncomfortable pressure to bear, but you are strong. Resist him, I beg you, and keep on resisting until he is obliged to give up the idea of your marrying Max, or until some other lucky occurrence should intervene to release you. No matter how long it may take, I swear this to you. I will never stop working to free us both so that we can be together again, this time as man and wife...

Such were my promises to Eliza, made from my heart in hopes of fortifying her for the difficulties ahead.

That evening, I bribed the girl who brought up my supper tray to deliver the missive. And the next morning, when the same girl brought me breakfast, I was able to confirm – by the expedient of an answering note – that she had done so. It was only a few lines, obviously scribbled in haste.

My dearest Christopher,
I depend on you so. I do not know how I shall manage if, as you expect, we are soon parted. It would be too cruel a fate by far! But I will try to be strong and remember what you have said. All my love, always...
Eliza

Not much, but it was a little something for me to hang onto when I was indeed sent packing the next morning with no chance of saying goodbye to Eliza face to face.

I was going to my sister's house in Suffolk, my father informed me. Clarissa and her husband, who could not yet know of the plan, would receive the happy tidings by an express message the day before I arrived on their doorstep. They would, by the same means, be strictly charged to look after me – in short, to do whatever was necessary to keep me there until such time as my father notified them that I was allowed to go free.

"How long will that be, sir?" I asked with as much defiance and disdain as I could muster.

"How long will depend entirely on your cousin," he said, continuing the business-like tone he had taken with me that morning. "The sooner she is married to your brother, the sooner you may be at liberty again."

"And if she should not ever consent to it?"

"Then she will be a very miserable creature, and you may have seen the last of her and of your home both. For she will never be allowed to leave Delaford, and you shall surely never be allowed to return, until after Eliza is made your sister-in-law."

~~*~~

My brother-in-law's estate in a remote part of Suffolk is called Freshings, and there I was, days later, delivered by my father's coach under the guard of two of his most loyal footmen. No doubt they had been enticed by promises of reward for their success (and probably dismissal if they failed), because I found them most immovable. Whatever private sympathy they might have felt for my plight, their own interests prevented them from making the slightest deviation in my favor. And I, of course, had no money to tempt them to do so; my father had seen to that as well. It seemed he had thought of everything.

Under other circumstances, I should not have been sorry to be coming to stay with my sister. I had seen her but rarely in the five years since her marriage, but I retained a strong impression of her kindness to me from earlier days. Of her husband, I knew almost nothing. He was nearly old enough to be my father, and those few times I had seen him, he had remained aloof and distant. Consequently, I could not imagine he was very keen to have me thrust upon him now, to have a rebellious lad of seventeen placed in his charge for an indeterminate length of time.

And indeed, Sir Stanley Vincent, baronet, looked none too pleased to see me when I arrived. He greeted me civilly enough, however, and then left me to my sister, who showed me upstairs to my assigned guest apartment to wash and change.

"Oh, Christopher!" she said after I returned to her below and she had settled us both in a sitting room with some refreshments. "What a hornet's nest you have stirred up at Delaford! Did you really try to elope with our cousin? Do take some tea, and then tell me all about it."

She handed me a steaming cup, and I drew a long draught of it, feeling the welcome burn run down my throat to warm my belly. It had been a long and difficult journey, not only because of the ordinary discomforts of travel, though those had been plenty enough. They had been compounded by the burden of anxiety for Eliza and myself that I carried all the way from Dorset. Although never entirely forgotten, our troubles would from time to time hit me afresh when I least expected it. I have been to the seaside and experienced the power of a cold wave to overwhelm, knocking the unsuspecting bather off his feet, pressing him down nearly to drowning. That is what I liken the feeling to. One minute I thought I was keeping my head above water, and the next I found myself going under again.

My sister must have read some of this in my countenance. "Poor thing," she said. "What you must have suffered, and Eliza too, of course."

Her compassion – and her mention of Eliza's name – only made worse what I felt at that moment, dredging up more unwelcome sensibilities from the well of my soul. When I at last gained mastery over myself again, I spoke, pouring out to my sister the whole story over the course of the next half of an hour. I held nothing back; there was no reason to. I had no secrets anymore. My misery was thus laid entirely bare before her.

"So you have no hope at all that our father will relent?" Clarissa asked with pity and concern when I had done.

"None whatever. You know how… how determined he can be. Eliza is to be sacrificed to his avarice for the sake of keeping Delaford afloat."

"And what of Max? Can he do nothing about it either?"

"Perhaps he could. I am convinced he will not, however. Although he cares nothing for Eliza, I believe he does care for securing his financial future and consequence. He knows he must marry an heiress, and here is one captive and conveniently close at hand."

I may have gained my sister's sympathy through this exhaustive account, but as she explained, she could not help me with my real object – returning to Delaford to rescue Eliza. She and Sir Stanley were under my father's most vehement constraint to act as my firm if benevolent keepers. As they knew perfectly well, he was not a man to be crossed.

~~*~~

I soon discovered that I had comparative freedom at Freshings. I could do as I liked so long as I made no attempt to leave. No locked doors or armed guards barred my way. Such precautions were unnecessary. My highly effectual jailers were the remote location and my abject poverty. With no way or means to travel (for I was denied access to the stables as well), I was highly unlikely to fly. It was well over two hundred miles from Freshings to Delaford, and I could hardly set out on foot with no money for food, transportation, or lodging. As desperate as I was to return to Eliza, even *I* could see it was hopeless.

I could only pray and bide my time, making myself useful and agreeable to my sister and brother-in-law in hopes of winning at least their respect, if not some eventual concession in my favor. On the grounds of needing something to do, I soon taught my sister to call on me for every trifling errand or chore. I was always ready to provide another hand at cards of an evening, or an alternative musician at the piano-forte when my sister preferred to be spared. Sir Stanley soon found I was an adequate opponent at billiards as well.

None of these tasks were irksome to me, for having no employment at all would surely have been the severest punishment. Under my current strain, I needed to keep occupied or run mad.

Becoming acquainted with my three-year-old nephew was the most surprising compensation during this period of detention. Calvin was a precocious lad, full of mischief, and I devoted many hours to his amusement – both in the nursery and out of doors. He liked games of all sorts, so long as none of them lasted above fifteen or twenty minutes. Then he must be on to some new entertainment. Clarissa repeatedly professed her gratitude for my help with the energetic child, but I believe it really was the beleaguered nursery maid whose undying devotion I earned. Pity *she* was in no position to assist me.

In this manner, my first month at Freshings passed away. Although I never gave up hope that I would hit upon some scheme to achieve Eliza's freedom and my own, when I marked her seventeenth birthday on the calendar, I could not help but feel a certain desperation, for I knew that now the pressure upon her must begin in earnest. I could only imagine what I much later learnt to be true of my father's cruel tactics. While she refused his demand that she marry my brother, he browbeat her relentlessly, allowing her no liberty, no society, and no amusements, not even books or music. A sensitive creature like Eliza was not born to live in such blankness. Her lively mind needed stimulation, company, and conversation as much as her body air to breathe. Yet I prayed she would be strong and persevere until I could come to her.

Had it been possible, I would gladly have traded places with her, for I believe I could have tolerated those conditions better. In any case, I should have been willing to spare her the punishment she endured. By comparison, my lot was far too easy. My greatest suffering derived from the suspense that preyed upon my mind – not knowing how things stood at Delaford and especially how Eliza fared.

As it happened, however, the suspense of those questions did not last as long as I had expected, nor even so long as I could have hoped. For after only another month, a letter from Delaford arrived for Sir Stanley, and inside it was tucked a note to me from Eliza herself. The handwriting I instantly recognized; the signature I did not.

Dear Christopher,

    I know you will think me very weak, and I daresay I am, but I could not hold out against your father's persecution for long, not without you by my side to support me. So I have done as he wanted; I have married Max, placing my fortune entirely in his hands. It is a marriage of conven-ience only, as you know, for neither his heart nor mine is presently engaged in the union. But I have been persuaded to hope for the best. Perhaps in time some mutual regard may grow between my husband and myself.

    In any case, the deed is now done, and your pardon is achieved. That is the one consolation upon which I depend, that you will soon be home – my friend once again and now my brother as well. Although much less than we hoped for, it is something to be salvaged from the situation. It will be

enough for us, I pray. It must be. Alas, we are obliged to
henceforth abandon all other thoughts and former designs.
My dearest friend, please forgive me.
Mrs. Maximus Brandon

What must be the effect of such a letter on one so young and so violently in love? To be called 'friend' and 'brother' only, with no hope of anything more, was a stabbing bolt to my heart. To think of Max, who I knew could sometimes be nearly as brutish as my father, being Eliza's lord and master, ruling over everything she did and said, having the right to treat her as he liked, to take his pleasures without any regard for her wishes...

After reading this dreadful missive and feeling the full impact of the words therein, I ran outside to the shrubbery to be sick.

~9~

I had not thought it possible that I could return home to Delaford with a heart even heavier than when I left it less than three months earlier, but such was the case. Before, there had at least been a shred of hope to hang onto, an outside chance that Eliza and I would find a way to be together in the end. Now even that feeble possibility had been dashed. The undeniable facts were that Eliza was married to my brother, and it could not be undone. Indeed, it would be wrong to even wish for it – the failure of their union or Eliza's release from it, only achievable by Max's death.

No, I told myself that I must become reconciled to what had happened, and for Eliza's sake, put the best possible construction on the situation. Max would grow to love Eliza – how could he not once he knew her as well as I did? – and they would be happy together. It was my duty to do everything possible to promote rather than endanger that favorable conclusion. Coming between them would be a sin. Berating Eliza for weakness and what felt like a personal betrayal would be pointless, even cruel. Thinking and speaking of what might have been would not avail a thing. Instead, I must wish them both well and find myself a different path from what I had previously imagined; I must find something else worthwhile to do with my life.

All the long trip home by post, I repeated these sentiments in my mind, trying to convince myself that they were not only true but reasonable.

At last I arrived at Delaford, but it was nothing like the homecoming that I had imagined so many times while I was away and still hoping for a better outcome. There were no fervent embraces with Eliza – or with anybody else, for that matter – no tender words exchanged. It was not even the less elevated reunion I had prepared myself for since receiving Eliza's letter, where she had spoken of at least sharing mutual consolation. No, it was far worse than that, for Eliza would barely speak to or look at me.

As for my father, he took no particular interest in my return, which did not surprise me. I would not have expected him to, other than perhaps to crow about his success over me. I *was* surprised, though, that he did not look as if gaining his principle object had resulted in much gratification. In fact, he appeared a bit... a bit off, perhaps a bit faded. He had developed a cough, as well, and seemed rather thinner than when I had last seen him.

When I later asked my brother about it, however, he only said, "He *is* well beyond fifty now. What do you expect of such an old man, except that he should be in decline?"

I had no opportunity at all for private discourse with Eliza that first day. The next, after I had breakfasted alone, I came across a stranger standing in the front hall – a respectable looking man of neat but not quite genteel appearance with a number of parcels piled on the floor beside him. "Good morning," I said. "Can I help you?"

"Good morning, young sir," he replied crisply, with an accent distinctly French. "I am Monsieur Armand, and I am here to paint a lady's portrait – your sister, perhaps? In any case, the help I require is already on its way, I trust."

Indeed, just then Eliza and two footmen appeared simultaneously. Eliza stopped short when she saw me, and then proceeded to welcome Monsieur Armand and direct the footmen in the disposal of the artist's things – his supplies to the conservatory and his portmanteau to the bedchamber assigned for his use.

"Robert will take you to your room first, if you like, Monsieur," she told him. "And then he can show you the way to the conservatory. I will meet you there shortly."

"Very good, Mrs. Brandon," he agreed, and then he and the footmen went off about their business.

Hearing Eliza being addressed by that name – Max's wife and not mine – grated on my nerves, but I would not waste whatever little time we might have together thinking about that. And yet at first we just stood there like two statues, six feet apart, arms at our sides, staring at one another.

I broke the silence. Unable to say any of the things I wished to say to her, I merely asked, "You... you are having your portrait painted?"

She nodded. "It was your father's idea. Your mother had her likeness taken on the occasion of her marriage too." She dropped her eyes at this.

"Yes, of course – the one that hangs in the gallery upstairs."

"He intends that mine will hang next to it. I am honored."

"My mother would have liked that. You know that she had a great fondness for you." We were both silent again, until I went on. "Monsieur Armand is to stay until it is completed?"

"That is correct. I am to sit for him daily, in the conservatory for the light. But it will probably take above a week, I understand, maybe two."

"I will look forward to seeing your portrait when it is finished."

We continued standing there awkwardly another minute, and I could not help being shocked – shocked and dreadfully saddened – at the change in us. Once we had been the closest of friends and confidantes. We had had no secrets between us, no thoughts withheld one from the other. No restraints. There could have been no two hearts more in tune, or so I had believed. Now we were reduced to this: stilted conversation about things of no importance across an unbridgeable gap. A perverted barrier had arisen between us, and I had to do something to break through it.

"Look at me, Eliza," I began desperately, taking one step closer to her.

She did look up and meet my eyes then. Before I could continue or she respond, however, somebody else spoke.

"She is 'Mrs. Brandon' to you, little brother," said Max, approaching and taking hold of her elbow, "and I would be very much obliged if you would remember that."

I stepped back again. "Of course," I said, suppressing my consternation at the reproof and the untimely interruption. "Please pardon my mistake, Mrs. Brandon, Max."

He then steered her away from me and down the corridor.

As I observed Eliza in those first few days, she made a credible show of playing the dutiful wife to my brother, whether by free choice or under some kind of compulsion, I could not be sure. I only knew that much of the light had gone from her eyes, the former spiritedness of her nature sadly tamed. I considered that these changes might be merely the unavoidable consequence of giving up one's childhood and its fanciful dreams in order to accept adult responsibilities and the realities of life. No doubt an astute observer would see the same changes in me.

In any case, Eliza seemed resigned to her fate. Perhaps that was just as well, I thought. Much as my vanity would have been flattered by a tearful demonstration that she could not live without me, it would have done more harm than good to us both. Acceptance of the situation must be the first necessary step, the foundation upon which to build something worthwhile and sustainable for the future. After all, in order to move forward, one must give up constantly looking backwards to the past. That applied equally to us both.

I hoped these resolutions were true, for her if not yet for myself. I could not always resist seeking Eliza out, though, especially since I now knew where she could be found for the better part of each day: in the conservatory with Monsieur Armand, probably unguarded except by a maid's attendance.

I came in silently at the back more than once, just for the satisfaction of looking at her for fifteen minutes while she posed for the artist. She sat regally in a high-backed wicker chair with palm fronds arching over her head. She wore her pale yellow gown of satin and lace – the exact one that she knew I favored because it brought out the flecks of gold in her eyes. *Had she chosen it for me?* Her honey brown hair was swept up on top of her head, exposing that exquisite neck. One hand lay in her lap, holding a fan, and the other rested on the arm of the chair. Her head angled slightly away and up, as if she might be following the movements of a butterfly on the wing.

She looked enchanting. An angel, even if perhaps a slightly dejected one.

My first two visits to the conservatory went undetected. I slipped in and out again without being observed by anybody, not even Eliza herself. Luck failed me on my third attempt, however. I had not been watching for above five minutes when Monsieur Armand told Eliza, "You may relax now, Mrs. Brandon. We are finished for the day."

While he set about cleaning his brushes, Eliza unbent herself, stood, and stretched. Even this was fascinating to me, and so I remained in my imperfectly concealed location longer than I should have. Looking about the room, then, Eliza noticed me. A frown, not a smile, creased her face, and she signaled with a jerk of her head that I should meet her off to the side of the room.

"What are you doing here, Christopher?" she asked in an impatient whisper.

"I merely wished to observe for a few minutes," I said quietly in my own defense. "I would never have interrupted your concentration or Monsieur Armand's progress."

"Nevertheless, you should not be here. If Maximus knew of it…" She stopped abruptly.

"What if he should? I am doing nothing to be ashamed of, am I? Unless you mean we are never to meet at all without him present, as if he… as if you cannot trust me to behave honorably."

She hesitated. "He would not like it; that is enough. Really, Christopher, you will only make things more difficult for me by trying to see me. Please stay away!" she implored.

I could hardly believe my ears. "Very well," I said slowly. "If that is truly what you want."

"It is. Now I must go." And she hurried off.

Spurred on by this disheartening exchange, I decided then and there to move forward with a tentative plan that had been forming in my mind. So instead of leaving the conservatory myself, I had a word with Monsieur Armand. I asked him to paint a miniature of Eliza for me alongside the full-sized portrait commissioned by my father. Now that I was home again, I had access to some funds of my own, out of which I could pay him. After agreeing upon a sum between us, I paid him a bit extra for saying nothing about the miniature to anybody else.

Eliza's words had reminded me of my earlier resolution to promote rather than endanger the success of her marriage. If my presence would only make things more difficult for her, as she said… If I was not to be allowed any friendly talk with her but was, on the contrary, to be always on my guard lest we be found accidentally together… What kind of a way was that to live? No, it would be better to be gone from Delaford altogether.

In the meantime, the best I could do was to keep mainly to myself and try to make a plan for my future elsewhere, one that did not include Eliza.

I was obliged to endure the discomfort of family dinners every evening, however. These consisted mostly of my father and brother discussing estate matters while Eliza and I ate in silence, occasionally catching each other's eye, but never lingering as in former times. She would always drop her gaze first, breaking any connection. There was none of the private communication we had enjoyed as children in the schoolroom and beyond. No nods, winks, or pulling faces. No handholding or kicks beneath the table.

"When do the workers arrive?" my father asked Max at dinner a week after my return home.

"Monday, a fortnight hence," Max said in brief reply.

When no further clarification followed, I asked why workers were coming to Delaford.

"Repairs to the roof," my father explained. "You know it has needed attention for years, and now..." Here he turned to Eliza with an artificial smile. "...thanks to my dear daughter-in-law, we are finally able to move ahead. The crumbling chimney pieces in the south wing are to be restored as well."

They had certainly wasted no time putting Eliza's coveted fortune to use. My belly burned at the thought, and I looked across the table to see how *she* bore it. But Eliza remained composed. It was not new information to her, of course. Then I remembered something else. "If there will be workers here for the roof, Father, I hope you will send them round to Mr. Jones's place as well."

"Mr. Jones's? What are you speaking of?"

"I thought perhaps you would remember, sir, but Mr. Jones's cottage has a leaky roof. When I was there before – before I left for Suffolk, that is – he asked me to remind you about it."

"Oh, that," he said dismissively, with a wave of his hand. "Yes, of course I remember. Perhaps, if there is time."

I was silent for a moment but then felt compelled to speak again. "The matter appeared rather urgent to me, sir. It seems they have been waiting for months already, with the rain coming in. Surely we have a duty to our tenants..."

Father interrupted me, harshly. "I heard you before, Christopher, and I will attend to the matter in my own good time. Now leave it! I do not need you to tell me my duty. Do you understand?"

"Yes, sir." I dropped my eyes to my plate again.

A little older and a little thinner he might be, but my father remained firmly in control.

10

I was no closer to a solution to my dilemma about my future when a few days later my father dropped an interesting bit of news over dinner.

"Sir Nugent Middleton has invited us to Barton on Wednesday, and I said we would come. It seems John has taken a commission in the army and is soon bound for the East Indies. By way of a sendoff for him, they are convening a little house party. We shall go and stay two nights."

I glanced at Eliza to see how she received the news, which in former days, I was sure, would have animated her excessively. Her face had always revealed so much about the contents of her lively mind. And not long ago, I had known her every subtle twitch of muscle and nerve, every mood and thought. Now, her expression was inscrutable. I was entirely shut out. She might be as indifferent as she seemed, or she might have lately learnt to school her features, hiding her true feelings behind those blank eyes. I no longer knew.

As for myself, I was far from indifferent about the invitation to Barton, but then I wondered. "Am *I* to be of the party, sir?" I asked my father, thinking that I might be denied on the grounds that I was still being punished for my recent rebellion.

"You may go," he answered. "Not that you deserve any special diversion, mind, but better you should be included than that I should be asked why you were not allowed to come. There can be no occasion to speak of our recent... our recent unpleasantness before such respectable friends as the Middletons. See that you remember that."

The other reason I was to go to Barton, I later suspected, was to be sure I was kept separate from Eliza. I learnt that she was to remain behind to finish her portrait with Monsieur Armand. Considering all that had gone before, it would have no doubt been judged imprudent for the two of us to be left together in the house without my father's or my brother's presence to serve as a deterrent to bad behavior.

I wanted to go to Barton in any case. Not only did I desire relief from the bleak outlook at home, but I was also intrigued by my friend John's decision to enter on a military life, so much so that it immediately sparked my own imagination.

When we arrived at Barton, I wasted no time cornering my friend. Although five years my senior, and therefore closer to my brother's age, John had always got on much better with me. Max had no interests in common with John and no patience for his frivolous ways. In contrast, John's light, good-humored manner – as well as his willingness to give consequence to a younger boy like myself – had exactly suited me during that stage of my life. Had we seen each other more often, we might have been very close indeed. Even so, I felt more of a kinship with him than with my own brother.

"What's this about your going to the East Indies, John?" I asked him at once. "I never figured you for a military man."

"Ah, it is the adventure of the thing, my good fellow! The travel to exotic ports! The romance! How could I resist it? There is little enough to hold my interest here, after all. Since I returned from Oxford, I have been about going out of my mind with boredom in this rural outpost. No balls. No parties. No company. Why, you cannot imagine the lengths to which I had to go just to get my father to finally agree to this little house party! When I inherit Barton, it will be different. I shall have the place full of lively people at all times."

"But to go all the way to India? That is a bit extreme, is it not?"

"Nonsense, my boy! The distance is part of the adventure, you know. And one must do these things with a bit of style, after all."

"Style? I hope you have not chosen this path simply for how well you will look in a uniform!"

He pulled himself up a little straighter, admiring his reflection in the glass of the nearest window. "So you think I *will* look well in uniform? I cannot help but agree with you there. Cut quite a dashing figure, I daresay. Just the thing to impress the ladies. Perhaps then I may have my pick for the future Lady Middleton, eh?"

"You might have anyway, with the promise of this estate and a title. Consider what my suit will be compared to yours, not that I ever intend to marry. Not anymore." I added the last under my breath.

"Ah, yes," he said, placing his hand on my shoulder. "I was sorry to hear about your little Eliza. Very sorry indeed. Married to your brother, too! That is particularly hard. But you will live to love again, friend. You must! There are plenty of other fish in the sea, as they say. And since I mean to catch a very pretty one for myself, it will not hurt to sweeten the deal a little. I am convinced that the added consequence afforded by military honors will be just the thing. Well worth a little discomfort in the end."

A little discomfort? I had read enough to know that the conditions in the Indian subcontinent were more than a little uncomfortable for the average Englishman: the long voyage there to start, then the unrelenting heat, the blood-thirsty insects, and the tropical diseases. That was not even mentioning the very real possibility of falling in a military conflict. I wondered if John was really robust enough to withstand it all. I also wondered at his father's willingness to let him go. John was his heir, after all, followed by four girls before finally a spare son had been born. But that boy was presently only a lad of eight.

"Your father does not mind your going?" I asked.

"Mind? Not a bit of it! He will be glad to have me out from under foot, I should think. Besides, he says it will be the making of me. Served a short stint in the army himself when he was a young man, you know. Says it was the best thing he ever did." Then his eyes lit up, and he said, "Come with me! By heavens, that would be just the thing. Deuced, but we would have some fun together then. You must be eighteen soon, and surely your father can spare you."

There was no question of that; my father could spare me very well. And although the conversation moved on to other things, John and I frequently returned to this scheme over the length of our stay. I had no particular passion to see India, but a military life did hold some appeal. To serve one's king and country seemed very noble to me, and I was even more desirous to discover a sense of purpose and belonging, for I could have neither at Delaford. There was nothing for me there anymore.

By the time my father, my brother, and I were on our way home again, I had all but decided. I told them both of my plan and, not surprisingly, it received their ready endorsement. No doubt they were *both* pleased with the idea of being rid of me.

And so I returned to Delaford to wait for my birthday, after which I could take up a commission in His Majesty's army for service in India. Whether or not I would be so fortunate as to meet up with my friend there, I did not know.

Meanwhile, I passed the time riding a great deal, taking solitary walks, and reading everything I could find about the East Indies. And I stayed away from Eliza as much as possible, in accordance with her wishes. The family dinners could not be avoided, but if I chanced to come across her in the house or gardens at any other time, I did not linger. I would only acknowledge her with a nod or a "Mrs. Brandon" and move on.

Should I feel the need to see her face in between times, I could visit the picture gallery upstairs, where her glorious finished portrait now hung, or pull the miniature version from my pocket and gaze at it as long as I wished – something I found myself doing several times a day. Armand had done a fine job of it, and it embodied a true likeness of my darling friend. Unlike the real article, though, this Eliza belonged to me and not my brother. This one I could keep close by my side always. She would accompany me to India. She would never age or grow weary of me. And when I was in an unforgiving mood, I could imagine that the trace of sadness showing in her eye was from her regret for having given me up.

Although my father had seemed hale and hearty while enjoying himself at Barton, once we returned to Delaford it was not long before he began a shocking decline. The medical men called in could do nothing, and before many weeks had elapsed, he was dead and gone.

I cannot pretend to have been much grieved by the loss of him. If I cried, it was entirely for the anguish it caused me to think how close Eliza and I had been to escaping his tyranny. If we had only known… If we had but realized, I am convinced it would have made all the difference. That knowledge would have given Eliza the strength she needed to hold out a few months longer against him; I am sure of it. She never would have consented to marrying Max. By now, my father would have been buried, his autocratic demands with him, and she would still have been free. We might have then married as we had planned, if only…

I wondered if these thoughts tortured Eliza as well. I wondered if she suffered over them as I did. Perhaps she too had bitter sobs and grievances aplenty to stifle, with no means of relief. When I could no longer stifle mine, I took myself off to release them in the wilderness, miles away from everybody. To the deer and the woodcock I bitterly complained aloud. To the hare and the fox I shouted, bemoaning the injustice of it all. But mostly to God. How could He have allowed this to happen?

After one day nearly breaking my hand, trying to put it through a place in the wall where I imagined Max's face, I knew it was time to become reasonable again. Dwelling any longer on such regrets would surely drive me to madness or worse. And I had not yet so much despaired of life and hope as to welcome the end of everything.

I was eighteen by then, and all the arrangements were in place for my entry into military service. So after the funeral rites were completed, I was free to go. There was no earthly reason to linger any longer in the oppressive atmosphere of Delaford. It only remained for me to assemble my traveling kit and say my farewells, which I did with dispatch. Delay would only prolong the misery of going, of leaving her.

My brother – no longer the heir apparent but the heir in fact – had deftly slipped into my father's still-warm shoes the moment they became vacant, putting into immediate practice all he had learnt by the master's tutelage. I knew that under him things would go on at Delaford much as they ever had, with or without me. I could expect no change for the better.

Max did make one small alteration almost at once, however. He had Eliza's portrait brought down from the upstairs gallery to be hung prominently in the great hall instead. At first, I could not comprehend it, for I saw no other sign that he had developed a sudden passion for her. But upon further reflection, I understood.

The walls of the great hall were furnished with items meant to impress visitors as soon as they entered the house: hunting trophies, ancient armaments, and other displays of wealth and importance. In that vein, the picture of Eliza fit. Not only was it an expensive and impeccably done masterpiece, the subject herself represented a valuable acquisition. Max did not love his wife; she was simply another exquisite trophy, meant to impress.

I exchanged words with Max the night before my departure. Nothing of consequence, really, just what he thought every father figure should say on such an occasion, I believe. He told me to be careful with my money, to guard myself against the wiles of camp-following women, to fight bravely when called on to do so, and to keep the name of Brandon from being sullied or disgraced.

Then in the morning, with the carriage at the door and my bags already loaded into it, I stood gazing at Eliza's portrait while I waited for her and Max to appear for our final farewells. They came in together. I shook my brother's hand and then asked if I might have a private minute with Eliza before I left.

"Whatever you have to say to my wife, you can say in front of me." That was his firm answer, and so once again Eliza and I must part unsatisfactorily, unable to say to each other all that we wanted and needed to.

"Very well," I said. I turned and took her hand, wondering if this consolation too would be denied me. Max held his peace, however. I suppose he thought it could do no harm since I would be leaving in the next breath.

Looking into Eliza's face, I glimpsed a bit of the girl I had known before. Her eyes were not expressionless, as I had so often seen them of late. They were not doors closed to me. They were open and brimming with unshed tears. "I wish you would not go," she said in little above a whisper.

"It will be for the best; you will see. This is your house now – yours and Max's – and you will be better able to build a good life for yourselves here if I am gone."

"But what will become of you in that unfriendly, foreign place? I am afraid I will never see you again."

"We will meet again… when the time is right. I am sure of it. Please understand, Eliza. This is something I must do. A man must learn to make his way in the world, and this is my chance. When I see you next, I hope you will be impressed by how I have distinguished myself."

"I care *nothing* for such things," she sobbed. "I only pray you will keep safe."

"I thank you for your prayers. Know that I will be praying for you as well, my dear sister and friend."

Max cut in. "That will do, Brother," he said, mildly but firmly. "Off you go now."

I looked once more into Eliza's eyes, squeezed her hand, and released it. Turning, I strode quickly through the door, not allowing myself a glance behind. *Move forward,* I told myself. *Do not look back.*

11

I thought I was doing right by my sweet friend. Although I loved Eliza with my whole being, I believed it was the honorable thing to withdraw, to sacrifice my own desire to be near her in order to give her unfortunate marriage to my brother the best chance of succeeding. And now, all these years later, I am being called on to do the same again. I must deny my inclinations and step aside so that the woman I love can be happy with another.

I had lately returned from making arrangements for Eliza's daughter Beth to retire to the country with her own child – a healthy boy she named Henry. Then in London, at Mr. Palmer's, I was greeted by the information that the two elder Miss Dashwoods were arrived in town, staying with Mrs. Jennings.

My foolish heart leapt at the news. Though I had little enough reason to hope for any revolution in Miss Marianne's indifferent sentiments towards me, at least my hungry eyes would behold her once more. My soul would exult in her presence after long weeks of separation. That was something. I did not hesitate; I went at once to call upon them.

My first glimpse was of Miss Marianne coming excitedly towards the door. She took one look at me, and her face fell. Then she fled from the room. I had not expected her to be thrilled to see me, but I admit to being astonished at her abrupt behavior. I could only think of one explanation, one that would not bear mentioning before her sister. "Is your sister ill?" I asked Elinor instead.

"Good evening, Colonel," she said, avoiding my question for the moment. "What a pleasure it is to see you again, and I thank you for the compliment of your calling on us so promptly. It is delightful indeed to meet with such a friend as you in a place where I had thought to know no one."

Elinor seemed intent on doubling her civilities to make up for the share her sister had neglected.

"You really must pardon Marianne," she continued. "I'm afraid the strain of our three-day journey has fatigued her unduly. Just before you arrived, in fact, she began to complain of a headache and wanting to lie down for a short while. No doubt by tomorrow she will be recovered. Perhaps you will see her then if not later today."

I doubted that fatigue was to blame for Miss Marianne's look of crushing disappointment when she saw me, but it would have been impolite to seem to disbelieve Elinor, who was clearly doing her best at trying to minimize my own disappointment. So I said no more on that subject, instead moving on to the usual inquiries about their journey and the friends they had left behind.

"Have you been here in town all this time since we saw you last?" she then asked.

She could not have known what discomfort such a question would give me – the unhappy memories, the things I could not speak of. I answered as well as I could, saying that for the most part I had been. Elinor accepted my incomplete explanation with no further curiosity, just as I had accepted hers minutes before.

I doubted I would be so fortunate with Mrs. Jennings, who soon came in. "Oh, Colonel!" she said, with her usual cheerfulness, "I am monstrous glad to see you, and sorry I could not come down before. I do beg your pardon. But I have been forced to look about myself a little and settle my affairs. For it is a long while since I have been at home, and you know one has always a world of little odd things to do after one has been away for any time. And then I have had Cartwright to settle with. Lord, I have been as busy as a bee ever since dinner! But pray, Colonel, how came you to conjure out that I should be in town today?"

"I had the pleasure of hearing it at Mr. Palmer's, where I have been dining."

"Oh, you did! Well, and how do they all do at their house? I warrant Charlotte is a fine size by now!" – an allusion to Mrs. Palmer's expectant condition.

"Mrs. Palmer appeared quite well to me, and I am commissioned to tell you that you will certainly see her tomorrow."

"Aye, to be sure, I thought as much. Well, Colonel, I have brought two young ladies with me, you see." Then she looked about herself. "That is, you see but one of them now. There is another somewhere about – your friend Miss Marianne, which you will not be sorry to hear. Dear me, I do not know what you and Mr. Willoughby will do between you about her. Oh, it is a fine thing to be young and handsome! I was young once, but I never was very handsome – worse luck for me. However, I got a very good husband, and I don't know what the greatest beauty can do more than that. Poor man! He has been dead these eight years and better. But Colonel, where have you been since we parted? And how does your business go on? Come, come, let us have no secrets among friends."

"As I was just explaining to Miss Dashwood before you came in, I have been mostly here in town, about my business. I was obliged to go to Delaford for a few days, but unfortunately, it has never been in my power to return to Barton. Now there is no need, for most of my friends are come here."

"Very prettily said, Colonel. I suppose I shall have to be content with that for now. Ah, here is Miss Marianne. And the tea things too. Miss Dashwood, perhaps you would do us the honors?"

While Elinor made the tea, Mrs. Jennings talked on about other things, seldom requiring an answer from me. Although I saw no signs of a headache in Marianne, she was certainly not in spirits – not in spirits to talk to me, in any case. It was so obviously a different caller she had looked for.

~~*~~

My subsequent, almost-daily visits at Berkeley Street were of a similar character. Elinor was kindness itself, whereas her sister seemed always disappointed if not annoyed that I had come. If she would stay to see me at all, she sat in near silence with hands folded and eyes determinedly downcast, as if simply bearing the torment of my presence was the most she could do. Therefore, I was perfectly free to torture myself as much as I liked by gazing at her comely face and form whilst speaking to her sister.

I had not long been back in town, however, when I received the news I had been dreading – the intelligence that Marianne was indeed engaged to that much-pined-for other man, to Willoughby. The talk of it was everywhere.

So when I next called in Berkeley Street, I was not sorry to be received by Miss Dashwood alone. For I had not come to further torment myself with stolen looks at the fair Marianne, now completely out of reach. Nor was I hoping for light and congenial conversation with her sister Elinor. No, I was come for a very particular purpose; I was come to have my worst fears confirmed, to ask that good lady to deal the final, fatal blow to my dying hopes. Whatever else I may have had in mind when I came was of no consequence in the end.

"Good day, Miss Dashwood," I began upon being shown into the drawing room. "I hope my visit is not inconvenient," I added when I noticed pen and paper set out on the writing desk she had so obviously just risen from.

"Good day, Colonel," Elinor said cordially, coming towards me. "I had merely been composing a letter to my mother."

"Oh, I beg your pardon."

"Not at all. I was finished. Do come in and be seated," she said gesturing in the general direction of a settee and chairs.

I heard but did not act on her invitation. Instead, I looked about myself and, as if only just noticing Marianne's absence, I said, "Your sister... I hope she is well."

"Perfectly well, sir, I thank you."

"I thought she seemed... uh, somewhat out of spirits when I was last here."

Elinor made her excuses. "She is perhaps a little fatigued. We, neither of us are accustomed to the more hectic pace of life here in town."

I believed it more likely Marianne was simply not interested in seeing me, not when she only had thoughts and eyes for Willoughby. But I said, "Of course." Then once again I found myself at a loss for words. While I was distractedly considering how to begin, I felt a light touch on my sleeve. Elinor was looking up at me with a wrinkled brow.

"Colonel," she said gently. "Forgive me, but you seem agitated. Are you quite well yourself?"

"I? Oh, yes. Entirely well."

"I am so glad to hear it. Then please, do sit down. Perhaps Marianne will yet join us."

This time I allowed myself to be directed to a chair, and Elinor sat as well. "In truth, Miss Dashwood," I said, "I am not displeased to find you alone."

She accepted this with a nod and waited for me to continue. When I did not, she said, "You have something you wish to discuss with me? I thought that might well be the case. Pray, tell me what it is, Colonel, and I will do my very best to help."

I did not wish to abuse Elinor's kindness or try her patience overly, and yet I could not for the life of me think how to embark upon the real subject of my visit. The truth, I suppose, was that in my heart of hearts I did not genuinely wish to. As long as I remained in some ignorance, I might continue to deny the inevitable. I might continue to hope... And yet I had discovered that I could no longer live in such a state of awful uncertainty. That is why I had come, I reminded myself.

I rose, strode once across the room and back again, breathing deeply and regathering the disorganized shreds of my resolve along the way. Then, in a voice that I fear did little to disguise my perturbation, I said it before I could lose my nerve.

"Miss Dashwood, would you be so good as to tell me when I am to congratulate you on acquiring a brother?"

She frowned. "Forgive me, Colonel, but I do not perfectly comprehend your meaning."

"Doubtless you seek to kindly spare my feelings, Miss Dashwood, but there is no need to dissemble. Your sister's engagement to Mr. Willoughby is very generally known."

"It cannot be generally known," she returned with conviction, "for her own family do not know it."

I was truly taken aback by this. "Forgive me. I am afraid my inquiry has been impertinent. But I had not supposed any secrecy intended, as they openly correspond and their forthcoming marriage is universally talked of."

"How can that be? By whom can you have heard it mentioned?"

"By many, I assure you – by some of whom you probably know nothing and by others with whom you are most intimate: Mrs. Jennings, Mrs. Palmer, and the Middletons. Otherwise I should not have believed it, for where the mind is perhaps rather unwilling to be convinced, it will always find something to support its doubts. But with so much evidence now before me, I can no longer do so. Tell me then, Miss Dashwood, please. Is everything finally settled between them? You understand me, I know, and will tell me the truth. On your honesty and prudence I have the strongest dependence." When she hesitated, I sought to reassure her. "Do not be kind, I beg you; tell me straightaway that I would be a fool to continue to hope, that the endeavor of concealing my... that is to say, of preserving what is left of my dignity is all that remains to me."

Spent, I sat down again. My head dropped forward into my hands as I awaited Elinor's next words like a condemned man dreading the fall of the ax.

It did fall, as I knew it must, although the fatal blow was not as quick and clean as I had desired.

"Oh, Colonel, I *am* sorry," Elinor said. I could hear the dreadful pity in her voice as she attempted to soften the truth with one prevarication or another. But in the end, it meant the same thing; Marianne was indeed lost to me forever, pledged to my mortal enemy.

"And this marriage... this marriage is what she truly desires?" I asked when she had finished. "Do you believe yourself that this is what will make your sister happy?"

She paused, again constructing her answer carefully. "As to your first question, Colonel, there can be no doubt of it. As to the second, it would be nearer the truth to say that I cannot imagine Marianne should ever be happy *without* Mr. Willoughby, for her mind and heart are so entirely set upon having him."

I rose and steadied myself before speaking my parting benediction. "Then to your sister, Miss Dashwood, I wish all imaginable happiness; to Willoughby, that he may endeavor to deserve her."

I ignored Elinor's confused expression and left the house in haste.

I could not explain the reason for my scruples, not at this late date. Perhaps if I had said something earlier, before Marianne had become so deeply entangled... But no, by the time I comprehended the full extent of the danger, it was already too late. Any disclosure then would have been received as the desperate attempt of an unrequited lover to ruin his rival's character in the lady's eyes. And such an accusation would not have been very wide of the mark. However much I might try to plead my case – that it was Marianne's safety alone I was thinking of – there was undeniable self-interest involved as well.

Willoughby's accusations the day of the duel still echoed in my mind:

"For whose best? For Marianne's? I think not. It was for your own! It was done out of spite. You could not have her, and so you intended that I should not either. I have never heard of anything so selfish in my life. If you truly cared for her, you would not seek to spoil her one chance of happiness..."

When it came right down to it, I wanted Marianne to be happy. If this was her one chance, I would not ruin it for her. After all, men could change when sufficiently inspired. Since Willoughby apparently intended to acquire his pleasures honorably this time – by marriage – perhaps he already had.

And so, despite my considerable misgivings, there was nothing for me to do but to pray that those words of blessing I had spoken would come to pass – that Marianne would indeed be happy, and that Willoughby's behavior henceforth would be exactly what it should to deserve such a worthy lady's affection.

I knew I should now put Marianne from my mind and retire to Delaford to lick my wounds. I made ready to do so more than once. Still, as long as she was in town, I felt compelled to stand by – for what purpose, I could not even conceive – at least until she was well and truly married. After that, it would be nobody's right except her husband's to guard her welfare.

Until then, however, I resolved to wait. Perhaps there might yet be some small service I could render. If I was needed, I swore I would not fail her. Whatever the cost, I vowed to do better by Marianne than I had by Eliza or by Rashmi. Even if in the end it meant giving her up.

12

F ive days I waited at my London establishment for news. Five long days, hardly stirring from the house. Again and again I told myself to go, to leave town and Miss Marianne behind me, and yet I could not.

I have more care to stay than will to go.

That line from Shakespeare's great play came to my mind and stayed, circling round and round like a bee buzzing at the hive. What was it that followed? Oh, yes.

Come death and welcome. Juliet wills it so.

That was going too far. Though I was again losing the woman I loved to another man; though I was feeling suddenly very old and tired; though Marianne likely cared little if I lived or died; I did not yet despair of life entirely.

Finally, on the sixth day, when I grew too weary of my own company to remain isolated any longer, I so far broke out of my lethargy as to venture on a few trifling errands of business, one of these being to the stationer's shop in Pall Mall.

I was very far from expecting anything of great consequence to occur there. Yet, while the shop assistant assembled my order, I could not help overhearing the voluble conversation of two ladies who were apparently awaiting their carriage.

"…And so everything is now finally arranged between them?" the tall one with the tremulous voice asked the stout lady with the flamboyant hat.

"Oh, yes! So you see, there need not be any secrecy about it anymore, for the wedding is to take place as soon as possible, within these few weeks."

"How thrilling for Miss Grey! I have heard that Mr. Willoughby is very handsome."

"Fortunate for him that he is! That is what sealed the deal, I daresay. And a shrewd match he has made of it too. 'We might do much better than Mr. Willoughby as to fortune and consequence,' I told Frederica. However, it was no use reasoning with the girl; she insisted on having him, and I cannot argue but what he does cut quite a dashing figure. Such fine manners, too. He must be at home in anybody's drawing room."

"Lucky girl to get the man she wants for a husband. Will they go straight to Combe Magna after the wedding?"

"Yes, indeed. A very pretty property, by all accounts. And he is to have Allenham as well by and by, it is to be presumed, so they may have their pick of which estate to call home. Ah! Here is the carriage."

My astonishment at hearing this intelligence was beyond anything. It was so entirely contrary to what I had been expecting any local gossip to tell me, that I would not believe it – I could not – not without some creditable confirmation. After all, I knew neither of the women whose conversation had told me Willoughby was to marry a Miss Grey instead of a Miss Dashwood.

When they had gone, I turned to the shopkeeper. "Do you know the names of those two ladies who just left?" I asked.

"Not the thin one, sir," he said, "but t'other is Mrs. Ellison. A woman of means she be, too! She and her ward, Miss Grey, comes in every week or two, and they spend quite freely. Like I tells the missus, if only I had a few more Miss Greys and Mrs. Ellisons, I would be able to buy her that fur that she wants so much."

I thanked the man, paid for my parcel, and went out into the street, hardly knowing what to do next.

Mrs. Ellison must certainly be considered a credible source; she must certainly know the identity of the man Miss Grey was engaged to marry and would not speak of it so openly unless it were true. But how could it be? Had Willoughby broken his engagement to Marianne, or had all the other experts in town got it wrong – the Middletons, the Palmers, Mrs. Jennings and all the rest? – all those who had spoken of a definite engagement existing between the two, the engagement which even Elinor had declined to dispute? What could have happened to bring about such a revolution? However, the most important questions in my mind were, did Marianne know about Miss Grey, and how could she possibly bear the disappointment?

I decided to proceed to Berkeley Street at once, not because I was delighted with the prospect of being the one to impart the news that would break Marianne's heart, but because it seemed to me that the only thing worse would be for her to hear it mentioned in the street, as I had. I would spare her that mortification if I could.

When I arrived, however, I soon learnt from Elinor that they already knew of Willoughby's desertion... and the likely inducement; it seemed Miss Grey had fifty thousand pounds. Marianne had been indisposed all day and finally persuaded to go to bed.

"Marianne's sufferings have been very severe," Elinor told me. "I only hope they may be proportionally short. It has been... it *is* a most cruel affliction. Till yesterday, I believe, she never doubted his regard, and even now... Well, in any case, he has been very deceitful! And in some points, there seems a hardness of heart about him."

Now we were speaking of the man as *I* knew him. "There is, indeed," I agreed, firmly. "But perhaps your sister does not consider it quite the same way?"

"You know her disposition and may believe how eagerly she would still justify him if she could."

I opened my mouth to speak and then closed it again. There might come a time to tell what more I knew of Willoughby's character, but not now, I decided. At the moment, it would only be heaping shock upon shock for the Dashwood sisters, sorrow upon sorrow. I would not do that to them.

In any case, the opportunity for private discourse was lost at that point, and the subject necessarily dropped. I remained until after the removal of the tea things and the arrangement of the card parties, but I remained grave and serious with all that was on my mind and with the knowledge of the dear sufferer upstairs.

Before going away, I had occasion for one more private word with Elinor. "I am extremely sorry for your sister, Miss Dashwood, and would that there were something I could do to ease her suffering. If you think of any way I can be of service to either of you –

anything at all – do not hesitate to send to me. It would please me very much to be of some use to you." Then I left the house.

My own disappointment was forgotten; my mind was now entirely consumed with Marianne's pain, which reminded me again of those other ladies of my acquaintance who had also suffered at the hands of unscrupulous men. Once again, history seemed intent upon repeating itself. Could I not have prevented it? – any of it?

My heart ached for them all – for Marianne… for Beth… for Rashmi… and for Eliza, who was the first and foremost sufferer. My conscience still smote me for how I had been an unwitting contributor there, when, at eighteen, I left Delaford for the unfamiliar climes of the East Indies and a military life.

I went off to get myself out of the way. I went off to seek my fortune, with the expectation of distinguishing myself on the field of battle. I went off, as so many young men do, with idealistic notions of fighting for right and nobly serving king and country. I had much to learn.

With the influence of Sir Nugent Middleton and the calling in of certain other favors, I had been able to secure my aim: to become attached to the regiment of my friend John Middleton. Once the misery of months at sea had been endured – enough to put an end to any ideas of instant glamour or glory – there was at least that one point of familiarity to look forward to amongst a sea of new and foreign elements in the port city of Madras.

Our regiment was a unit of the British Army infantry on loan from the Crown to the Honorable East India Company, prepared to fight alongside the Company's own private forces to protect British merchant and trade interests in India. An alliance of strange bedfellows, it seemed to me, but I suppose it is often the case that affairs of state and private financial concerns go hand in glove, regardless of the geographical location.

The idea did give me some unease, however, especially as I learnt more about the Company's business practices – that they were far from above reproach. More than once I asked myself if it were just to use the king's army simply to enable corporation heads and stockholders to line their pockets through, among other things, an illicit opium trade with China. Or was it in service of another addiction altogether – the insatiable desire at home for tea and fine Indian muslins?

My youthful idealism would have been more comfortable with a clear and justifiable enemy to fight against, like the French, who had proved themselves the aggressors so often before. And indeed, sometimes it *was* the French with whom we traded fire, or the Dutch, for they also held territory in India and were never satisfied. But more often we were called in for some uprising of the local populace or to side with one tribal leader at the expense of another less favored. British policy in the East Indies, it seemed to me, was more often decided by consideration of profit and loss than of right and wrong.

Regardless, young men fought and young men died. This remained the one immutable law of any kind of war, just or unjust. I saw friends fall at my side. The so-called enemy too, at least one by my own hand. I try not to think of it. I tell myself it was not my fault; I was merely following orders. I remind myself that he would surely have killed me if I had not struck first. And yet I expect that man's dark and terrified face will haunt me as long as I live.

A complete account of my military years could fill a book, but I do not wish to dwell on these things. It is enough to say that through them I received a thorough education. I gained a more complete and accurate knowledge of the world itself: its tremendous size, exotic beauty, its diversity of landscapes and peoples. I was taught much about the character of man, witnessing examples of both the best and the worst of which human beings are capable. And I learnt a great deal about myself as well – of what I could accomplish and what I could endure. I left England a boy and returned a man.

I do not regret my military experience. I only regret – and will to my dying day – what my decision to go to India cost Eliza, for my being so far away ensured that she had no one to help her when her situation became desperate.

I received no direct correspondence from her while I was away, nor did I send any. My only letters came from Max – perhaps one every six months and much delayed by the transit time. He rarely mentioned anything about his wife, that is, until the devastating missive which arrived when I had been gone from home somewhat above two years. After a few notations of commonplace news, he wrote...

...You should probably know that Eliza is gone.

Gone? My heart thudded against the wall of my chest. Did he mean she was dead? *Oh, God, no!* I hastened on.

...She proved an inconstant woman and an unfaithful wife. Now, she has run off with her lover, I am sorry to inform you, and I have had no choice but to start the long process of divorce proceedings against her. Where she is at this time, I have no idea. Nor do I care. I only hope never to see her again...

The words on the page blurred before my eyes, and I had to sit down. I could not believe Eliza would ever behave in such an unchaste manner, not the tender innocent I had known. If it were true, I could only imagine that she had been driven to it by prolonged cruelty.

The shock of this news was so severe that it threw me into a deep and protracted gloom of spirits, one from which I believe I have never fully recovered. Its effects on me were even more devastating than when I had learnt of Eliza's marriage. For two days, I could not carry on my duties and had to claim illness until I was at least a little restored. Thinking of what my sweet friend must be suffering – what she must have been suffering right along without my knowing it... Considering the manner of life she had sunk to – a fall from which no recovery would ever be possible... It was too dreadful to contemplate. And there I was, thousands of miles away and completely powerless to help.

Indeed, it would be three more years before I was released from my military obligations and able to return home. I only got through those long intervening months with the support of my brother officers, including John Middleton, and by throwing myself into my work with more vigor and dedication. I also took every opportunity for kindness to an unfortunate soul, especially if it were a woman. If I could not assist Eliza myself, I would assist another in her stead, hoping that some kind person back in England might do the same for her, wherever she was.

When at last I reached home shores again, I should by rights have reveled in the joy of standing on British soil once more, in my return to a temperate climate, in the sight of familiar and beloved things. And yet, I could enjoy none of it until I knew Eliza's fate. So I went straight to Delaford.

The first thing I noticed upon entering the house was the empty place where Eliza's portrait had hung five years before. Considering what had happened since, it should be no surprise. The picture could not be counted a trophy anymore, and so, no doubt it had fallen, like the woman herself, from the place of honor it had previously occupied. Max had probably banished it to a dusty attic somewhere, I supposed. I hoped at least that he had not destroyed it.

Just one more reminder of the urgent reason I was there.

Informed of my presence, Max soon appeared. Either I had grown while away or Max had become somehow diminished, for I immediately noticed that I now looked down slightly to meet my brother's eye. We shook hands, exchanged the barest minimum of civilities as we made our way into the drawing room, and then, before we could even sit down, I came right to the point.

"Where is she?" I demanded.

"Who?" he asked as if uninterested.

"You know perfectly well that I mean Eliza."

"Oh, her." He rolled his eyes." I suppose she must have *somebody* to think of her, for I never do."

The bands of restraint snapped at my brother's calloused remark, and I struck him on his pompous jaw, knocking him to the floor. I then dragged him back to his feet, saying through gritted teeth, "You will tell me all you know about what has become of her. And if any harm has befallen her, let the blame for it be on your head, for I make no doubt that it was you who drove her out of this house."

Although no further violence occurred, several minutes of circling, glowering, and muttering of oaths followed before our tempers tolerably cooled and we could be rational.

For the sake of progress, I told him I would make no more accusations if he would in turn speak of our cousin, his former wife, with respect. Agreed on this, we sat down and I again enquired as to Eliza's whereabouts. Max claimed to know very little, and he held fast to that assertion no matter what pressure I brought to bear. In the end I was no better informed on the subject except for knowing the name of the man with whom he believed Eliza originally left Delaford – an alliance which had apparently not lasted.

"I heard the man returned to the area some months later without her," Max said. "I've not taken the trouble of verifying it, though."

"But what has she to live on," I asked, holding my head, which felt as if it might fly apart at any moment. "Has she any money at all?"

"An allowance... at least she did have. My attorney informed me several months ago that she made over the payments from it to another person. Perhaps an extravagance on her part left her in a tight spot, from which she needed some immediate relief."

"So now she has nothing! Is that the situation?"

He shrugged and held his hands palms up. He did not know. Neither did he seem to very much care.

13

Working on so little information, swift success was not to be expected, I suppose. I did what I could, however.

First, I undertook the distasteful task of seeking out and speaking to Eliza's original paramour – a Mr. Williams – who represented himself as entirely irreproachable in the case. He had not seduced the girl; on the contrary, it had been she who had come to him, very desirous to change her situation. They had gone on well enough together for a time, until Eliza once again became dissatisfied and moved on. To where and with whom, he knew not. Such was his story, which he admitted to only after I had liberally bribed and plied him with spirits to allay his fears of being sued for the trespass of another man's wife.

I went to the town where he said he had left her, and I questioned everybody I could find, from the clergyman of the parish to the ostler at the inn. Only a few remembered ever seeing her three years before, and nobody knew where she had gone. Time had passed, memories had faded, and so had any trail Eliza might have left behind herself.

Had Eliza not relinquished her claim to her allowance, I might have traced her whereabouts through Max's attorney, who had been charged with sending her the money. But now the payments went to a third party who was not inclined to be helpful. Thus, it became another dead end. The only thing I could think to do from there was to enquire, in person or by letter, in all the surrounding communities, on the slim hope that somebody had seen her. That, and wait in terrible suspense. I was finally near enough at hand to help Eliza and yet just as incapable of doing so as before.

Memories of that dreadful time ran through my mind again and again, keeping me awake, that night in London after learning Marianne had been deserted by Willoughby. I remembered the agony of not knowing Eliza's fate, and of how my ignorance of her whereabouts and recent associates had left me powerless to lend her any aid at all.

These were not the circumstances now, however, I realized. I knew exactly where Marianne was, and I had a great deal of information about her recent companion – the man who had hurt her – more than I had yet told anybody. So perhaps I was not as powerless in this case; perhaps this time I did have some resources that might help.

But, should my information about Willoughby be made known to Marianne? Would it ease her suffering or only increase it? These were the crucial questions, and I was no impartial judge. Fortunately, I could leave the ultimate verdict to another, to one who had known and loved Marianne much longer than I had: her sister. So I resolved to return to Berkeley Street the next day and lay my evidence before Elinor, trusting in her wisdom to determine what was best to be done. Only once that decision was made, did I finally sleep.

Not surprisingly, Marianne was nowhere to be seen when I arrived the following morning, and I already knew Mrs. Jennings was out, since I had happened to meet her on Bond Street. So nothing stood in the way of my making the intended disclosure except my own uncertainty, which deprived me of fluency when I tried to explain my purpose in coming.

"My object... my wish," I began to Elinor. "My sole wish is desiring that the information... I hope, that is, I believe it must be a means of bringing comfort. No, I must not say comfort. Not present comfort, at least, but conviction – lasting conviction to your sister's mind. My esteem for her, for yourself, and for your mother... Will you allow me to prove it by relating some circumstances, which nothing but a very sincere regard – nothing but an earnest desire to be useful..."

I finally ground to a halt and sighed, feeling I had made a very poor start. It was enough, however, for one as perceptive as Elinor. She eased my way.

"I understand you, Colonel," she said. "You have something to tell me of Mr. Willoughby that will open his character to us farther." Relieved, I nodded.

"Your telling it will be the greatest act of friendship that can be shown to Marianne. *My* gratitude will be insured immediately by any information tending to that end, and *hers* must also be granted in time. Pray, do let me hear what you know."

This was confirmation of everything.

"Thank you, Miss Dashwood. You shall hear it, although I'm afraid it is a long story. Will you not sit down?"

She did, but I could not. I have always thought better on my feet, and I needed all my wits about me then. So I set off to pace my way through the difficult story ahead.

"I hardly know where to start, Miss Dashwood. When I quitted Barton last October... No, I must go farther back, much farther." I stopped a moment to consider before beginning again. "You have probably entirely forgotten a conversation between us one evening at Barton Park. It was the evening of a dance, I recall, and I alluded to a lady I had once known, who, as I told you, reminded me somewhat of your sister Marianne."

"Indeed, Colonel, I have not forgotten it!"

I was pleased. Once again, Elinor had eased my way. And so, in order to come to my relationship with Beth, I recounted in brief my history with Eliza and her sad outcome.

"...She left to my care her little girl, whom she called Beth," I continued, "the offspring of her first guilty connection. Perhaps Eliza might have chosen better, for what did I, a single young man of four-and-twenty know about caring for a girl of three? But of course, there *was* no other choice, and I was glad to do it. It was a sacred trust and the only remaining service I could render the sweet friend of my youth, who had endured so much at the hands of my family. Still, with no home and no proper situation at the time, I was hardly in a position to keep the child with me. And so she was placed at school, and I saw her as frequently as I could. After the death of my brother, which happened about five years ago, and which left to me the possession of the family property, she frequently visited me at Delaford. I call her a distant relation and she calls me uncle, although I am aware that we are generally suspected of a much nearer connection.

"Last February, however, almost a twelvemonth ago now, Beth – Miss Williams, I should call her – suddenly disappeared. I had allowed her (imprudently as it has since proved to be) to go to Bath with one of her friends, who was attending her father there for his health. I could find out nothing from them when the trouble occurred, except that she was gone. The rest, for eight long months, I was left to imagine. You may guess what I thought, what I feared, as well as what I suffered on Beth's account."

"Good heavens!" cried Elinor at this point. "What are you saying? Do you mean Willoughby?"

"Be patient with me one minute more, Miss Dashwood. The connection will soon be clear." Collecting my thoughts again, I prepared to conclude my story. "The first news of my ward I received was the letter that came for me the morning of our intended excursion to Whitwell. It had been forwarded from Delaford, and its contents necessitated the immediate departure that seemed so strange to everybody.

"Little did Mr. Willoughby imagine, I suppose, when his looks censured me for disappointing the company, that I was called away to the relief of one whom he had made poor and miserable. But had he known, what would it have availed? Would it have pained him? Would he have been less gay or less happy in the smiles of your sister? No, I think not. He had already done that which no man who can feel for another person would do. He had left the girl, whose innocence he had stolen, in a situation of utmost distress, promising to return but never doing so."

I stopped before Elinor, who looked dazed. For a minute, she said nothing. Then she shook her head and exclaimed, "This is beyond everything!"

"The full picture of his character is now before you, Miss Dashwood. Knowing this, imagine what I felt on being assured that your sister was to marry him, moreover that she should never be happy without him. Imagine what I must have felt for all your sakes at your being so imposed upon and deceived by him. I came to you last week determined to know the truth and yet irresolute what to do about it. What could I do? I was convinced that I had no hope of interfering with success; no *right* to interfere. And sometimes I thought your sister's influence might yet reclaim him. But now…

"In any case, we may at least be thankful that your sister has come away far better than she might have, far better than poor Miss Williams. I do not mean to minimize Miss Marianne's sufferings, but fortunate is she to have nothing to reproach herself for. She will bear no lasting disgrace. Use your own discretion, however, Miss Dashwood, in communicating to her what I have told you – how much of it she should hear and when. You must know best what will be its effect."

"Yes, thank you," she said, getting shakily to her feet. "I will carefully consider it."

"I would not have troubled you with this account of my family afflictions, if I had not from my heart believed it might in time lessen your sister's regrets."

"I am sincerely grateful to you, Colonel. I appreciate that such a personal disclosure must have occasioned you some pain. But like you, I also believe the knowledge will be of material advantage to Marianne, if not immediately, then with the working of time. The lucky escape from a proven scoundrel must ultimately grieve her mind far less than the loss of the man she has continually tried to justify. Though now she suffers, I am sure she will soon become easier. Have you," she continued after a short silence, "ever seen Mr. Willoughby since you left him at Barton?"

"Yes," I replied gravely, "once. One meeting was unavoidable. Honor demanded it."

She looked startled and asked, "What? Have you met him to… Oh, what shall I call it? To challenge him?"

"We met by appointment, yes. I could meet him in no other way after discovering him to be my young ward's seducer. Unfortunately, even under such a compulsion, he still refused to do the honorable thing. And so it was left for me to exact some satisfaction from him, to mete out some little punishment for his heinous conduct. News of it never got abroad, however, since I came away unharmed and Willoughby's wound was minor." As I said this, I made a slashing motion below my ear to indicate the location of his injury. "Perhaps you have noticed the mark."

Elinor only shook her head and sighed. "Thank heaven neither of you were seriously hurt, but really, Colonel!"

Apprehending that my companion did not particularly approve of dueling, I redirected the conversation. "I have wondered, though, what must your sister have felt if I had been more successful in convincing Willoughby to marry Miss Williams?"

"I hardly think she would have blamed you, for Miss Williams certainly had a higher claim to be his wife than had Marianne. Nobody could dispute that."

~~*~~

When I called again at Berkeley Street a few days later, I was actually favored with Marianne's presence as well as her sister's. The same occurred upon my subsequent visits. Marianne joined whoever else was home at the time in welcoming me. She might not speak, other than to return my greeting and later my farewell, but I was glad to see her calm and in control. The violent irritation of spirits, which Elinor had described to me before, seemed to have passed, replaced by a more settled dejection.

The improvement was not all I could have hoped, but I took it as a good sign that Marianne no longer felt it necessary to actively avoid me. Perhaps Elinor had disclosed my information (something difficult to confirm, with her sister always present), and it had done some good – at least in her opinion of me. I thought this probable, especially after catching Marianne observing me with what seemed a compassionate eye. Did she now understand me better or only pity me? If she knew my sad history, could she fathom why I was often so grave and silent? I had not always been so.

Within a fortnight of Willoughby's desertion, he was married to Miss Grey. Everybody knew it, Miss Marianne included (by her sister's good information, I assumed), although no one would have dared to mention his name to her again. The next time I saw her, I expected some apparent setback, but she remained surprisingly composed. Then, when I asked how much longer the sisters intend-ed to stay in town, assuming it would be Elinor who answered, Marianne voluntarily stepped in instead.

"We shall remain some weeks yet," she said firmly, resignedly, looking directly at me. "My mother has written to say that is her wish."

I was amazed but tried not to betray it in my countenance or reply. "She is a noble lady, for in being willing to spare you so long, she must be desiring her daughters' interests and comforts above her own."

"That is exactly true," said Marianne. "She is the kindest creature in the world, although I could almost wish her more selfish on this occasion."

"Your own preference would be to return to your mother at Barton." It was a statement, not a question.

She nodded sadly and dropped her eyes.

Although I expected Marianne's unprecedented contribution to the conversation was likely at an end, I was not prepared to lose that connection or the sound of her voice just yet. I attempted to keep her engaged. "An excellent mother can be a great mainstay, I believe. You have been fortunate there, Miss Marianne."

I waited, but she made no reply. Finally, Elinor picked up the loose end. "Yes, we have indeed been fortunate in that regard, Colonel. You have not been as lucky, I think. At least that is my impression."

"No, I was not so lucky. My mother, though she was a good woman too, died when I was only twelve years of age."

This caused Marianne to glance up at me with that same compassion I had noticed in her eyes of late. I would have preferred to see love and admiration there, of course, but this was a step in the right direction. It was far better than her former contempt.

~14~

It was February now, and I was obliged to share the Miss Dashwoods with a growing circle of friends. The Middletons and the Palmers had been in town since January. Now Mr. and Mrs. John Dashwood and two young ladies of the name of Steele were newly arrived.

Mr. John Dashwood was Elinor and Marianne's brother by their father's first marriage, and therefore the inheritor of their former home, Norland. He clearly had a claim on their attentions. Through him, they had also acquired an association with his wife's family: people by the name of Ferrars. The Miss Steeles, whom I understood to have visited Barton after I left, seemed to be always underfoot at Berkeley Street, cultivating their newfound connection with Mrs. Jennings and her house guests.

All these were soon acquainted, enlarging their social spheres, mixing and mingling with each other very freely.

Consequently, I did not see the Miss Dashwoods as much as I had been used to. Or when I did see them, some of these others were of the party as well. It was not an advantageous change, from my point of view, for I preferred quiet talks with my intimate friends to the noise of large gatherings. But my own inclinations were of little importance. I could only hope that these wider diversions would serve as a valuable distraction for Miss Marianne, giving her something else to think of besides Willoughby and his desertion. There seemed little evidence of such beneficial effects, however.

We were all invited to the John Dashwoods in Harley Street to dine one evening, the unstated purpose of which seemed to be that we might have the honor of meeting the matriarch: Mrs. Ferrars herself. Mrs. Ferrars was a small, formally upright woman with a sallow skin and a sour aspect. I could see nothing in her person or manners worthy of the particular admiration we had been given to expect would overtake us. In her judgement, I could place no reliance at all, for it was soon clear to me that she preferred Miss Lucy Steele's less cultivated mind to either of the superior Miss Dashwoods, accepting the fawning attentions of the former while determinedly ignoring the very presence of the latter.

Moreover, I had the distinct impression that much was transpiring that evening to which I was not privy. A current of competition and animosity seemed to underscore everything done and said, especially between the ladies. At one point, I was called upon for my opinion of a very pretty pair of painted screens – the work of Miss Elinor Dashwood, I was told. No sooner had I given them my warm and honest approbation than Mrs. John Dashwood seemed to think it necessary to turn the attention from Elinor's artistic abilities to a Miss Morton, who apparently also painted delightfully.

"She paints beautifully indeed!" agreed Mrs. Ferrars. "But Miss Morton does *everything* well."

I had no idea who this Miss Morton was or why she should be set up in comparison to Elinor, but Marianne clearly could not bear to see her sister so slighted. "This is admiration of a very peculiar kind!" she cried. "What is Miss Morton to us? Who knows or cares for *her*? It is Elinor of whom we think and speak." She then went to her sister. Putting an arm round her neck and drawing close, she said, "Dear, dear Elinor, don't mind them. Don't let them make you unhappy."

What spirited sweetness was this! What a tender and amiable heart Marianne possessed that she should rush to defend her sister, when her own wounds were still so fresh! I honored her for it.

How strange, then, that after likewise witnessing this demonstration of brave affection, Mr. John Dashwood should have seen something entirely different. "Poor Marianne," he told me a little later in a low voice. "She has not such good health as her sister, and one must allow that there is something very trying to a young woman who has been a beauty, in the loss of her personal attractions. You would not think it to look at her, perhaps, but Marianne *was* remarkably handsome a few months ago; quite as handsome as Elinor. Now, you see, it is all gone."

I stared at him in disbelief. Her looks gone? Was he mad? In my eyes at least, Marianne had never been more beautiful.

~~*~~

I was reluctant to go, but with duties to discharge elsewhere, I judged it as good a time as any to briefly absent myself from London. And so I called at Berkeley Street to take my leave, fortunately finding nobody there on this occasion except Mrs. Jennings and the two Miss Dashwoods.

"Leaving London!" exclaimed Mrs. Jennings. "How can this be, Colonel? No, we cannot possibly spare you, for we are only just now gathering enough company about ourselves to make us merry."

"It cannot be helped, my good lady," I replied, "but I assure you I will return just as soon as I have completed my business."

"You will not stay away long?" Marianne asked unexpectedly. I was touched by her solicitude.

"You see there, Colonel," said Mrs. Jennings. "Miss Marianne cannot spare you either, and I daresay Miss Dashwood, here, feels the same. Now, do tell him to stay, Miss Dashwood."

She looked to Elinor, who said, "I should be very glad if Colonel Brandon would stay, but not at the expense of his duty or his wishes."

"There now, you see?" Mrs. Jennings continued, undeterred. "If you care nothing for the wishes of an old lady like myself, you must listen to my young guests. We simply cannot do without you!"

"You must forgive me, Mrs. Jennings," I said and then turned back to Marianne. "No, I will not be away long. No more than a fortnight, I hope. I must look in at Whitwell again, on behalf of my friend, and I have had a letter from my steward to tell me there are matters at Delaford requiring my attention, as well."

What I did not say, due to Mrs. Jennings's presence, was that I also needed to pay a visit to Beth and her infant to see how they were faring.

I discovered nothing out of order at Whitwell, where I went first, and so I moved directly on to Delaford. There I tended to my steward's concerns and also took the time to visit old Mr. Stinson at the parsonage house, whom, I had been informed, was ailing. I found Beth and her infant son well, though, when I later reached them in their country lodgings. The child was healthy and growing, and the mother was as cheerful as I could have supposed her to be. Still, I would have preferred to have them both under my own roof at Delaford, had it been an eligible arrangement. But a bachelor has no business keeping an unchaperoned girl, who is not his near relation, within his household.

On my travels, I carried with me the image of Miss Marianne turning her eyes to me the day I took leave, concern wrinkling her fair brow. *"You will not stay away long?"* she had said, as if she would truly miss me. Perhaps I had imagined more than was actually represented, but her words did give rise to a bud of hope as well as encouraging the swiftest possible completion of my business.

Although I had been gone from London no longer than I had anticipated, I soon learnt that events of great importance to my friends had taken place in my absence. A secret engagement between Mr. Edward Ferrars and Miss Lucy Steele, both of whom I had become acquainted with by this time, had come to light in a most unfortunate manner. Mr. Ferrars's mother, who apparently held full control of the family fortune, had demanded he break off the engagement on pain of disinheritance, which, as a man of honor, he refused to do. He had therefore lost nearly everything irrevocably to his younger brother.

My compassion for the injured young couple was immediately aroused, as well as my indignation against Mrs. Ferrars, who had thus borne out my original unfavorable impression of her. There was just enough similarity in the case to my own sad history with Eliza – the autocratic parent, the attempt to part and punish two young people long attached – that all my energy and emotions were engaged in the business as well. At first, however, I could see no possible way to help or interfere. Then I received a communication from Delaford saying that old Mr. Stinson had died, and I knew I had some help to offer after all.

I went at once to Berkeley Street, intending to ask Miss Dashwood's opinion of the idea, but I was met by still more news instead. The Miss Dashwoods were intending, along with Mrs. Jennings, to go to the Palmers at Cleveland for Easter. This part of the plan seemed to please everybody, including myself, for I was to be included in the party as well. The difference of opinion arose from what was to happen afterward.

"Ah, Colonel!" cried Mrs. Jennings upon my coming into the room. "You must assist me! I do not know what you and I shall do without the Miss Dashwoods, for they are quite resolved upon going home to Barton from the Palmers. How forlorn you and I shall be if we cannot change their minds! Lord! We shall sit and gape at one another as dull as two cats."

The picture this painted in my mind was indeed dreary. I turned to Marianne, however, to attempt to ascertain her sentiments. Although her countenance gave nothing away, I believed she and Elinor had long been desiring some eligible means of returning to their mother. If they would indeed benefit by this plan, I could not on the whole regret it myself, and so my answer to Mrs. Jennings was not all she had hoped.

I still had the other matter on my mind as well, that which had brought me to Berkeley Street in the first place. When I noticed Elinor moving away towards the window, I followed to where she stood regarding a print.

She turned and smiled at me. "I mean to attempt a copy of this for a friend of mine," she explained. "I hope I may do it justice. Now, Colonel, I trust your business went well, the business that took you from town."

I nodded. "And now it will soon be *your* turn to leave."

"Yes, we have been away from our mother long enough. Marianne, especially, is impatient to be at home again."

"Then I am glad for you both."

"Thank you. I could have wished for a more direct route, but it is a relief to finally have an eligible plan for our departure in place."

"Miss Dashwood, I came today in hopes of speaking to you about something else, in fact. I have heard of the injustice your friend Mr. Ferrars has suffered – that he has been entirely cast off by his family for persevering in his engagement to Miss Steele. Have I been rightly informed? Is it so?"

"It is indeed."

"The cruelty, the impolitic cruelty of attempting to divide two young people long attached to each other is abominable! Mrs. Ferrars does not know what she may be doing, what she may drive her son to do. I have seen Mr. Ferrars two or three times in Harley

Street – not enough to be yet fully acquainted, but enough to be pleased with him. And especially as a friend of yours, I wish him well."

"Thank you, Colonel. I believe he is truly deserving of your esteem."

"I am glad to hear it, but I wish him to have more than that. My esteem will not go far; I wish to give him some practical relief as well. Since I understand that he intends to take orders, I should be pleased to offer him the living at Delaford, which has just become vacant. I only wish it were more valuable. Although it is certainly capable of improvement, it cannot, I fear, at its present rate of two hundred pounds a year, afford him a very comfortable income. Such as it is, however, my pleasure in presenting it to him will be very great. Pray, will you inform him of it?"

I could see that I had quite astonished her, and for a time she did not speak. Then she burst forth – in warm gratitude to me and in further praise of Edward Ferrars's character as meriting every friendly assistance that might come his way. Once I had convinced her that I really did prefer that she be the one to impart the news to him, she graciously accepted the commission.

"I believe Edward is still in town," she said. "In fact, I have had his address from Miss Steele, and so it should be in my power to inform him of your offer in the course of the day."

"I hope he will find it of use. I should be fortunate indeed if he should accept the office – to have secured for the parish a respectable gentleman as the new rector, and for myself such an agreeable neighbor. If I find I can do more for him by and by, I certainly will."

We discussed a little further the size of the rectory and whether or not the living would be sufficient to allow Mr. Ferrars to marry. But in the end, we had to leave it for the man himself to decide. He must know his own needs and assets better than anybody else could.

Miss Dashwood was prompt in her communication to Mr. Ferrars, for later that very day, he presented himself at my door in St. James's Street, overflowing with thanks and compliments that I turned aside as well as I could. He, no doubt inadvertently, left me with the impression of some discomfort, however, and that his joy, though expressed, was not fully felt. I put it down to the awkwardness of our being so little acquainted, and I believe I finally convinced him that it was an arrangement that would work to my benefit as much as his.

I was gratified indeed to have been in a position to do Mr. Ferrars a good turn, all the more so, I think, for having been so frequently in the past powerless to help where help was needed.

~15~

Very early in April, the party for Cleveland prepared to set out. The ladies – Mrs. Palmer with her new infant, Mrs. Jennings, and the two Miss Dashwoods – departed London first at a leisurely pace. Mr. Palmer and myself followed a few days later, traveling more expeditiously.

Cleveland is a spacious, modern-built house with tolerably extensive grounds. Like every other place of similar importance, it has its open shrubbery and wood walk, a road of smooth gravel and a lawn dotted over with fine timber. Our hosts soon proved themselves not deficient in their attentions either. Nothing was wanting on Mrs. Palmer's side that friendliness and good humor could supply. As for Mr. Palmer, I was by then accustomed to his odd ways. I found him perfectly capable of being a pleasant companion when he chose, and only prevented from being so always by often fancying himself as much superior to people in general as he must feel himself to be to Mrs. Jennings and his wife.

We arrived to a very late dinner and found the ladies well settled in. I was uncommonly pleased to be reunited with the Miss Dashwoods, though it had been only a matter of days that had divided us.

"The grounds are delightful," Marianne told me in response to my inquiry as to how she liked Cleveland so far. "There are some very fine walks as well. In the morning, you will see a Grecian temple on a distant eminence that fairly beckons one to come visit it. I could not ignore its call, and so I went nearly at once when we arrived. From there, I discovered, one can see a great distance…"

Here she abruptly stopped, and I wondered if she was thinking of Combe Magna, which was reportedly no more than thirty miles from Cleveland. Had she looked for Willoughby's home from the top of that hill, considering that by now it should have been hers as well?

"Perhaps tomorrow you will show me the way," I said gently.

She ignored this, saying instead, "I meant to go out again after dinner, all over the grounds, but Elinor prevented me."

"Marianne!" Elinor objected. "That is hardly fair! It was the rain and not I that prevented you. Although you are indeed a very intrepid walker – no one can dispute that fact – even *you* cannot fancy that being chilled in a heavy, settled rain would be pleasant."

"Perhaps not, but another time I will go just the same."

"Not when you have a cold already."

"Are you unwell, Miss Marianne?" I asked in concern.

"It is nothing at all, Colonel Brandon," she said. "Nothing that I regard. Only the smallest stuffiness in my head, which will do better with fresh air and exercise than by being cosseted inside. Elinor is overly fastidious."

But two days later, after insisting on going out twice more for "delightful twilight walks," Marianne's cold was decidedly worse. Although she had promised to keep to the dry gravel of the shrubbery, Elinor suspected she had ventured far beyond, for she came home with her shoes and stockings very wet indeed.

Marianne denied her illness as long as she was able. First, she claimed she was not really unwell at all, and then it was nothing more than what a good night's sleep would cure. Only after a day spent shivering by the fire, holding a book she was unable to read, did Marianne finally submit to the necessity of retiring to bed and the expedient of her sister's nursing.

Although I was by this time feeling real alarm on Marianne's account, Elinor remained calm, trusting to the efficacy of sleep and proper medicines to work the necessary amendment in her sister. I tried to quiet my anxious solicitude by telling myself that Elinor's superior knowledge of her sister and of caring for the sick must give her a clearer view of the situation. But it did no good, especially when the next day, after Marianne had reportedly spent a very restless night, brought only a worsening of her symptoms. I was informed that she now had a high fever, a violent cough, and a sore throat, as well as pain and heaviness in her limbs. Nobody, not even Elinor, could any longer dispute the fact that she was very ill indeed.

The apothecary, Mr. Harris, was summoned at once. After examining his patient, he cheerfully encouraged Miss Dashwood to expect that a few days would surely restore her sister to health. However, by pronouncing that the disorder did have a putrid tendency and also allowing the dreaded word "infection" to twice pass his lips, he ultimately gave more fright than comfort.

The household was thrown into immediate alarm. Mrs. Palmer and her infant were to be removed from the premises at once for their own protection, the father to follow soon afterward. Mrs. Jennings, however, steadfastly resisted her daughter's entreaties to likewise decamp. She declared her resolution of not stirring from Cleveland as long as Marianne remained ill, to assist Elinor with the nursing duties, and by her own attentions to supply to them both the place of the mother she had taken them from. It was a promise she tirelessly fulfilled in the coming days, to her very great credit.

I felt particularly indebted to Mrs. Jennings for this because there was nothing I could do for Marianne myself but pray. I could not carry any of the burden for the others either. Useless and helpless once again, I could not see, speak to, or minister to the dear invalid in any way, since naturally I was not admitted to the bedchamber where her feverish body lay. Instead, I was forced to rely on the little information I periodically received from the ever-optimistic apothecary or from a fretful Elinor. And to imagine the worst. Marianne might be said to be improving one minute, but the improvement never held. Finally, even Mr. Harris was forced to admit that the prognosis was grave.

Oh, how my fears preyed upon my mind! I had seen vile fevers in the Indies, with the most dreadful results. From the little that had been told to me of Marianne's condition, I could picture her writhing in pain and delirium, her cheeks flaming with aberrant heat, her bedclothes drenched from her fight against the forces of infection that had invaded her delicate frame. How would the battle end? There again, my mind drew a terrible picture: a death-like pallor, and a stillness that would soon be death indeed.

It required no great stretch of imagination to supply these images, for I had seen the face of death many times before. The only difference was the identity of the person wearing death's cruel mask. This was no ancient relation, no hardened warrior fallen on the battlefield, not even a brother soldier by my side. This was one so young, so fair, so defenseless that it should have been inconceivable that death could find a victim in her. And yet it was not inconceivable to me, for this, also, I had witnessed before. Years before. This particular horror – watching the life inexorably drain from the woman I loved – I had personally experienced.

Marianne's seeming approach to death very naturally sent my mind reeling back to Eliza. Hour after hour, as I waited in excruciating suspense through the crisis of Marianne's illness, I had nothing but time to relive what had happened to Eliza those many years earlier.

~~*~~

When I returned from India, I had followed every lead, every clue that came my way, in an exhaustive effort to discover the whereabouts of my lost friend. All to no avail. Six full months passed without my uncovering a trace of Eliza, and if I could not find her, I could not help her. I could not make up for the abuse she had suffered at the hands of my family. Nor could I atone for my own mistakes.

Then, from an acquaintance, I heard of one whom I *might* do something for. Winston, the faithful coachman from Delaford, who had always been so kind to me, had apparently fallen on hard times after being dismissed from my brother's employ without even so much as a small legacy to provide for his old age. He was as a result now detained in a workhouse for an unpaid debt. And so I made my way to the ghastly place at once, determined to achieve Winston's release and comfort if I could.

Seeing the warden first, I had to exert myself greatly to control my anger, outraged as I was that an honest man, who had worked hard all his life, should lose his freedom over such a trifling sum! Needless to say, I paid the debt and went to find my old friend, to see what else I might do for him. I was not a wealthy man, but thanks to frugality during my years in the army, I had some savings at my disposal.

"Bless you, Master Christopher!" Winston exclaimed when I found him and told him he was free to go. "You was always a kind lad."

The old man looked far from well, but I had to smile at his calling me what he always had, as if I were still a boy of twelve or thirteen. "Never mind that," I said. "It was the least I could do after all your years of faithful service. Now, collect your belongings and let us get you out of this dreadful place at once."

He hesitated, which puzzled me. Considering the filth, the stench, the overcrowded conditions, one would have to be mad to linger any longer than absolutely necessary. The uneasy look on Winston's face, however, made me pause as well. "What is it, Winston?" I asked.

"Pardon me, Master Christopher, but do you know about the young lady?"

"What young lady do you mean?" I asked with no apprehension of what was to come.

"The young lady you was so sweet on – five year ago, before you went away. Mrs. Brandon, I suppose I should call her, though it never did seem right she married Mr. Maximus."

My heart gave a great lurch. "Miss Eliza, do you mean?" I hurriedly demanded. "What of her? Do you know where she is?"

"Yes, sir. She must have fell into misfortune, like me, for she be right here in this same spunging-house. Seen her with me own eyes, so I did. Much changed, but it was her, right enough."

I left Winston collecting his things while I hurried back to the warden's office to redeem Eliza as well. When I was then taken to her, though, I nearly told the matron who escorted me that she had made a mistake, for I could not at first reconcile the sickly, faded creature crouching before me with the vital young woman I had known. But when I looked closer, there was a brief glimpse of something familiar. "Eliza?" I said, still unsure.

She did not answer; she only looked dully back at me with haunted eyes.

I fell to my knees then, a moan escaping my lips when the devastating truth struck full home. This pitiful figure before me was indeed Eliza. This shadow, this melancholy shell was all that remained of the beautiful, blooming girl who had been my childhood companion and soulmate not so long ago, the love of my youth upon whose sweetness, innocence, and liveliness I had once doted! How was it possible? What pain, what prolonged suffering must have been hers in order to have worked this terrible alteration?

Eliza then broke into a series of racking coughs, and I swiftly concluded that my questions must wait. I had to get her out of that depressing place to somewhere safe and warm, where she could be cared for. Later – perhaps much later, when she was better – would be soon enough to seek the explanations my mind cried out for.

She was too weak to walk, and so I carried her to my carriage, leaving the matron to bring Eliza's meager belongings and the little girl who was with her. Winston I deposited at the home of a relative, as he requested, slipping a little money into his hand as I bade him farewell. Then I saw mother and child – for so they turned out to be – placed in comfortable lodgings with a respectable woman to attend to all their needs. I called in a physician, too, to see what if anything might be done. My hopes were not high, but I was still unprepared for his verdict. Eliza was in the final stages of consumption and would not live long.

~16~

Another drowning wave of guilt washed over me that day. My motives had been right and honorable when I withdrew from Delaford in order that Eliza and Max could build their marriage without distraction. And as young as I was, I believe I could have recovered and reconciled myself to my loss, if their union had been a happy one. Or at the very least, I should not now have lamented it for *her* sake.

But what did any of that matter now? What mattered were results, not motives, for the sum total of all my good intentions had not saved Eliza from disaster. All I had succeeded in accomplishing by my five-year military absence was to ensure that poor Eliza had no one to turn to in her hour of need. Wretched, wretched mistake! – one that I would never cease to regret.

It was one failure after another where Eliza was concerned. First I had failed with my plan to spirit her away from the danger at Delaford when I had the chance. I failed to protect her from my father's machinations and then my brother's calloused treatment. Then, to compound my sins, I had all but deserted her, failing to be there to rescue her when she needed me most.

Now at last, I would take my place at Eliza's side, and no one would prevent me. For whatever time remained to her, I would stay to ensure she received every possible comfort and attention. It was an act of love, certainly – love for the girl of the past and what we had once meant to each other. It was also an act of penance, for my conscience told me I had much for which to atone.

And so I visited Eliza every day at her new lodgings, and I at least had the gratification of seeing how much benefit she derived from kindness, comfort, and proper nourishment. If the illness could not be beaten, then perhaps it could at least be robbed of some of its inherent cruelty.

By the second day under better care, Eliza was more coherent and aware of her surroundings. She was more aware of my presence, as well, and I knew she heard me as I held her hand and apologized again and again for what had befallen her. Knowing I did not deserve it, I begged her forgiveness anyway.

"You have it," she said in little more than a whisper.

I exhaled, and part of the weight I had carried with me for three and a half long years lifted from my soul. Though I could not yet forgive myself, I was extremely relieved to have her absolution before it should become forever too late.

Gradually, then, bit by bit over the course of the next several days, Eliza's story came forth. Though our conversation was frequently interrupted – by coughing spells and her lapses into slumber – at last I pieced together a fairly clear picture of what had transpired during the previous years.

My brother, who never had any true regard for her, had been unkind from the start – ignoring, belittling, and verbally abusing her as his changeable moods directed. His behavior only grew worse after our father's death and my departure, when it was no longer tolerably checked by anybody else. Max made free to take his pleasures how and where he liked, completely unrestrained.

When Eliza could bear her unhappy situation no longer, she clutched at the only way of escape she saw open to her – the man I had met and questioned, the man who had subsequently fathered her child. He eventually left her, however, worse off than before, and easy prey for the next man who seemed to offer her a scrap of kindness. It became a downward spiral, one that eventually left Eliza so desperate as to sign away her only lifeline: her legal allowance payments. And so she and her little girl ultimately ended where I had found them.

The child was often in the room during my visits – a shy, quiet thing who, when she was not snuggled up with her mother, sat on the floor playing with a few simple toys.

One of those first days, after watching her come to her mother and kiss her, I asked, "How old is the girl?"

Eliza smiled wistfully. "She is almost four and the apple of my eye. I call her Beth."

"She is named after you, then: Elizabeth."

"Yes, poor thing, to have such a mother and no father at all."

"The man has no interest in his daughter, then?"

"Worse than that; he pretends not to be her father. When I told him I was with child, he accused me... Well, never mind. What he said to me does not bear repeating. I suppose that when one is known to have been guilty of unfaithfulness, one should not be surprised to be accused of being so again. In any case, that was his excuse to leave me without any support."

"And his own child as well," I added.

"Yes."

Our eyes being naturally drawn to the little girl, we silently watched her play with a doll, holding it close as she wandered about the room warbling a nonsensical song to it.

"Promise me, Christopher, that you will look after her when I am gone. Not that I expect you to raise her yourself necessarily, but to see that she is safe." She fought down her emotions before continuing. "I do not mind leaving this life so very much, except for her. If I know she will be well cared for, I can die in peace."

I was momentarily overcome. The idea of being responsible for the small creature before me was not a welcome one, for I had no experience with children whatsoever. "Surely, not," I said without thinking. "There must be someone else better qualified."

She just looked at me patiently.

No, of course there was nobody else. Eliza had been an orphan to begin with, and she was now irrevocably cut off from her only remaining relations... save for me. And so I said, "I will, I promise." I had no idea how I would keep that vow; I only knew that, after failing Eliza in every other way, I could not fail her in this. I could not refuse her dying wish.

In our slow and broken fashion, we talked about many things, but mostly happier times. We reminisced over our shared childhood – the stories we had composed together (*Remember the one about Freddie the Fox?*), the games we had played, the frequent tricks on our tutors (*Poor, Mr. Loshbough...*), our unrestricted rambles over the grounds of Delaford, the flower garden we had planted and tended ourselves one summer, the indulgence of every other youthful diversion we had been able to devise, and our expectations that we would be together always. These were bittersweet recollections, in light of what had ultimately become of our pleasant plans.

Sitting at Eliza's bedside, the melancholy days crept by in a strange tension between longing for the painful ordeal to be over and yet not wishing her to die. Above all, though, I reminded myself that these hours were to be treasured, since they would be the last we spent together. They were holy hours, too. The parish clergyman came more than once to assist us as my cousin lay poised between this world and the next, administering all the important services and prayers to prepare her for what was to come.

I would not have given up those exquisitely painful final hours with Eliza for all the world. By them, my memories of her were reinvested with their original value and more. The heartache that had followed lost its power to mar, and their beauty was restored. By them, it seemed we were able to put back together something precious we had lost for a time, the pieces of which had been rent asunder through the trials of the intervening years.

Perhaps it was in light of this restoration that I briefly imagined a restoration of Eliza's health as well. She looked so much improved to me one day that I momentarily entertained a grain of hope that she would eventually recover, in defiance of the physician's prediction. The moment did not last, however. An honest assessment with a more objective eye told me that she continued to waste away. Her breathing became more difficult by the day. She was feverish, and the cloth she kept in hand to cover her cough was now tinged with blood: all signs, the doctor warned me, that the end was near.

"Are you in much pain?" I asked her, trying to keep my voice steady.

She grimaced slightly. "Not much," she answered. "Not anymore. At times, it has felt like a full grown man was sitting on my chest, crushing my lungs. But perhaps now I am beyond even that." Her eyes left mine to scan the room and ceiling. "Now I seem to be more aware of this host of attending angels than the pain of this world."

I had no reply to this surprising statement. Was she in earnest, or had her mind begun to slip?

She smiled weakly. "What? Can you not see them? I am not surprised. You always did have your feet too firmly planted on solid earth to notice things made of less substantial stuff. But I assure you, old friend, they are here with us now."

A chill ran across my shoulders, but not an unpleasant one. "I'm glad," I said, wishing I had the vision to see angels too.

For a while, we, neither of us spoke. It felt as if we had already said everything that needed to be said between us. For once, we had been given enough time and privacy for a proper goodbye.

But then her voice came again, quiet but steady. "I am sorry, Christopher."

I leant closer and asked, "What do you mean, dearest? What have you to be sorry for?"

"I have made my peace with God, but I must with you as well, if I can. I know I should have been stronger those years ago, as you urged me." She paused to gather enough breath to continue. "I should never have given in and married Max. If I had only held out against your father a little while longer... Can you forgive me, Christopher?"

I hesitated a moment before answering, not because I still harbored any resentment for what I had once seen as a personal betrayal. I did not. If she had wronged me, she had paid a very high price for it – and was still paying. I would not add my punishment on top of what she had already suffered. And so my first impulse was to tell her she had done nothing that required my forgiveness. Then I thought better of it. She deserved the same relief she had given me days earlier.

"I forgive you, Eliza," I simply said. "I did so long ago."

The brief tension in her countenance eased. She rested back against her pillows, and she was soon asleep. I stayed another quarter of an hour, gazing at her pale, waxen visage, watching the rise and fall of each ragged breath. I knew it could not be long now. Eliza was truly on the threshold, but judging by the serenity of her face, it did not trouble her. She slept the peaceful slumber of a soul whose sins had been pardoned by a much higher authority than me. She said she had made her peace with God, and I tended to believe her. It seemed her burden was gone; her stained and filthy robes had been washed clean by the blood of Jesus the Christ.

When I went to see Eliza the next day, she was gone. Somewhere in the night she had cast off her mortal coil, exchanging it for the glories of heaven. I shed tears for myself at being left behind, but I was glad for her. By the time I had found her, the enchantment of life had already lost its sway over her. It offered nothing more to Eliza beyond the chance to prepare for death – a chance she had not wasted.

In time, I learnt to view Eliza's passing as a merciful release from suffering for one who had no future. But when my mind came back to the present with a painful jolt, I could not apply the same comforting logic to Marianne. *No, may it never be!* Marianne had suffered as well, but her situation was not nearly so hopeless, her outlook not grim at all if she survived. Her reputation was neither ruined by dishonor nor her place in society forfeited. Her young life still held unlimited promise. It would not be fitting or fair for it to be cut down by illness, as Eliza's had been. Surely that could not be God's will.

And yet I knew she lay upstairs in very similar straits to what I had witnessed in Eliza shortly before her passing.

After my brief recess, reliving past traumas, I resumed pacing Cleveland's drawing room like a caged animal, which I had taken to doing for lack of any more productive occupation. I only knew I should go mad if forced to sit still in my current state of extreme perturbation. Then, looking more beleaguered than I had ever seen her, Elinor came in, and my insides turned to stone.

17

"How is she?" I asked before Elinor could speak, though I was not sure I could bear to hear the answer.

"Oh, Colonel! What can I tell you? She is not at all herself! I suppose it is the fever, but she is crying out for her mother and talking wildly. Nonsense, really. It is quite alarming."

"She's not seeing angels, is she?"

Elinor looked confused.

I shook my head and waved off her unspoken question. "Never mind. Tell me what I can do."

"I must send for Mr. Harris at once, but I believe my mother should come as well. As soon as possible, in fact, to comfort Marianne or at least... at least to see her before..." She broke off mid-sentence.

I solemnly nodded my comprehension.

"I hoped you might advise me on the swiftest way to bring her from Barton. Perhaps a message could be sent by express?"

"No," I said at once, immediately knowing what should be done. I could not alleviate Elinor's fears, which were all my own as well, but I could obviate her other difficulty. "I will go myself," I told her.

Relief flooded her face. "I probably should object to putting you to so much trouble, Colonel, but I will not."

"It is no trouble to me. On the contrary, you will be doing me a great favor by giving me some better occupation than pacing this room. Now, while I make my preparations to depart, Miss Dashwood, do sit down and compose a few lines to your mother. She is already aware of your sister's illness?"

"Yes, I wrote when we were still quite sanguine about Marianne's prompt recovery. She will be wondering now why I have not written again, I suppose. And worrying. You are the very person to reassure her when she hears the news, to keep her company and soothe her fears on the journey here. God bless you again and again for your kindness, Colonel Brandon!"

I bowed. "I am only too pleased to be of service, Miss Dashwood." And I meant it.

I set aside the unruly personal feelings of the moment before, in order to perform my assigned duty with a clear head – something I had learnt to do in the midst of military campaigns. With firmness and utmost dispatch, I made the necessary arrangements, and as soon as the horses were ready, I pressed Elinor's hand and left without delay. It was then about midnight.

If only that state of consuming activity could have been maintained! Then might my mind have continued uncluttered by emotion, with no leisure to think and worry. But there were hours and hours alone in the carriage to be got through before I arrived at my destination. Without the distraction of something less dangerous, nothing could have prevented me perpetually dwelling on my fears for Marianne. And so I deliberately picked up the thread I had recently left off. Not Eliza's death this time – there was no safety in that – but what followed afterwards.

My first duty after Eliza had passed was to make the arrangements for her proper burial, which I did with a heavy heart. Then I set about the even more difficult task of finding the right situation for little Beth.

By this time, I was tolerably accustomed to the idea of her being my responsibility, as well as a bit acquainted with the little girl herself. That being the case, I would gladly have fulfilled my promise to Eliza in the most straightforward manner, taking charge of Beth's care and education myself, had my circumstances allowed it. However, having no permanent home and no family to support me in such an undertaking, I judged it best not to attempt it. And so, after an exhaustive search, I placed her in the most ideal situation I could discover: with the rector of a parish on the outskirts of London, where I could visit her frequently. With no children of their own, he and his wife had opened their home as a kind of school for a small number of orphaned children, like Beth. There she would have a much more settled life than I could have provided for her myself.

When these necessities were accomplished, I felt constrained to one more duty before my responsibility to Eliza could be laid to rest. And that required my returning to Delaford... to my brother. Max had not only been Eliza's relation but her husband, at least after a fashion. He had a right to know what had become of her, and she had a right to expect him to be told.

I admit that my initial motives in this were anything but pure and noble. The fact is, I wanted to confront Max, throwing Eliza's death in his face like a full glass of port. I wanted to watch him absorb the blow, reeling from the shock of it. And I wanted him left forever stained with the guilt of what he had done, never able to forget it. After all, the consequences of his actions were unquestionably permanent as well. Nothing could bring my sweet Eliza back, restored.

It was not at all a Christian sentiment, and to persist in it would place me in the wrong as well. And so, along the way I prayed that my unholy anger against my brother would be tempered, that God would grant me the grace to eventually forgive him if he asked, even as Eliza had freely forgiven me, and to leave the rest in the Almighty's hands. "*To me belongeth vengeance and recompense,*" God said in Deuteronomy. And so I must not take those things upon myself.

I was tolerably composed by the time I arrived, no longer breathing fire or seeking my imagination's version of retribution. But even so, Max did not look at all pleased to see me. I could not blame him for that, considering the last time we met I had knocked him to the floor. Since then, I had thought of doing much worse. To his credit, though, he did not refuse me entry, even though he seemed to anticipate the reason I had come.

As soon as we were closeted in the drawing room by ourselves, he poured us both a drink and then asked, "Did you find her?" His tone held the trepidation of a man expecting bad news and dreading it.

"Let us sit down first," I said. Then I told him everything I knew: why Eliza had run away in the first place, her progressive descent into degradation and want, the ultimate outcome being a pitiable death. I also told Max about little Beth, left to my charge, and the arrangements I had made for her.

I could not keep a certain intensity of sadness from my voice, but God enabled me to speak calmly and without undue censure. No doubt my brother's conscience did the rest, for I saw genuine pain in his countenance by the time I finished my recital, as well as the distinct shimmer of tears forming in his eyes. Gone were the calloused attitude and false bravado that had so angered me on my previous visit. There was none of that in evidence any longer.

Max was entirely silent for some time, head hanging and eyes downcast. Finally, he stood, breathed a heavy sigh, dragged his hand through his hair, and exclaimed in a miserable groan, "Oh, God!" He then walked to the windows, peering out and continuing his confession – not to me, necessarily, but more to himself or to the universe at large. "I am so desperately sorry. I wish…" Another sigh. "Lately, I wish a lot of things had been different – that I had been more humane to her, or that I had refused my father's demand for me to marry her in the first place – anything but what has actually happened."

I said nothing, but I tended to believe his remorse was genuine.

Presently, Max turned, looking around the room and to the ornate ceiling overhead. "Her fortune saved this grand old place, as the old man intended, but…"

At what cost?

The unspoken words hung in the air between us. My father's insistence on Eliza and Max marrying had cost us all dearly, even Max. Although he was far from blameless – *very* far – he was in a way a victim, too. I could see that now. Before me stood a broken and lonely man. He had a fine house but no family to fill it with life, warmth, and laughter, no sons to carry on after him. Without that, what good was it? While I could not yet forgive him – that would come in time – I could sincerely pity him.

I stayed a week at Delaford, and we spoke of these and other things again. It was the beginning of a certain degree of reparation between us. The past was not forgotten, but we tacitly agreed to put it behind us. Max's behavior to me became more civil after that, and I could come and go to Delaford as I liked without wondering if I would be welcome or not.

Poor Maximus. His reign at Delaford was short and unhappy. He did not marry again. He never begat a family of his own and a son to inherit. I can only hope that he was at peace when he, still a young man, died in a riding accident, leaving me his heir.

I have often wondered since, if he had known he had so little time, would he have made better use of it? Would he have been kinder to Eliza from the beginning and made himself a proper husband to her? Perhaps he might then have left behind an honorable legacy. Instead, his ten or eleven years as lord of the manor accomplished little.

Of course, it remained to be seen if I would do any better. After five years at the helm, the estate was fiscally sound and respectable, but it was still without a family. The house still had no mistress. The halls were still devoid of children's voices. And the current master was a lonely old bachelor. Still.

18

My mission to fetch Mrs. Dashwood transpired with the barest minimum of difficulties. When that good lady first espied me, however, her face fell and I feared she might collapse altogether. So I made haste to reassure her that her daughter, though very ill, yet lived. Then I pressed Elinor's note into her hand to complete the explanations.

"I see. I see," she said nervously, reading it. "Yes, Elinor says I must be strong and go with you, and pray we are not too late." She refolded the note and looked up, her chin trembling. "Oh, Colonel," she sobbed, "your coming to me just now is the greatest kindness in the world! I had grown so alarmed, thinking about Marianne's illness, that although I knew not how I should manage the journey on my own, I had determined to set out for Cleveland this very day! I have already packed a bag, in fact, and the Careys will be arriving at any moment to fetch Margaret, for I was unwilling to take her with me lest she should also become ill. Now you have come to make everything easy for me."

"I hope indeed that I may, Madam," I said. And as soon as Margaret was off with the Careys, we were off as well.

One may imagine that this was hardly a journey to be filled with talk of trivialities, as Mrs. Dashwood and I might have done quite happily under ordinary circumstances. Instead, we both had one thing and one thing only on our minds: Marianne. It would have been impossible to pretend otherwise.

I kept my own counsel at first, not wanting to allow my fears to add strength to Mrs. Dashwood's. I perceived that she fought to keep her worries under wraps as well, no doubt in deference to Elinor's appeal that she should be strong. And yet that was asking too much of a lady of Mrs. Dashwood's elevated sensibilities. Her anxiety for her beloved child would bubble to the surface and overflow from time to time, despite her efforts to prevent it. Then I must hear a tearful recital of all Marianne's excellent qualities and the dread that her darling presence might be lost to us forever.

I knew my duty was to quiet her fears, to console the distraught mother who despaired for her child. That is what I had envisioned and what Elinor almost certainly expected of me. But has not the would-be lover nearly as much right to be desolate as a parent? Mrs. Dashwood's fears were my own as well, and I doubt that she was deceived into believing otherwise.

No, instead of my presence quieting her effusions, the opposite was often true. I became caught up in them, at least internally. Then, quite without premeditation, I opened my mouth and my true sentiments about Marianne began flowing forth.

"Mrs. Dashwood, I see that we are in complete agreement," I told her calmly. It was a statement of simple fact, as was everything else that followed. "Your daughter is just what you say. She is all that is lovely: sweetness and light, open and artless, kind and generous with herself. She is to me, as you yourself said a moment ago, the dearest creature in the world."

I had her full attention now, no doubt having amazed her by such a confession. As I had surprised myself. I was not sorry for having said what I did, though, for it was very relieving. I only wondered where I might go from there. I had come too far to turn back, I perceived, and so I decided I might just as well make a clean breast of it.

"Be not alarmed, Madam, for I have no expectations, I assure you. But the truth is I have a very great regard for Miss Marianne. In fact, I love her, and I have for a long time. I love her with an earnest, tender, and constant affection. And so you may believe that I enter wholeheartedly into your celebration of her character and your agonies over the prospect of losing her. Not that she is mine to lose, of course. You alone can claim that. I merely claim to be your friend and hers, to take a strong interest in your family's general wellbeing and hers in particular. I only wish to be of service where I may, and I expect nothing in return. Above all, I desire to know that Marianne is alive, well, and happy. That must and will be enough for me."

My companion looked as if she felt obliged to say something, probably to express kind regrets. I could not bear her pity, and so I hurried on.

"I do not tell you these things, dear lady, to burden you or to excite your sympathy on my behalf. No, not in the least. I did not mean to tell you at all, and it might better have been left unsaid, for there is nothing to be done about it. Even if her heart were free, which at present it is not, I am too old and too serious for Marianne. She has made obvious, by her previous choice, the sort of gentleman she can love. And though Mr. Willoughby has proved he never deserved her, one day a much better young man will come along to capture her heart. When that occurs – and may God grant that it will – I shall sincerely rejoice in her happiness, as everybody who loves her must."

Now I had done. The words had poured out, and I was glad to have unburdened myself to such a ready friend, one who I knew could entirely appreciate my feelings.

"You have overwhelmed me, Colonel," Mrs. Dashwood said. "My goodness! I am honored that you should feel free to open your heart to me. And of course I could never disagree with you that Marianne is deserving of your admiration and affection. As to whether there might be any hope…"

I interrupted, shaking my head vigorously. "No, I cannot even think of such a thing now, and I do not ask it of you either. I have spoken as to a sympathetic friend, not in application to a parent. Believe me, my only prayer is for Marianne's recovery."

"I do believe you, Colonel, and once again, we are of the same mind."

And so we left it for a long time. The miles rolled on. We periodically stopped for refreshment and change of horses. Then by and by, Mrs. Dashwood resumed the topic over my objections.

"No, Colonel, you must allow me say my piece as you said yours. You have shown me and my daughters true, active, and unselfish friendship, and I have the greatest respect for you in the world. Should Marianne recover, as I trust she might, I could wish for nothing better than to see her married to a man like you."

It was a very kind sentiment, but one I could put no faith in. Mrs. Dashwood's wishing it would not make it true anymore than my own wishes had. Besides, my mind was still in terror of there being no future for Marianne at all, let alone one with me.

We travelled on, the weather deteriorating as we went. As dusk came upon us, so did a storm. The temperature dropped enough that I offered Mrs. Dashwood another rug to keep warm, and I could feel the wind buffeting the carriage. For the sake of safety, our progress from that point on would necessarily be slowed, I knew, our arrival at our destination further delayed. Therefore, likewise prolonged would be our period of awful uncertainty over what we would find there. It seemed an inauspicious sign.

As we drew near to Cleveland, the suspense built to an unbearable level, with Mrs. Dashwood's fears again leading the way for my own.

"We must prepare ourselves," she suddenly cried out in an agony of spirits, "for I am now persuaded that Marianne is no more!" Coming up the gravel drive, she lamented, "Oh, my darling child, how I have loved you. And that you should have suffered and died without me by your side..."

The carriage rolled to a stop, and I helped a quaking Mrs. Dashwood out. In an instant, the front door opened and Elinor came rushing toward us, calling, "She will be well, Mama! Take heart. Marianne is out of danger, and she will be well!"

Tremendous relief and thanksgiving flooded through me. I believe I could literally have leapt for joy. But Mrs. Dashwood began to sink, her spirits as overcome by happiness as they had been by her fears the moment before. Elinor and I supported her into the house and to the drawing room, her copious tears now overflowing from the depths. Unable to speak, she embraced Elinor again and again, turning periodically to silently press my hand as well. In her eyes, I read deep gratitude – to God for His mercy, no doubt, and perhaps a little to me as well. There was something else, however, which I interpreted as a knowing kinship of spirit. Thanks to my revelations in the carriage, she knew I fully shared the profound bliss she now experienced.

Presently, though, Mrs. Dashwood was recovered enough to go to the dear invalid, which she did at once, escorted by Elinor. I was left on my own to raise an earnest prayer of thanks and then collapse into a chair, my strength gone. My fortitude had lasted as long as, but no longer than, was absolutely required.

~~*~~

For the next few days, I lived for the periodic reports I received from Elinor and Mrs. Dashwood of Marianne's steady and reliable improvement. She continued to mend day by day, Elinor repeatedly assured me, her quiet composure adding credence to her words. Mrs. Dashwood's information came in a more effusive style. The brilliant cheerfulness of her looks proved her to be, as she repeatedly declared herself, one of the happiest women in the world.

Although I delighted in the restoration of the dear lady's spirits and in hearing about Marianne's improvement, I could not receive all her other confidences with such unmitigated pleasure.

In one instance, returning from her latest visit with Marianne, Mrs. Dashwood came to sit beside me. We were quite alone. She patted my hand as a mother would and said conspiratorially, "Time, Colonel. Mark my words; that will do the trick. Time is all that is wanting, and perhaps not so very much of that."

Though the words themselves were ambiguous, I was confident that I understood her meaning, for this was not the first time she had alluded to my earlier confession that I loved her daughter.

"You are very kind, Mrs. Dashwood," I replied. "But really, you must not encourage me to hope."

"And why not, I should like to know? Your rival is gone and you are still here. One day soon, Marianne will look about herself and recognize her own good fortune."

"You will forgive me if I disagree. Miss Marianne's heart was – and no doubt still is – powerfully engaged. A person does not recover from such an attachment soon if ever, Mrs. Dashwood. We should not expect it of her."

"Tut-tut. That is why I say a little time is needed, but not much. Young people are very resilient. Marianne will recover from disappointment more quickly than you or I would. Then she will be ready to love again, and there you will be, waiting, you see."

I knew better, however. I had been deeply in love with Eliza when I was exactly Marianne's age. I had not recovered quickly, nor had I learnt to love again for years and years. But I would not argue the point. "Even were that to be true, dear lady, it does not follow that I would be your daughter's choice. She will want – and she deserves – somebody younger and more spirited like herself, as we discussed once before."

"I cannot agree with you, Colonel Brandon. You are too modest. You underestimate your own merits... and Marianne's good sense, as well! She is neither so headstrong nor so whimsical as to make her unteachable, you know. Yes, she made a mistake with Willoughby; everybody acknowledges that, even she herself. But she will learn from it! She will learn to choose differently and more wisely next time. Do not speak to me of your age either, my dear colonel, for it is only so much beyond hers as to be an advantage, as to make your excellent character and principles, which we have all seen for ourselves, quite fixed. It means she can depend on your constancy, that her future will be safe in your hands. Your person and manners are entirely in your favor as well. And as to your more staid disposition, I am convinced it is exactly the thing to make Marianne happiest in the end."

How could I argue against all this without sounding churlish? I submitted gracefully and thanked Mrs. Dashwood for her good opinion.

Some of what she had said was certainly true; Marianne could indeed rely on my constancy. As for the rest? Well, I only wished Mrs. Dashwood's reasoning would prove accurate. In any case, it was flattering to be assured of the mother's approbation, for whatever weight that might eventually carry with the daughter. And in spite of my own cautions against it, I began to cherish a small hope for the future. Perhaps when I at last saw Marianne for myself, I would be able to judge if optimism might be at all justified.

19

Within four days of my return to Cleveland, Marianne was enough improved to leave her bed for the more sociable atmosphere of Mrs. Palmer's dressing room, making it respectable for me to finally visit her. I was invited to do so. I was told, in fact, that the patient herself had particularly requested it. Elinor escorted me upstairs, and both she and her mother remained.

My anticipation was naturally running high. The woman I loved had asked for me to come – a circumstance most gratifying – and I hungrily longed to see her beautiful face again. That is what I was unconsciously expecting, I think, that she would look just as lovely as ever. But when I entered the room... Oh, what were my emotions upon first beholding Marianne so altered? Pity me, for at once the image of the dying Eliza was before me again! The hollow eyes, the reclined posture of weakness, the pallid, sickly skin: these things, added to the general resemblance between the two ladies, gave me a dreadful shock. If this was Marianne improved, what must have been the mournful sight her sister had beheld at the darkest hour?

I recovered in no more than a moment, but I fear not quickly enough to avoid revealing to the ladies some of what I had felt.

"Colonel Brandon," said Marianne, holding out her pale hand to me.

I took it with the greatest care, almost afraid it might break like the white porcelain it appeared to be. I held that delicate hand long enough to bow over it, and then released it unwillingly, saying, "Miss Marianne, are you well?"

A faint smile curved the corners of her mouth. "I may not yet look it, but I am, thank you. Or rather, I soon shall be, I promise."

I mirrored her feeble smile, which was all I could manage at the time, and nodded. "Your mother and sister have told me it is so, but still, I am exceedingly glad to hear it from your own lips."

"Will you not sit down for a few minutes?" she asked me.

I hesitated. "I would not wish to tire you by staying too long."

"You needn't worry. I will tell you – or more likely, Mama will – when I need to rest again. But I did particularly wish to speak to you without further delay."

So I pulled a straight-backed chair forward and sat.

"Good," she said. "Now, allow me to sincerely thank you for all you have done for me and my family during my illness, especially in bringing my dear mother to me. You cannot imagine how keenly I have felt your kindness and how grateful I am." She stopped me before I could object. "No, no, I see that you would refuse to hear it, but you must. I have determined to live a better life from now on, and that means, among other things, acknowledging my debts and repaying them as well as I am able."

I shook my head, distressed that she should think herself beholden to me in any way. "You owe me nothing, Miss Marianne, and neither does your family. Please believe me, I was only too glad to be of service."

"You are too modest, sir."

"Not at all. Friends help in times of need, without wanting or expecting anything in return. Is that not so?"

"Yes, so it is," she agreed.

"And I hope I may count you among my friends… and I among yours."

A deeper smile warmed her face, and a bit of the former brightness enlivened her eye. "Yes, Colonel, I would be pleased to call you my friend. A dear friend."

When I quit the room five minutes later, it was with an unprecedented sense of hopefulness, thinking that perhaps Mrs. Dashwood's theories might not be entirely wrong after all.

The following day, Marianne was strong enough to be helped downstairs and sit with us for a time. And with even more improvement the next, Mrs. Dashwood began to talk about going home to Barton.

My feelings upon the occasion were mixed. As delighted as I was to see Marianne looking noticeably better day by day, it would soon mean losing the chance to see her altogether. Once she was recovered enough for the Dashwood ladies to return to Barton, I could not imagine I would be wanted or needed any longer. There would be no reasonable excuse for my going with them to Barton Cottage only to impose on their hospitality at an inconvenient time. Nor did I wish to go to Barton Park, not with Sir John and Lady Middleton still away in town. The inescapable conclusion was that we must part, however reluctant I was to do so.

All that remained was to convince Mrs. Dashwood to accept my carriage to convey them home. With Mrs. Jennings to support me, and arguing on the grounds of Marianne's comfort, that was soon accomplished.

"Very well, Colonel," said Mrs. Dashwood. "Have it your own way. I will accept the generous offer of your carriage, if you will allow me in turn to set the conditions of your redeeming it. Once we are settled again, you cannot refuse to stay with us at least a few days when you come."

I bowed, saying, "With the greatest pleasure, dear lady."

Thus it was settled, and yet I could not be satisfied with merely the prospect of more time with Miss Marianne at some future date. Although before I had told her mother, God, and myself that I would be content if only she would recover, I had apparently been lying. Having finally been given a small taste of Marianne's attention and approbation, I was now hungry for more. And so in the dwindling days left at Cleveland, I looked for an opportunity to sample her company again, preferably alone. She herself – with a little help from her mother – provided it to me.

"Might I go outside?" Marianne asked her mother the afternoon of the last day before their planned departure. "The weather is particularly fine, and I am certain the fresh air will do me good."

Although stronger by the day, Marianne was still far from returned to perfect health. In the meantime, Mr. Harris's medical advice said she should be kept indulged and quiet. So her request posed a conflict. Was it more advisable to keep her sitting quietly in the house or to indulge her desire to go out? Mrs. Dashwood had a solution.

"Perhaps it would be safe if you were to wrap up warmly and go out on Colonel Brandon's arm, only as far as the terrace. And you must promise to return as soon as you are the least bit cold or tired." Turning to me, she added, "Colonel, you will not mind, will you?"

I could almost swear she wanted to wink at me. In any case, I was glad to have Mrs. Dashwood on my side, although I hoped her preference would not become too obvious, since we rarely want what we are told we should. "Not in the least, I assure you," I said, being careful to keep my tone and countenance from betraying my delight at the prospect. "I would be very pleased to do so."

Marianne accepted my arm and leant heavily upon it as we went, saying nothing along the way. The terrace was on the south side of the house, and so even though it was not yet May, hours in the sun had warmed it to a very comfortable temperature by this time. A footman hurried out ahead of us with a diminutive chaise longue for my fair companion, which he placed according to my direction. I helped her into it and then seated myself on the adjacent stone bench.

"Are you comfortable, Miss Marianne?" I asked her.

She sighed and closed her eyes. "This is heavenly," she answered, "to breathe fresh air and feel the sun on my face again. There can be no felicity sweeter."

I felt a bit awkward. "Perhaps I should leave you, then," I suggested. "You may not desire company and would prefer to rest."

Her eyes popped open again. "No! Please stay. I have done nothing *but* rest these many days. Read to me, Colonel," the appealing invalid ordered, as appealing invalids are allowed to do. "Or tell me a story, if you prefer."

I was intrigued. "A story? What kind of story?"

"Oh, you know: once upon a time, a faraway kingdom, brave heroes rescuing fair maidens and saving the day, happily ever after. That sort of thing."

An idea occurred to me, but I hardly dared to act upon it. So I delayed, saying, "A fairytale, then, rather than a true story?"

"I suppose, although it would be even better if it were true."

"The only *true* story I know – and it is quite a long one – is about a more ordinary sort of man. Not at all the hero you have in mind, I'm afraid."

"Is he brave and honorable at least?"

"Hmm. You must be the judge of that, but I can tell you this much. He does earnestly *desire* to save the day – and the fair maiden too, of course. And he does not sit idly by; he acts on his convictions. However, circumstances – and his own feeble nature, I suppose – conspire to prevent him from achieving all he had hoped. He is a very poor sort of hero, you see." Hearing no response, I added, "One might even be tempted to call him a failure."

"And what is his name?"

This was the point of no return. Should I tell her the truth and risk losing her interest altogether or carry on in the manner I had begun? I decided upon the latter. "His name is Colonel Charles Dunston," I said with barely any hesitation, grabbing hold of the first name that came to my mind.

"Someone from your military days, then?"

"Yes, in India, so there is your *faraway kingdom*, at least."

"True."

"I spent a great deal of time with the man, for we sailed together and then served in the same regiment. What I did not witness for myself of his story, he confided to me in detail and without reservation. So I think you will find my information quite complete. Do you wish for me to begin?"

"Tell me what Colonel Dunston looks like first, or at least what he looked like at the time."

This required some quick thinking. "Oh... What he looked like..."

"Yes, so that I can picture him while you talk."

"I see. Well, then, I imagine you would like me to tell you he was tall and very handsome. But he was not. The truth is, he was a very ordinary man in every way, including his appearance."

"That tells me nothing useful, Colonel. I need specific details if I am to form any sort of picture in my mind."

"Very well. Let me think. Hmm. I would say he was of average height or perhaps a little taller, with a narrow face, regular features, straight brown hair, and dark eyes. Anything else you wish to know?"

"Yes. How old was this Colonel Dunston at the time, and how came he to be in the army in the first place?"

"He was just eighteen when he left England. As to why, I suppose it was the usual inducements: a younger son needing a profession to make his way in the world, the lure of adventure, the idea of doing good and distinguishing himself by service to king and country. Most of us could have said the same, only Dunston had the additional persuasion of a broken heart to send him abroad."

"Oh, no! What happened?"

"The lady he loved married another."

Marianne was silent and grave.

"I'm sorry," I quickly added when I realized what I had said and how she must have felt it. No doubt I had just succeeded in reminding her of Mr. Willoughby and her own pain at losing him to Miss Grey.

"Not at all, Colonel," she said presently, lifting her chin. "These things do happen, and there is no need to pretend otherwise."

I was eager to move on. "So considering what I have now told you about Colonel Dunston, what do you think? Could you be interested in that kind of an inferior hero, Miss Marianne? Could his story even be worth listening to?"

She looked at me, eyes clear and unsuspicious. I felt a slight qualm, but there was no turning back now.

"It is my experience that the right storyteller can make anything worth hearing," she said. "And as to that, I do like the sound of your voice, Colonel. I find it…" She paused, pensive. "I find it pleasant and easy on the ear."

This was new information.

"…So if I must sit quietly, as Mama insists, I may as well listen to your story."

"Very well," I said cautiously. "I shall make a start of it today, and then you can decide for yourself if you wish to hear any more. One other thing you should know, though; I will not embellish to make Colonel Dunston more heroic or his tale more entertaining. I shall stick to the absolute truth. How else can you decide for yourself if the man is someone you can admire or not?"

"As you wish," she said agreeably. "So long as it ends well. I will condition for nothing less." She settled back into her chair and closed her eyes.

"Yes, of course," I mumbled. "We, all of us, desire our stories to end well." That was the best I could say, for the end of this particular story had not yet been written.

20

A nd so, with Marianne looking to me in childlike expectation, I took a deep breath and began.

"Colonel Dunston and I both sailed from Portsmouth in March of 1779 aboard the *Duke of Grafton* – a British merchant ship belonging to the East India Company and captained by Samuel Bull. After stops in exotic places like Madeira and Madagascar, the ship finally docked in Madras eight months later, in the middle of November.

"I suppose these details cannot be of much interest to you, Miss Marianne, other than to demonstrate that my memory of these events – and also of Dunston's account of them – is under good regulation. What *is* important for you to realize is that by taking a commission in the army, Colonel Dunston – like all others bound for the East Indies – had to first, for several months, become a sailor. We were told we had been lucky, for the voyage might easily have taken much longer or we might never have arrived at all, since the seas off the Cape of Africa are particularly treacherous."

Marianne looked at me in some alarm. "Oh, dear! Is it really as dangerous as all that?"

"It can be. I certainly found it so. *The Duke of Grafton* came close to sinking on more than one occasion, tossed by storms and violent waves. Although Dunston was neither drowned nor killed by a tropical disease on the voyage, still, he suffered enough, I think."

"In what way?" she asked.

"By various insults to body, mind, and spirit. In the main, however, it was this: he discovered within the first two hours of leaving England how little sailing agreed with his constitution. But there was no turning the ship back. Perhaps, Miss Marianne, you have noticed the unsettled feeling continuous motion can give – feeling unwell when travelling some distance in a carriage, for example." I paused for her response.

"Oh, yes. That is to say, occasionally I have felt a little of what you mean. It was a good deal worse when I was a child. My parents were always careful to be sure I rode facing forward and able to see out of the window if we were going very far."

I nodded. "Ah, yes. Then you have received a small taste. Unless a person has actually been on a ship at sea, however, it may be difficult to imagine what Colonel Dunston experienced. It is easily ten times as bad as a long ride on a hot day in a poorly sprung carriage travelling a rough road. And it goes on and on. Having nothing solid under one's feet for weeks or months at a time is not a natural condition for a human being. We were not designed for that, I am convinced. The deck heaves and rolls in every imaginable direction, it drops out from under one's feet without warning and then unexpectedly shoots up again, as the ship is tossed about by the waves, which can sometimes be as high as a house. The horizon constantly bobs and shifts before one's eyes, or even disappears entirely…" I shook myself out of the reverie I had fallen into, remembering. "Well, suffice to say that it plays havoc with one's insides, and the rougher the seas, the more one feels it."

Marianne studied my face then. "Colonel, you sound as if you suffered the same malady as your friend. In fact, you look like you recall it all too clearly."

"Indeed, I do, as if it were yesterday, though it has been a long time ago now. I was not a good sailor either. Some men learn to tolerate the constant motion, but I never could. It was eight months of pure misery, held a virtual captive aboard a ship that was every minute carrying me farther and farther from home."

"But surely you must have stopped from time to time. You mentioned your exotic ports of call a moment ago."

I was gratified that she had paid such close attention. "As you say, the ship docked from time to time to take on fresh supplies, and yet that was not as much relief as you might think. The action of the waves on a ship is minimized in the protection of a good port, of course, but it never ceases completely. So if one stays aboard, one does not leave the vile motion behind altogether. And yet if one goes ashore, there is never enough time to recover completely. One might finally adjust to feeling solid ground beneath the feet, only to be told it is time to cast off again. Being forced to board once more after a brief reprieve was nearly as bad as having no reprieve at all." I took a moment to remember. I had tried both options and found them equally unsatisfactory. "Do you know what the worst part was?"

She shook her head. "Truly, I cannot guess."

"Speaking only for myself in this case, the worst was the knowledge that I would have to endure the same prolonged misery a second time at a later date if ever I was to see England again. That was always in the back of my mind during my years in India."

"Oh, dear! That would be a torment to the soul – wanting to be at home again but knowing what you would have to endure to get there. And were you of a similar age when you went abroad, Colonel?"

"Yes, exactly the same; I was just eighteen when I left England."

"Only a bit older than I am now," she said thoughtfully.

Yet another reminder that I had lived a lifetime since I was her age.

"You must have been very brave to undertake such a thing so young," she continued.

"Brave? No, it is only bravery when one knows enough about what lies ahead to be afraid, and then chooses to go anyway. I believe you might more rightly call my state when I boarded the ship 'the ignorance of youth.' But enough about me; let us return to Colonel Dunston."

"Oh, yes, of course. To Colonel Dunston."

I went on to tell Marianne in some detail of 'Colonel Dunston's' ports of call – which, not coincidentally, I had shared – trying to attribute as many of my personal experiences and impressions as possible to my fictitious friend. I described the landscapes, flora, and fauna, so different from those she would be used to; the dark-skinned people with musical languages we could not begin to understand; the spicy, unfamiliar foods we sampled some of which we never learned what they contained, and some we might have been happier not knowing. All the while Marianne gave me her rapt attention, causing me to ask, "Do you think you should like to visit these places I have described?"

"Oh, yes! That is if I could reach them in perfect comfort and safety, I would, for it is a sorrow to me that I have travelled so very little and only in England. When I think of the world – how big it is and all the wonders it contains – it seems a shame that anybody should know only one tiny portion of it. But I could never endure the voyage! Your accounts will have to do for me."

"You need not rely exclusively on my information, Miss Marianne... or Colonel Dunston's either. There are paintings and books that might help quench your appetite for a wider knowledge of the world, all without leaving England. Perhaps a visit to a picture gallery when next you are in London. And of course, you would be welcome to borrow anything you like from the library at Delaford. There are a few fine volumes I could recommend, if you desire to learn more about foreign lands."

"How kind you are, Colonel. I do love books of poetry and stories, and I always mean to embark on a course of more serious study, but somehow I never do. I like listening to your descriptions, though. It makes these places seem more real than only staring at words on a page can do. Please go on."

Before I could do so, however, the footman who had helped us earlier reappeared to say that Mrs. Dashwood desired Marianne to return to the house.

After he had delivered his message and gone, Marianne complained to me, "But we have not even arrived in India yet! How can we interrupt Colonel Dunston's story now, when it could be weeks before we may continue?"

"So, you *do* wish to hear more?"

"Certainly! Perhaps..." She stopped abruptly.

"What is it?" I asked.

"Oh, nothing. For a moment I thought of suggesting you could write to me – just to tell more of your story, you understand." Her eyes dropped. "But that would not be proper, I suppose, and I have vowed to learn from my past mistakes."

I considered the idea. While I would be gratified to continue our discourse in any way possible, I would on no account wish to involve Marianne in anything disreputable again. I was no Willoughby.

"Your scruples do you credit, Miss Marianne. While a single gentleman may not write to an unattached young lady, it might be possible for me to send something to you through your mother – a continuation of Colonel Dunston's story, I mean. I will speak to her about it if you would like."

"Yes, that is an excellent notion! I am sure Mama will agree to it."

I was relatively certain she would too, since she had stated plainly that she would do whatever she could to promote my suit with her daughter. When I proposed the idea to Mrs. Dashwood later, it was as I had expected; she could not have granted her permission with more alacrity and enthusiasm.

"That will be just the thing, Colonel Brandon! How clever you are to give Marianne something to look forward to, a reason to anticipate pleasure at next seeing or hearing from you. And there can be nothing at all improper with your writing to *me!*"

So it seemed I had an excuse to maintain some communication between Marianne and myself, even during the upcoming separation. Whether or not it would be of any avail in the end remained to be seen. It seemed I had succeeded in garnering the lady's interest on behalf of my alter ego, but would that ultimately help or harm my own case, once the truth was revealed? Only time would tell.

21

The day of separation and departure arrived.

Marianne had said she was now determined to live a better life. Though I was hardly the one to find any fault with her before, I believe she was indeed changed by her brush with death, as evidenced by the manner in which she took leave of Mrs. Jennings. At the door of the carriage, she tenderly pressed that lady's hand and showed her a very particular respect that may indeed have been lacking in the past. Marianne's gratitude for her service and kindness was clear and earnestly expressed. Then she turned to me with similar cordiality.

"Good bye, Colonel, and thank you again for all you have done," she said warmly. "I hope we shall have the pleasure of seeing you at Barton Cottage again very soon."

Such simple but earnest solicitude on my account would have been unimaginable only a few short weeks before. I bowed slightly, covering the rush of sentiment her words produced with my own efforts at attentiveness.

"Here, Miss Marianne, do allow me to help you," I said handing her into the carriage. "And you must take the seat facing forward, to spare yourself feeling unwell from the motion. I am certain your sister and mother would agree with me." The other ladies murmured their assent and allowed me to hand them in as well.

Oh, how I wished I could accompany them – to see Marianne safely settled and comfortable again at home, to know for myself that she continued to improve and would soon be strong and flourishing as before. But it was not only Marianne's health that I wished to see continuing to improve; it was also the better understanding between us, which so far had only time to establish a slim foothold.

Small though it might be, I *should* have been happy with the unan-ticipated progress we had made. And I was! At the same time, that slight encouragement from Marianne made me much less fit to go home to my bachelor's life again.

But that is what I did; I had no choice. As soon as the carriage containing the Dashwood ladies was gone from my sight, I took leave of Cleveland myself and made my solitary way back to Dela-ford on horseback.

Once at home again, it became a matter of trying to keep myself occupied. There was always something to do, especially after hav-ing been away. This time was no exception, and yet nothing seemed to absorb my interest adequately. Nothing filled my mind sufficient-ly to prevent it wandering hither and yon, especially over recent events and their possible implications.

Several times that first day I thought of writing, as Mrs. Dash-wood had given me leave to do. But something held me back. It would be better to move slowly at first, I believed, as I had always found worked best with skittish horses. Be gentle, show them steady kindness, and win their trust. Then they would forever be your faithful friends. After all, my hope was that Marianne would feel a growing affection for me, not coercion *from* me. My desire was that she should come to me willingly in the end, or not at all.

Passing the music room later that day, I stopped abruptly, backed up a few paces, and gazed in. It was a beautiful room, tastefully appointed, with one of the finest instruments available claiming pride of place at the center. I could find no fault with what the room contained... only with what it lacked. My mind's eye easily filled in the missing article: Marianne seated at the piano-forte. Next, my imagination contrived so well as to provide the notes to something I had heard her play and even the sound of her voice to accompany it.

Then later, as I ate my dinner alone at the monstrous table meant to accommodate as many as thirty, I could not prevent myself from considering how much pleasanter it would be to have at least one companion – a wife? – sitting opposite me, someone charming with whom to exchange fond looks and gentle conversation. And there can be no mystery as to the familiar visage my brain supplied for this pleasant companion.

These were my more optimistic moments. But too often my thoughts tended in the opposite direction. Especially in the long evenings after I returned, my concentration would fail. My mind would stray from the book I was attempting to read towards darker ideas. I did not have to look far to find fodder for gloomy reflections; the subject was readily furnished by the truth of my circumstances – that I was hopelessly in love with a girl half my age. Hence, I was left to meditate many hours upon the unbridgeable gap there existed between thirty-six and seventeen.

I hoped that Mr. Edward Ferrars would come to divert me into more productive lines of thought. In fact, I had sent him a letter of invitation to do so. Surely the gentleman would be curious to view Delaford, the church, and the parsonage house that would soon be home to himself and his betrothed bride, Miss Lucy Steele. It seemed only reasonable that he would. Then we could begin making plans together for what improvements were needed, setting the work in motion at once for the early accommodation of the happy couple. Yet, unaccountably, he did not come. There had been that little reticence on his part, I remembered, which I had put down to the surprise of receiving the offer of a parish living from a relative stranger. Still, I thought we had tolerably overcome that awkwardness before we parted in London. Perhaps not.

When I had been idling away my time at Delaford a bit over a week, with very little to show for it, I was heartened to receive a letter from Mrs. Dashwood:

Dear Friend,

Be assured that we are all well and settled back into our comfortable cottage here at Barton. Margaret is happily restored to us and we to her. She claims to have vastly enjoyed her time with the Careys, and yet she cannot quite hide how much she missed her sisters.

Marianne continues to steadily recover her health. (I know this is what you have really been waiting to hear!) I daresay it can be only a matter of weeks before she is quite herself once more.

I want to thank you again and again for the role you played in restoring my daughter to me, Colonel. I should like nothing better, believe me, than to show my gratitude one day soon by giving her back to you as your wife. I continually pray for that felicitous outcome, and I firmly believe it would be the making of her happiness as well as yours.

In the meantime, remember your promise to spend no less than a few days with us when you come to retrieve your carriage. Come as soon as you like, for as I said before, we are already well settled and ready to receive you at any time now. Think no more about delay or that by coming you will incommode us in the slightest. Nothing could be further from the truth, I do assure you! Consider that there can be no circumstance in the world to make us more comfortable and happy than the company of a person who has forever proven himself our kind and valuable friend.

Yours, etc.
Mrs. Henry Dashwood

PS – Marianne has not forgotten your promise to continue relating the story of your military comrade, begun at Cleveland. She speaks of it frequently and is eager to hear more.

Despite the encouragement of Mrs. Dashwood's letter, I did not rush to Barton Cottage at once. I would take my time. Move slowly, as I had already determined to do. And yet it seemed as if a letter was necessary, not only to carry on the story but to apprise my friends of my plans so they might know when to expect me. To neglect that basic courtesy would be unspeakably rude.

Dear Mrs. Dashwood,
I thank you for your kind letter, informing me that you arrived safely at home and are comfortably settled, with Miss Margaret restored to you. The news has set my mind at rest. Naturally, I am also very gratified to hear that Miss Marianne rapidly continues recovering her health. I daily pray for the time she is fully restored.
I certainly have not forgotten your invitation to Barton Cottage, nor my promise to come to you soon and stay some days. In fact, you may believe me when I tell you that I anticipate my visit amongst you all with the greatest pleasure.

Alas, pressing business here at Delaford will not allow me to be away again at once. Please pardon this unavoidable delay. I anticipate that I shall be with you by the middle of the month, however, or perhaps a day or two before.

In the meantime, I have written out and enclosed a bit more of Colonel Dunston's story for Miss Marianne's amusement. The rest of you should make free to read it as well, of course, should you find it of any interest.

Regards and best wishes for your continued health and happiness,

Col. Christopher Brandon

Writing this brief missive was the easy part. Telling more of Colonel Dunston's story was the more arduous task, and I had already begun to regret having promised to do so. Not because I begrudged the time or the effort it would require, for I admit I would gladly have taken on any exertion necessary in order to please and entertain Marianne. No, it was nothing as simple as that but a more complex combination of sentiments, difficult to put into words.

I knew what lay ahead – the things that had happened to me in India – and I was hesitant to open those old wounds again. I was loath to expose my failures there to the woman I cared for, even under the guise of a different name. That deception in itself accounted for a large portion of my uneasiness, I realized. Sooner or later the truth must come out. There might be no need – and no harm done – if nothing ever developed between Marianne and myself. However, if the best should occur – if our friendship advanced to more… Well, then, eventually I would have to confess. Would it spoil everything when I did? Would she blame me for deceiving her? I had no way of knowing, but I could see that she might.

What I had thought a harmless diversion at the start was now taking on more serious implications. Nevertheless, I forged ahead, telling myself that surely Marianne would understand, at least I prayed that she would.

So I wrote to her about the arrival in Madras, which was accomplished at last, for I could speak from my own experience, not pretending to be anybody else, only adding an occasional word or observation "from Dunston" – anything I thought would be of particular interest to the Dashwood ladies. Also, it was a time I could speak of without distress. The moment of release from the ship was near ecstasy, in fact. I felt like a long-forgotten prisoner miraculously loosed from his chains at last. I knew enough not to expect the world to feel solid underfoot immediately, but it would come, and this time to stay.

Meanwhile, there was much of novelty and interest to claim my attention: first and foremost, the oppressive heat. It was not that I had been unaware of the change of climate and temperature as we had sailed south from England, round Africa, and then north again toward the equator. Of course I had noticed, and yet at sea, there were often moderating breezes. Once on land and a short distance from the water, the breeze died, leaving only the inescapable, baking heat. Although I felt I could tolerate it better than seasickness, I could not help mentioning it now and again. Such complaints, I soon discovered, were much more likely to be met with laughter than sympathy from more seasoned men.

"You think this is hot, do you?" said Major Becton, the officer who met our ship. "Ha! This is only November! Wait until April and May, and then you shall see. Then, and not before, you may claim to know what true heat is."

As we newly arrived soldiers followed the major in the direction of the army encampment that first day, we passed through the raucous marketplace, which was a veritable cacophony. I felt the tremendous crush of colorfully dressed people pressing about me, all of whom seemed to be shouting at once, trying to be heard above others as they bargained for the array of unfamiliar goods and produce on display. There were small troupes of marauding monkeys who did not take so much trouble; they simply stole the fruit they wanted and scampered away again. I saw cows of an unusual breed loose in the street, unfettered and unmolested, and was told that they were venerated as holy by the local Hindu people. And everywhere, I breathed in exotic smells. The sweet scent of tropical flowers mingled with pungent spices on the warm air. The tantalizing aroma of mysterious foods frying wafted from open booths, taunting the noses of hungry soldiers with the promise of pleasures just out of reach.

It was all somewhat overpowering, I admit, and yet such a welcome change from the long months aboard ship that I could not regret it. On the contrary, I welcomed it. I absorbed it through all my senses, ready to embrace this astonishing place where my new life was to begin. In comparing Madras to things familiar, indeed there seemed no point of reasonable resemblance. This place had little in common with London, and even less with the English countryside where I had been born and raised. And yet, people were born and raised and lived and died in Madras too, halfway round the world, as ignorant of my style of life as I had been of theirs.

These ideas filled me with wonder at the time, and I hoped to convey at least some part of it to Marianne by what I wrote.

I easily filled two pages closely written, front and back. Judging that sufficient to fulfill my obligation, I went no further. When I saw her again at Barton Cottage would be soon enough to come to the heart of Colonel Dunston's story – my own, in truth, mine and Rashmi's. And so I did not write of my first seeing her walking through the marketplace with her entourage the day I arrived. I did not mention how beautiful she was and how our eyes met and held for the briefest moment, leaving me wondering who the exquisite lady was and what was her story.

No. I folded and sealed the letter, setting it aside to be posted. Not so easily, however, could I set aside the memories of that time, now that they had been stirred up again. But I refused to think of Rashmi. Not yet. Instead, I smiled, recalling the moment I joined my regiment.

"Brandon!" I heard somebody shout across the grounds of the military compound.

I turned to see John Middleton pushing towards me through the jumble of other soldiers about one task or another. He crashed against me with a brief but violent embrace. "By Jove, but it does my eyes good to see you!" he exclaimed.

He could not possibly have been any happier at seeing me than I was him. I nearly sank to my knees with relief. At long last, a familiar face, a sign of home after months away with nothing comfortable to hang onto. I could not even speak at first; I believe I just stared at him stupidly with my mouth hanging open.

"My father wrote that you were coming, and now you have finally made it!" he continued. "How was your voyage? Bad as mine? I cannot say you look at all well, old friend. But never mind that. A week or two of rest and good food will soon set you right; you will see." He clapped me soundly on the back once more. "I daresay the deck is still rocking beneath your feet, eh? Poor fellow. I remember it well!"

"John," was all I could manage in return, and then he was off again.

"Capital to see you, Brandon. Quite a shockingly different place, is it not? But I know you will soon love it here as I do. So much to do! So much novelty and excitement! And I assure you that our fellow officers are excellent men. Wait until you meet them. Look," he said pointing. "There is Lieutenant Hancock across the way. Hancock!" he shouted, trying to hail the man, to no avail. "Ah, well. You shall meet him another time. I suppose what you really want right now is some victuals and a bunk to lie down on, eh? – one that does not buck and sway like anything! Come with me; I will show you the lay of the land."

I shall be eternally indebted to John Middleton for how he took me in hand that day – and for many days afterward – seeing me safely though the hazards of adjusting to India and to military life. Whereas I went in at the rank of a major, John was a lieutenant colonel when I arrived, and he was therefore in a position to protect and direct my path, seeing to it that I came to no harm. I needed protecting at first too, I freely admit. Later, though, John's laudable desire to continue in that same role had unintended consequences. Devastating consequences.

22

S towing away these memories for another time, I returned to my work at Delaford and to making preparations for soon being gone again. Another week and a half, and I was on my way to Barton.

A man may not be aware of how dim the light has grown with the gathering clouds until the sun breaks through again in bright contrast. So it was with me. I was not fully aware how much my spirits had gradually faded over those three weeks alone at home, not until I arrived at Barton Cottage and the contrasting warmth of affectionate company burst upon me afresh.

Margaret had seen my approach, waved, and then run inside to alert the others. And so Mrs. Dashwood and Marianne also emerged from the door in time to meet me. A very light rain had just commenced, to which they seemed to pay no heed.

After I had dismounted and tied my horse, Mrs. Dashwood came forward and offered me her hand, which I took and bowed over. "Oh, Colonel, you have come at last!" she said.

A quick glance at Marianne had satisfied me that she was well, and so I schooled myself to focus on her mother first, as was only right. "Mrs. Dashwood, how good it is to see you again. You and your daughters are well, I trust."

"Oh, yes!" she exclaimed gaily. "We are all extremely well. Margaret is as you see her. And look how much color Marianne has now. That is an improvement since we parted at Cleveland, I think. The sight of you today has done her a deal of good, I daresay, as it has me."

With this permission granted, I did indeed turn my attention to the Miss Dashwoods. "Miss Margaret," I said with a nod and a smile to her. Then I rested my longing eyes on her sister. Her color was indeed high, but whether from health or embarrassment at her mother's remarks, I could not judge. Her countenance was pleasant and open, though, so I saw no reason to suspect she was unhappy to see me. Presently I said, "Your mother is quite right, Miss Marianne; you are looking especially well. I hope you are feeling so too."

She smiled. "I am in good health, Colonel, I thank you. Welcome back to Barton."

"Now," said Mrs. Dashwood, "shall we all go in before we are soaked through to the skin?"

We did so without further delay and then dispersed ourselves in the cottage's cozy parlor. I had expected to find Elinor awaiting us there, but she was nowhere to be seen. "Is Miss Dashwood well also?" I enquired after I sat down.

Mrs. Dashwood exchanged a playful look with Marianne. "Elinor is very well indeed, Colonel. In fact I daresay she has never been better in all her life!"

"I am glad to hear it," I said, a bit mystified by her manner. "Is she from home at present?"

"She is," Mrs. Dashwood replied, "but only in the sense of being off somewhere on a long, pleasant ramble in the hills. I do hope this rain will not interfere with that plan. Ah, it looks as if it has stopped now. See, the sun has come out again, so we need not fear for her."

I dutifully looked at the window and agreed conditions had improved, as Mrs. Dashwood said. I wanted to ask if her daughter had gone out alone, which did not seem like something the prudent Elinor I knew would do. But instead I held my peace and waited to see if more information would be forthcoming. What I heard surprised me exceedingly.

"Oh, Colonel," the mother continued, laughing. "You must forgive me. I see that I have puzzled you, but I will leave you to wonder no longer. You cannot think how much has happened since I wrote to you, and what news we now have to share!"

"Happy news, I trust."

"The best news of all, I assure you! It is simply this: Elinor is engaged to be married!"

I was momentarily struck dumb. An engagement should indeed be happy news, but it concerned me that it had apparently come about so quickly. I had only been three weeks apart from them all, and there had been no indication of such a thing in the offing before that time, no one paying Miss Dashwood court that I was aware of. Could she really have met some worthy gentleman here in this rural place and committed to him so swiftly? Again, it hardly seemed consistent with Elinor's prudent character. It was not my place to voice such apprehensions, however, which would have been too late in any case. "My congratulations, Mrs. Dashwood," I said. "May I know the fortunate gentleman's name?"

"Of course!" she said with a girlish giggle. "He is none other than Mr. Edward Ferrars, whom you have already met in London."

Now I was more confused than before. "Yes, Madam, I do know Mr. Ferrars, but how can it be as you say? I believed Mr. Ferrars to have been engaged to marry Miss Lucy Steele. Indeed, I know it was so. What could have occurred to produce such a surprising alteration?"

Mrs. Dashwood then commenced her animated recitation of all that had transpired. According to her account, Elinor and Edward had fallen in love when they had been often in each other's company at Norland, before the Dashwood ladies had left that place. The lovers could not acknowledge their attachment, however, much less act on it, because of Edward's prior engagement to Miss Steele, which had been kept secret until it accidentally burst forth while we were all lately in London. That was the only part of the business I had been aware of. But it seemed that after Edward had lost his inheritance, Miss Steele abandoned him in favor of his newly rich brother Robert Ferrars, whom she had subsequently married.

Suddenly Mr. Ferrars's reluctance at my offer of the Delaford living made perfect sense. While his good manners constrained him to thank me for the presentation, his heart could not be truly grateful for a gift that only enabled him to do more quickly that which he did not wish to do at all: marry a woman he no longer cared for.

I was quite shocked for Edward's sake at hearing all this. It appeared terribly heartless and particularly disloyal of the newly-weds – Edward's long betrothed lady and his own brother – to have behaved towards him in such a fashion, and I said as much to Mrs. Dashwood.

"…Is not Mr. Edward bitter at losing his inheritance to his brother for nothing?" I asked in conclusion.

"I daresay he has every right to be," she answered, "and I am quite indignant with Mrs. Ferrars for treating the dear boy so ill. But Edward acts as if his mother has done him a great favor by taking his money away. All he seems to care for is that he was made honorably free to marry Elinor. He wasted no time in coming here to secure her either, I can tell you!"

"Indeed." Now I had my answer for why I had not yet seen Mr. Ferrars at Delaford.

"They may be rather poor, of course," Mrs. Dashwood continued, "that is if Mrs. Ferrars remains set against them. But I cannot help thinking she will come about in time. What mother could truly deny her own son and wish to see him impoverished when she has the power to prevent it? Her firstborn, too! Meanwhile, Edward and Elinor will have each other and enough to live on, thanks to you, Colonel, and they claim that is all they really want or need. I am convinced they will do very well together. Elinor has a good head on her shoulders; she will know how to make a small income go a long way, as she has had some practice doing recently. And they will have a very kind and considerate neighbor in you!"

"I believe I shall be the fortunate one," I said, considering that it was exactly so. Elinor was to become Mr. Ferrars's wife. *She* would be the one living at the parsonage with him, not the former Miss Steele. The gentleman had made an excellent exchange, to nearly everybody's satisfaction, apparently. Now I was even more pleased with my impulsive act to offer Mr. Ferrars the Delaford living, for it would benefit dear Elinor as well.

Something else became clear in that moment. I always had the impression that Elinor shared something of my experience of disappointed love, and here was the explanation. For all the months I had known her, she had been secretly pining for Edward Ferrars! And yet no one might have suspected it from her manner, which bespoke only dignity and restraint. Her exertions must have been great indeed to hide so well what she was feeling all that time. But now her suffering was over, and I was very glad for it.

If I had needed further proof of her happiness, it soon arrived in the form of the lovers themselves, returned from their long walk together – a bit damp and cheeks flushed with color, no doubt thanks to an intoxicating blend of outdoor exercise and prosperous love. I rose at once and crossed to them when they came in.

"Allow me to wish you both joy," I said, taking Edward's and Elinor's hands in turn. "I hear you are to be married. My sincere congratulations."

"Thank you," said the former through the smile that seemed now permanently affixed to his face.

"I see Mama has wasted no time in sharing our good news," observed Elinor, also smiling.

"She has told me. I suppose this explains why I have not yet seen you at Delaford, Mr. Ferrars," I said. "You had more important business to attend to."

"Yes, do forgive me, Colonel. Seeing my future home, although of great consequence, could not compare to the importance of who would be sharing that home with me. Now that that question is so agreeably settled, I would be very glad for the chance to view the parsonage house as soon as may be."

It was shortly decided between us that Mr. Ferrars would accompany me when I left for home a few days later. But I was in no hurry to go, having now the fresh reminder of the difference between my cold, solitary existence at Delaford and a home with the benevolent warmth of human companionship. God had said it in the beginning, right there in Genesis. *It is not good that the man should be alone. I will make him an help meet for him.*

After Eliza, I had all but given up the idea that God had made any other helper suitable for me. Now, however, gazing across the room at Marianne as the others chattered on excitedly about wedding plans, my heart dared to hope again. I prayed once more, perhaps for the thousandth time, that I and the vibrant, responsive beauty sitting by the window would someday be joined.

Therefore shall a man leave his father and his mother, and cleave unto his wife; and they shall be one flesh…

Marianne's eyes darted my way, as if she had sensed I was looking at her. I was caught, but at least she could not read what my thoughts had been at that moment. In any case, I hoped not.

She smiled, though, and moved to sit nearer to me. "Thank you for your letter, Colonel," she said. "Mama shared it with me and then asked me to read out to her what you had written of India."

"I hope it did not bore you, Miss Marianne. Some people find such descriptions tedious."

"Not at all! To be transported to a place I have never been and never will be... What could be more glorious than that?"

"My words had that effect?" I questioned, never having considered they could do so much.

"Oh, yes, at least for me. Mama said it must be partly my imagination too, for she could not so easily picture the scenes you described, or to feel what it must have been like to be there."

I pondered this a moment. "Yes, I think your mother is correct in saying so. That is the way with all kinds of storytelling, I believe. The teller can only do so much; part of the responsibility for success rests with the listener. Your cooperation in being a willing participant was vital to your own enjoyment of what I wrote, Miss Marianne. In a way, you created your own amusement."

"I never thought of it in exactly those terms, Colonel. Do you mean to say that even Shakespeare would not be brilliant without my help?"

Seeing mischief in her eye, I half smiled. "Perhaps that is taking it too far. I only meant that what *I* wrote was certainly not a work of genius; it was your generous interpretation that may have made it seem so."

"Teamwork, then. That is the key – teamwork between reader and writer, listener and storyteller."

"Precisely."

"Then when shall we team up again? When shall I have the next installment of your story, Colonel Brandon?"

"Of Colonel Dunston's story."

"Yes, of course. That is what I meant, and yet you are doing your part as well."

"We shall make time for it whilst I am here, I trust, for there is still much more to tell."

I had never seen Mrs. Dashwood looking more pleased. It seemed nothing could be so felicitous to her as having more company than what her house would hold. Although I suspect if her company had been boorish relations instead of single gentlemen in love with her daughters, the case might have been significantly altered. Mr. Ferrars, as first comer, was granted the privilege of keeping his place at the cottage. I very happily walked every night to my habitual quarters at the Park, despite the fact that the Middletons were still away, and then returned each morning, early enough to interrupt the lovers' first tête-à-tête before breakfast.

Spending all day every day at the cottage allowed time for conversation in every combination. Naturally, the newly engaged couple reserved their greatest share for each other, but I took some opportunity to advance my acquaintance with Edward, and likewise my good opinion of him. Confirming my early view, I found him a sensible, principled, and good-humored young man. And his preferring Elinor to the former Miss Steele attested to his very good taste.

I looked for the chance of a few private words with Elinor as well. We had spent so many hours together, consoling each other while on the outside looking in at the enjoyment of others, that we had developed a deep bond of friendship between ourselves. That, I hoped, would not change with her marriage.

"You must know how sincerely delighted for you I am," I told her upon my first opportunity. Edward was outside playing some sort of game with Margaret, and the other ladies were in the kitchen at the time. "You were very circumspect about your affections, though. All the hours we spent in conversation, and I never suspected."

"Oh, Colonel, I do beg your pardon. You cannot know how many times I wished to confide in you," she said, looking a little ashamed. "Here I knew all your secrets and I was not at liberty to return the favor."

"I expect my secrets were more of a *burden* for you to bear than a favor. And even now…"

Elinor picked up where I had trailed off. "Now there is reason for optimism, at least I believe that is so. Your case cannot be more hopeless than mine was, and see how well that has turned out. God does still perform miracles; Edward and I are proof of that."

I laughed sardonically. "Is that really your view of what would be required to convince your sister to accept me? A miracle? I had not thought my chances quite so slim as that. After all, she can now look at and speak to me with only a hint of the former grimace."

"Colonel, for shame! I think you know that is not what I meant at all. It is just that our situations were very similar, though you did not know it at the time. In both our cases, a former attachment that stood in the way of our happiness has been removed. Which of us can claim credit for that?" She paused, but I had no rebuttal. "So you see, we all need a little help from the One who is more powerful than ourselves. And for my share, I am glad to receive it."

"You are exactly right, Elinor, which is why I pray every day for a seeming impossible outcome – one over which I know I have very little control."

"Marianne can change; she is already changed!"

"Not too much, I hope. As I believe I once told you, I would hate to see her thoroughly disenchanted with life, her youthful innocence completely lost. After all, I fell in love with her as she was, and I found little fault with her then."

"Ah, yes, there is the rub," she said with a bubble of laughter. "Marianne was perfect as she was… oh, except for the fact that she failed to appreciate you! You would have that one flaw changed but nothing else. Come now, Colonel, do be reasonable. My sister herself acknowledges her flaws and the role they played in her troubles. She sees this recent illness as a blessing in disguise, for it has given her the time and opportunity for serious reflection. She has resolved to improve her temper and learn to govern her feelings better. Her feelings are not to be eliminated but regulated – 'checked by religion, by reason, and by constant employment.' Those were her very words, I believe. It will not make her a different person, simply a better version of herself, the better self she was designed by God to be. Such an amendment will surely bode well for her own happiness and for the gratification of those who love her."

My friend's rationale was sound, but for some reason I resisted immediately giving in to it. Then, with a spark in her eye, Elinor added one more thought. "It will also make her more fit to assume the adult responsibilities of wife, mother, and mistress of her own home."

I said nothing, just looked my gratitude for her implied support of my wishes concerning Marianne. Yes, Elinor was a dear friend, and soon she would be living at Delaford Parsonage. I could easily see the great benefit of having such a sensible and agreeable neighbor. Not only that, but her proximity would seem to invite an even nearer, more permanent connection between our two families. There was nothing wrong in hoping.

23

It was not until the third day of my stay at Barton that the right opportunity presented itself for continuing my story with Marianne. I had offered earlier, when Mrs. Dashwood was by, since she had professed a keen interest in what I had sent by letter before. But she said, "Oh, good heavens! It is very kind of you to think of me, Colonel, but I could not possibly sit still to hear it, not now with a house full of company and wedding plans on my mind. You had much better tell it to Marianne, perhaps on a walk. Yes, that would be the very thing, and you know this changeable spring weather is bound to clear by tomorrow."

I suspected she simply preferred to promote a chance for my spending time alone with her daughter, to which I had no objection. And luckily the sun did come out the next day.

"Did you wish to walk, as your mother suggested yesterday?" I asked Marianne after breakfast. "Your strength may not be fully restored, and I would not wish to tire you."

"I must surely get out to take the air, Colonel," she replied. "Perhaps just a short walk, and then we can sit in the sun while you continue the story. I know just the place."

I nodded my assent to the plan and motioned for her to lead the way.

Like Mrs. Dashwood had, Edward and Elinor professed to be far too busy to join us, and Miss Margaret was prevented from following by her mother's tactful intervention. So we were quite alone as we set out.

So much privacy was hardly necessary. I had vowed to proceed slowly and thus I had no plans to frighten Miss Marianne by making violent love to her or declaring myself her suitor. Nor did she contemplate a lover's tryst. Still, with the weather so fine, it would be pleasant to wander about the gentle hills surrounding the cottage, and then to talk together without the sensation that all our well-wishers were listening to every word.

We took an established path into the hills at first, eventually departing from it toward the place Marianne had in view. Once along the way, she paused and stared at a spot some yards from our route, remaining long enough that it prompted me to enquire, "Are you quite well, Miss Marianne? We can turn back if you are tired, and do take my arm." I held it out to her.

She was roused from her musings and smiled faintly. "Thank you, Colonel Brandon," she said, moving her hand to rest lightly on my offered arm. "I am perfectly well. I was only remembering... You see, that is the place where I fell all those months ago, on that low mound over there," she said, pointing with her other hand.

"Where Mr. Wi... Where you twisted your ankle?"

"You need not be afraid to speak his name, Colonel. I am quite inured to hearing it now and more than reconciled to what has happened. I wish for no change. I never could have been happy with Mr. Willoughby, not when I learnt, as I must have done eventually, of his treatment of Miss Williams. No, I have nothing to regret – nothing but my own folly in the affair. I only stopped to remind myself of that. It is best to remember our mistakes. To forget is to risk repeating them. Do not you agree?"

"Of course, but there is also risk in carrying the remembrance of our failings too far. God forgives us, and then we must move forward and not continue to wallow in false guilt."

I spoke the words, hardly knowing from whence they came. And I heard them too, which was perhaps more important, for I had the eerie sensation that they were meant for me as much as for Marianne. Was God speaking to me out of my own mouth now?

"Colonel?" said Marianne, calling me back from my brief reverie.

"Oh, yes. Pardon me. What I meant to suggest is that you not dwell too much or too long on past failures or perceived indiscretions. Yours are not to be compared with *his*."

"Perhaps not, but they are bad enough. Much of what I suffered can rightly be put down to my own account, and by that knowledge I have been properly chastened."

Before I could decide how to reply, Marianne smiled again, removed her hand from my arm, and walked decisively onward, signaling that the topic was closed.

We spoke no more until we reached our destination, a natural stone-lined alcove near the top of a hill. As soon as we stepped into the protected recess, the chill breeze died away, replaced by the warmth of the sun reflecting off the light-colored rock faces. I took a moment to enjoy the view as well. From that elevated vantage point, I could look far and wide and back over our path, all the way to the cottage below, now off at some distance. "I can understand why you like it here," I said.

"It is my own special place. I've brought no one here before."

I was touched and looked at her. "Thank you for sharing it with me."

She held my gaze a few moments before dropping her eyes. "Yes, well, it is the least I can do. You have brought the story; I must contribute something too. Shall we begin?" she asked, sitting down on a small, flat-topped boulder where she had no doubt rested many times before. "We have just arrived in India and experienced all the sights and sounds. I am impatient to hear what happens next."

"Very well," I said, looking about for a seat and settling on an outcropping across from her, near but not too near. Since I had already spent hours considering what I would say and how to begin, I was as prepared as I could be. And so, after taking a deep breath, I plunged in. "First you must understand that there is much to learn for a newly arrived officer like Major Dunston."

"*Major* Dunston? Forgive me, but I thought he was a colonel?"

"Indeed, he left India a colonel, after being twice promoted, but he was a major when he arrived."

"Oh, I see. Do go on."

"As I was saying, Dunston had much to learn. You mustn't imagine that he or any other man was ready to be sent out on military missions at once. There was a good deal of drilling and training to be got through first. And even at that, I doubt he felt sufficiently prepared when his time came to lead out a company of men, not knowing what kind of trouble they would encounter.

"It is nothing like battle in a traditional war must be, where there are two sides and a uniform makes clear to all who is friend and who is foe. We were essentially an occupying force in a much disputed land. One day we might be protecting British claims against the encroachment of another foreign power, and the next, dealing with some uprising of the local population. India itself is not like the sovereign nation of England, organized around a central government with one king, a single language, and a common religion. It is rather a collection of territories and ancient dynasties with shifting boundaries, ruled by various kings, sultans, and chiefs, speaking dozens of different languages, and subscribing to nearly as many different faiths. Add to that the East India Company – a commercial corporation behaving more like an occupying force itself, with its own standing army and its own currency – and it is difficult to get a clear understanding of who is in charge and who is the enemy."

"I understand," Marianne said at first, and then, "Well, I suppose I don't really. It seems very complicated."

"It was indeed. But that is where the army simplifies everything. Ordinary soldiers do not have to understand any of it; they only have to do as they are told – follow their immediate superiors, who in turn receive their commands from those above them. Soldiers are not invited to think for themselves, you see, only to obey orders.

"I give you this general background information just to set the stage, so that the story I mean to tell you will make more sense. But I will not try your patience any further. I will get to the heart of Dunston's story now. It concerns a woman, an Indian woman. And you will remember what I told you before – that Dunston was nursing a broken heart."

"Oh, yes, Colonel. Poor man. Please proceed. You have my full attention."

And so, using Dunston's name instead of my own, I told Marianne about how I met Rashmi.

Upon my arrival in Madras, I happened to see a particularly exquisite Indian woman as I passed through the marketplace. All was noise and disorder, and yet somehow she seemed to rise above it. Her manner was calm and her countenance serene. From her fine clothing and the number of her entourage, I knew she had to be a lady of wealth and consequence.

She was nothing like the dear one I had left behind in England, of course, not in person or dress. But perhaps that was part of her appeal. If she had borne any similarity to Eliza, it might have seemed disloyal to my lost love to admire another woman less than a year later. But instead, I was merely appreciating a creation of rare splendor, much as I would a picturesque view or the sight of a magnificent thoroughbred flying down the track.

In any case, I was much struck by the woman's exotic beauty – her fine, regular features; her smooth, brown skin; her large, thickly lashed dark eyes; hair so black it was almost blue; and then the vibrant dress and jingling jewelry, which completed the picture. Catching and holding her gaze for a moment before she passed by, I could not help wondering who she might be. But then I soon forgot about the fleeting encounter altogether, caught up in the business of my new life.

It was only months later that I saw her again, recognized her, and learnt the answers to my earlier questions. Her name was Rashmi, and she was the young wife of a rich and influential local man at least forty years her senior.

I learnt all this when I was invited, along with my fellow officers, to dine with that particular Indian gentleman – one of the many elite who found it useful to curry favor amongst the British. He used all resources at his disposal, including his beautiful wife, to please and impress the men who came to dine with him that evening.

The food was superb, with a vast array of Indian dishes spread before us on a long, low tables out of doors. Although some local dishes were still too spicy for me, my tastes had adjusted by this time, so that I could thoroughly enjoy most of what was offered that night. We sat on cushions on the ground and ate, while a handful of musicians played for us on instruments that I had yet to learn the names for. There was a flute of some sort, a stringed instrument played rather like a guitar, a type of drum, and a horn that sounded a bit like an oboe. Altogether, the effect was quite enchanting, but nothing like the music one might hear played by a quartet at an English country dance.

Rashmi was apparently there solely to entertain, for she ate nothing herself. Instead, she moved from table to table, being friendly and attentive to her husband's guests. Obviously well educated, she spoke to the higher ranking officers in accented English with sultry tones and flattering words, some of which I could hear from my position farther down the table. And then, after dinner and at her husband's command, she danced for us.

If every man present had not been half in love with her already, the dance must have done it. The newly arrived officers, like myself, had never seen anything of the kind before, certainly not in our home country. And so perhaps we could have been forgiven for falling under her influence when her hips swayed back and forth to the foreign-sounding music and her lithe arms beckoned seductively.

At first, I looked away, feeling uncomfortable watching the alluring young woman dance in such a provocative manner. After all, she was married, and had I not sailed thousands of miles to separate myself from the pull of the woman I loved because she was now another man's wife? But then, this was a different culture, I reminded myself, and different rules applied. Her husband had provided the dance to entertain us, and it might be seen as an insult to reject his goodwill offering.

And so, giving myself this excuse, I was soon drawn in and staring quite openly, along with all my fellows. I could not seem to help it. She was the most bewitching creature I had ever come across.

After the dance, Rashmi continued to charm the guests. Though I was one of the junior officers, even *I* was not overlooked completely. My nerves jumped when I saw her coming my way, and I leant back ever so slightly. I needn't have worried, though, for the rich man's wife maintained a careful distance when she gracefully knelt across from me at the low table where our dinner had been served.

"Did you enjoy the dance?" she asked.

I felt my face grow hot with guilty embarrassment, as if I had been a naughty child caught stealing sweets or cheating on an examination at school. Before I could recover enough to reply, she continued.

"You did not seem to like it at the beginning, for I noticed you would not look at me. But later you did."

"Yes," I said self-consciously. "I am sorry if you thought I was displeased. I was not. Your dancing was very beautiful. Captivating even, although I cannot imagine my opinion should matter to you, madam. I am a man of very little importance."

"Not so. My husband and I care very much that everybody should enjoy himself tonight. Perhaps you are a little shy, though yes? What is your name?"

"Major Brandon."

"I am very pleased to meet you, Major Brandon. You may call me Rashmi. I wondered if we had met before."

"We have not been introduced or spoken before, but we saw each other once a few months ago, in the market."

A glint of recognition appeared in her eye. "Yes, now I remember. I thought there was something familiar in your face. It is a very good face, Major."

"Yours also," I said and then cursed myself. Not only was it probably too forward; it sounded juvenile as well. But the words had escaped my lips before I could stop to think. Rashmi did not seem to mind, though. In fact, she smiled.

"It is very unlike the faces of the ladies you know in England."

"Yes, but no less lovely for it." I could not seem to keep from saying such things in her presence.

"You are very kind, Major. Do you have a wife or a sweetheart waiting for you at home?" she asked.

That sobered me. "No. There is no one," I said, not wishing to elaborate on the painful subject.

Perhaps she sensed some of what I was feeling, for she apologized. "I am sorry, but I think that will not always be the case. I am very glad to know you, sir, and I hope we shall meet again." And then she moved on.

Nothing of particular significance had occurred, and yet this brief encounter made a deep impression on me, answering some questions but filling my mind with more. To begin with, how had this young beauty ended up married to such an old man? Money, I supposed was the answer; it usually was. The man was rich and his wealth had bought Rashmi for him, one way or another. The idea was repugnant, but not all that foreign, for some version of the same scenario often happened even in England. Could this pair really be happy together, though? Had Rashmi's upbringing prepared her for this life? And what kind of future could she look forward to in such an uneven match? Years and years of widowhood most likely, which seemed a terrible shame. Although perhaps she would marry again – someone nearer her age next time, I hoped. Not that it was any of my business.

Thoughts of Rashmi lingered long after that night, fading and then resurfacing, especially when I would happen to catch a glimpse of her in the town – with or without her distinguished husband.

Six months after the first dinner invitation, a second arrived. Again, it meant an enjoyable evening of excellent food and entertainment for the officers of our regiment. I went, of course, wondering if I would have the chance to speak to Rashmi again.

She smiled when she saw me before the dinner began – a smile of recognition that led me to imagine she was genuinely pleased to see me. Then later, she came to talk with me at the table as before.

"Major Brandon," she said at once. "How good it is to see you again."

"And you, madam. How is it that you remember my name, though? You must have occasion to meet so many people."

"Ah, yes, but not all of them have a face like yours. It is a good face, as I told you before, and so I have made a point of remembering the name by which it is called."

"You are too kind. I hope you have been well, you and your family."

"I have been well, indeed. My family… Other than my husband, that is, I have no family in Madras. I am from the north, you see, and there my family remains. I have not seen my parents or any of my brothers and sisters for nearly three years – ever since I was sent to Madras to be married."

"I'm sorry. You must miss them."

"Of course, but they are happy – and honored – my father especially, to have me married to such an important man. You are far from your home as well, Major. You must have family you miss and who are missing you too."

"Very little. My parents are dead, but I do have two sisters, a brother, and… and a cousin. They will not much miss me while I am gone, however. They are all married and have their own families now."

"And this makes you sad?"

Either she was very perceptive or I had been too transparent. "Not at all," I said. "I must be happy for them to be all so well settled. I will miss *them*, though… some more than others."

"Of course."

I was sorry when Rashmi moved on to give similar attentions to others, for I felt as if we could have talked together for hours if permitted. That was probably only the effect of her skill as a hostess, however, making all her guests feel special and important.

In any case, I hoped I would see Rashmi again. I did, in fact, but under very different and far less pleasant circumstances.

~24~

"So Major Dunston saw this lady, Rashmi, from time to time?" Marianne asked after my narrative had progressed this far. She had been listening intently without interrupting.

"Yes... and so did I occasionally," I told her, thinking it for the best that I should confess this much. "I had been at those dinners too, you see, seated near enough to my friend to hear the conversations I have related to you."

"Then she must have spoken to you as well, since it sounded as if she was careful to take notice of *all* the guests."

"I... That is, yes, she did... just a few inconsequential words in passing," I said, momentarily stumbled. Then I quickly moved on. "But the next event in the story is that, a few months after the second dinner, we heard that Rashmi's husband had died."

"Oh, then she *was* made a very young widow, just as Major Dunston had predicted. Did he have any thoughts of pursuing her himself after that?"

"I cannot say how far his mind might have leapt ahead, had it been given leisure to do so. What I do know is that he was immediately seized with deep concern for her. Not knowing if she had loved her husband or not, he wondered how she fared. Was she distraught? Would she be well cared for, or would her husband's wealth pass immediately into different hands? Might she even be cast out of her home with no means of support? He was still very ignorant of local practices, including what was likely to happen in such a situation.

"And so he enquired of his commanding officer that same day if he might have leave to make a condolence call on the widow. That permission was flatly denied him, however. Furthermore, he was warned in the most emphatic terms to stay away, ordered to do so, in fact. It seemed the official policy – of the East India Company and the British Army as well – was not to interfere in local customs or religious affairs at such a time.

"No additional explanation was given him, but the ominous tone of the warning left Dunston feeling quite uneasy. And so he presently asked a few other men – those who had been in the country much longer – what was likely to happen to Rashmi, now that her husband had died."

Here I paused, dreading what would come next.

Marianne sat forward. "What did he learn, Colonel?"

"In truth, Miss Marianne, it is something difficult for me to speak of. It may be likewise difficult for you to hear." I sighed. "Perhaps I should not continue. No, perhaps I ought never to have begun at all. I apologize."

"Now, Colonel, this will not do. You must indeed continue! I am no shrinking violet, I assure you. I can bear it, whatever it is."

"Very well, then," I said after further consideration. Another sigh and I did as she bade me. "There is a Hindu custom called *sati* or suttee. Have you ever heard of it?"

Her brow furrowed. "No, I do not believe so."

"I thought not. It is a subject unfit for drawing room conversation, and I was unfamiliar with it myself before going to India. In any case, you may be aware of the belief – common to many of the religions of India – of reincarnation, the idea that after death, people will be born again into a new life, higher or lower than the previous one according to how well they have lived, how much karma they have earned. Suttee is said to be the ultimate way for a wife to honor her husband after his death. She can gain a great deal of karma while proving her eternal love and loyalty to him by… by sacrificing her own life, throwing herself on his funeral pyre."

I had tried to say it gently, but still Marianne gasped.

"Heavens!" she exclaimed. "But surely Rashmi would not have done such a thing. She could not have been married to her husband long, and it was unlikely to have been a love match, as you yourself have said."

"Yes, but her husband was a very important man, doubtless considered one to whom much honor was due. There is a great deal of pressure brought to bear on the widow in such a case, I understand."

"And if she still refuses?"

"The grim truth is that she may be taken against her will and cast into the flames by force."

"Barbaric!" cried Marianne in dismay. "Cannot something be done about it? What better use of the British military power could there be than to put an end to such brutal practices?"

"Suttee has been and is strongly discouraged by the British, and individual officers have occasionally taken it upon themselves to intervene. Such heavy-handed tactics anger the local populace, however, inevitably increasing tensions. So, in the name of diplomacy, the official British policy, at least at that time, was not to interfere."

We sat in somber silence for a minute before I asked, "Do you wish me to continue?"

I waited for her answer, and at last, she nodded solemnly.

And so I proceeded, attributing what was really *my* story to Major Dunston as before, as well as omitting certain details, including any mention of the name John Middleton. That he was involved in the business was not mine to reveal.

~~*~~

I was nearly frantic after being told of the suttee custom, with the implication that it might be the horrible fate awaiting Rashmi. And yet there seemed nothing I could do.

I had seen the house where she lived, or more accurately, the compound. A high wall surrounded it, and the place teamed with servants, many looking more like bodyguards than domestic help. If she were truly a prisoner there, her protective compound had become her jail. If she were not, then she did not need my help.

One lone man, attempting a rescue, would almost certainly accomplish nothing beyond getting himself killed. And anybody who might be foolhardy enough to join him in the venture, would be risking life and career as well. Even so, if I had been certain Rashmi's life was in imminent danger, I might not have been able to restrain myself. I might have charged in despite the danger and direct orders to the contrary.

As it was, though, I did not know the true situation. Rashmi might be perfectly safe, not under any threat or compulsion at all, neither requiring nor desiring interference from me or anybody else. Unless or until I had more information, I could not act.

It was as well that I was assigned to patrol the boundaries of the army encampment that night, for in my state of mind, I was fit for nothing but pacing back and forth in any case, going through the motions by rote while continuing to worry over Rashmi.

Half an hour into this duty, my attention was drawn by a slight noise in the brush, along with the impression of movement at the corner of my eye. Leveling my pistol in that direction, I demanded, "Who is there? Show yourself at once."

I held my place several moments, looking and listening intently. Nothing further occurred, and I had nearly decided it had only been a small animal or my imagination playing tricks, when I was startled to hear my own name spoken in something above a whisper. Then a slight figure rose from the brush and came forward into the moonlight. I recognized her at once; it was Rashmi. "You must help me, Major Brandon," she said in a quavering voice.

My amazement at seeing her there was only exceeded by my relief at knowing she was safe, at least for the moment. I looked about to be sure we were not being observed. "Of course I will," I said, "if I can. Tell me what the matter is, Rashmi."

Before she could reply, voices and laughter erupted from another part of the camp. She glanced about fretfully and drew back into the shadows. Then, in a lower voice, she said, "I am in a great deal of danger. You will have heard that my husband has died, yes?"

"Yes, I did hear. My condolences, madam."

"Thank you, but now my husband's friends and family, they intend to force me to join him in his funeral fire! They say I must do the *sati* in his honor. You know this word?"

I nodded solemnly, too distressed to speak.

"And so I run away from them. Some will say that I am a very wicked woman, that I shame myself and my husband. But you will not think so, Major Brandon, will you?"

She extended a trembling hand towards me, which I took and held. "Of course not."

"I know the Englishmen do not believe in such treatment of widows, and so I come here and I wait. Then I see you and remember your kindness. I tell myself, 'He will help me.' If I go to my friends in the north, perhaps I will be safe. But I cannot do it alone. I have no money, you see, and a woman cannot travel by herself only. I have nobody else I can turn to, nobody I can trust to not betray me."

My mind had already been hard at work, searching for an answer to Rashmi's dilemma, which had now, with my promise, become my own as well. That I must help the lady before me did not admit a doubt. I believed it was my duty – as well as my desire – to do so. The question was how. Money, I had; that was the easy part. The way to accomplish her escape was more problematic. Rashmi was not the only one who would need to be secretive; I was under direct orders not to interfere in the case. There seemed no way that I could obey both: my superior's orders and what my conscience required of me.

I looked right and left again to be sure my unusual behavior had not drawn unwanted attention. Instead of moving in a continuous patrol as I should have been, I had stopped several minutes in one place, apparently conversing with only the sultry night air. There was nobody about, however. Luck was with me so far, but I would need much more than luck if I were to succeed. I was still fairly new to India, and there was so much I did not yet understand about the way things worked in this part of the world. Then I thought of John Middleton.

"You were right to trust me," I told Rashmi. "I will help you somehow. Stay here out of sight while I see what arrangements can be made. Do you need anything while you wait? Food? Water? This may take some time."

"Thank you, Major. You are very kind, but I need nothing at present. Do hurry, though."

I nodded and tried to smile encouragingly. Then I squeezed her hand before letting it go and quickly making my way to where I thought to find John Middleton. I was relieved to discover him alone.

"Have you lost your mind?" he retorted after I had explained Rashmi's situation and my intention to assist her. "I understand your desire to help the lady, Brandon, and your compassion does you credit. But you would be throwing away your promising military career on a girl you barely know."

The face of another imperiled young woman then flashed before my mind's eye: my friend and cousin Eliza. Unlike Rashmi, Eliza I had known as well as I knew my own right arm. And yet, when trouble came, I had utterly failed in my intention to save her. Perhaps that was why it seemed so imperative that I should do something for this girl, though a stranger.

John was continuing. "Probably all for nothing, too, for like as not the attempt would meet with disaster. It simply cannot be done!"

"Nevertheless, I mean to do it. Get me a guide, and I will escort Rashmi north myself. Confound it, man! I will not turn my back on another lady who asks for my protection!"

"Now Christopher, you are not thinking of Eliza again, are you?" he said more gently. "You did everything you could there, and it cannot be so horrible a fate to be mistress at Delaford, after all. But you see what I mean; this situation is beyond your control just as that one was. Do not sacrifice yourself to a hopeless cause, I beg you."

"I appreciate your concern, John, but you can save your breath; my mind is made up. Now will you assist me or no? Either way, you are sworn to secrecy."

John sighed and then looked heavenward, wagging his head back and forth – beseeching the heavens for aid or debating with himself what to answer me. I knew not which.

"Very well," he said at last. "If you are determined to go forward with this daft plan, I suppose I must do what I can to see you come to as little harm as possible."

I stepped forward and firmly clasped his hand. "Thank you, old friend. I knew I could depend on you."

"Do not thank me; if I were any kind of a friend, I would talk you out of this insanity."

What he did instead was offer to send for someone he knew to guide the expedition. "Conner Baldwin is your man," John told me, "and luckily, I happen to know he is here in Madras at the moment. He is just the fellow for this kind of thing. Been everywhere. Knows everybody, European and Indian. More important, he knows how to get things done in this backward country... for a price, of course. He will not sell his services cheaply, I warn you."

"I do not regard the expense."

"Well, no doubt he will be happy to hear that!"

"Is the man trustworthy, though? Will he do what I ask and keep his word? That is what I wish to know."

John waved off my questions. "Oh, as to that, you need have no scruples. Baldwin is as good a sort of fellow as ever lived, I assure you. So what do you say? Shall I send for him?"

I hesitated, feeling the import of this decision. I was not normally a man to act in haste, and the need to do so now made me uneasy. But Rashmi was waiting, huddled in the jungle, perhaps even at that moment in mortal danger. And it would be light in a few hours. There was clearly no time for thorough investigations or interviewing other candidates. I was obliged to rely on my friend's judgment in the matter. What other choice did I have? I had to move quickly and decisively if we were to get away before daybreak, before we were found out and prevented.

I gave a sharp nod. "Do it," I said.

While I waited for the guide, Mr. Baldwin, to arrive – which I could only hope he would, and without delay – I packed together my few personal possessions and whatever else I might need for the journey. I had no idea what would happen to me when I returned to camp, how severe my punishment would be for disobeying orders and being absent without leave. But I could not think of that then. I had committed to helping Rashmi escape, and I was not about to go back on my word, regardless of the consequences. If I could save her, I reasoned, then my life would have had some meaning after all.

Baldwin did come, ready to take on the job, and John brought him to my tent. My first impression was that he seemed a rough sort of man, not like somebody I would normally gravitate towards as a friend. But then I considered that was probably what the occasion required. A drawing room style gentleman who was afraid to get his hands dirty would not serve the purpose at all.

The barest of introductions completed, Baldwin named his price without compunction. It was high. Very high, in fact. It would cost me virtually every farthing I had at my disposal, with only a little to spare for my return trip. But I was in no position or mood to quibble. "Very well," I said. "I will pay you half now and the other half when you have seen me and the lady safely to our destination."

He rolled his eyes and held out his hand, rubbing his fingers together as if literally itching to feel the weight of the silver in his palm. "All of it now or I don't go a step." When I did not promptly comply, he added. "Look here, Major, I have plenty of other, more profitable things I could be doing. It is only as a favor to your friend here…" He poked a thumb back over his shoulder at John Middleton. "…that I come at all. So let's not mess about. Pay me the money and we'll be on our way. Right?"

I looked at John. He was nodding with an expression that said *this is the way things are done here.* And so I paid the man and we went out into the night to collect Rashmi.

~~*~~

At this point in my narrative, Marianne and I were interrupted by a flash and a clap of thunder, drawing our attention simultaneously skyward. When the dark clouds had rolled in, I knew not. The diminution of the light had gone unnoticed by me, probably because in my head it had been the black night of India.

"We had better return home at once," I said – needlessly, for Marianne was already on her feet and moving.

"What a shame about our story," she called over her shoulder as we hurried down the hill. "Just when I feel sure we were nearly to the most exciting part, too!"

By then, as the rain began to pelt down upon us, I had a different concern in view. "Mind your step, Miss Marianne," I called back. "And will you take my hand? I would not suggest it except for the exigence of the situation."

We were approaching the very spot where she had fallen before, and by the change in her countenance, I believe she understood my intent, which was to do what I could to ensure a safer descent this time. No doubt that was the only reason she complied so easily. We clasped hands and raced on with as much speed as the steep terrain allowed. When we had attained the garden gate, I reluctantly released her, and then we swiftly passed on into the house itself.

Marianne was laughing by this time, as if she had found great sport in the escapade. I, too, had enjoyed our time at the hilltop as well as the run for home, although I imagine my own lightheartedness had more to do with my companion than the activity itself.

"At last!" exclaimed Mrs. Dashwood upon our entrance. "Did you not notice the darkening sky?"

"My apologies, madam," said I. "I should have taken more care to observe the change in the weather."

"I am perfectly well, Mama, as you see," said Marianne, her laughter beginning to subside. "No sprained ankles this time; Colonel Brandon has seen to that." She sent me a smiling glance. "In any case, it was well worth getting caught in the rain to hear more of Major Dunston. I was so absorbed in his story that it took the sudden storm to call me back to myself."

"No doubt that was very pleasant, child, but I will not have you taking a chill, especially so soon after your other illness. Now upstairs with you at once to change out of those wet things."

"But the story, Colonel! We were interrupted before we could finish."

"Never mind that, Miss Marianne," I interjected. "It will keep. Your health is more important."

"Upstairs, now," Mrs. Dashwood ordered her daughter, pointing that direction. After Marianne had turned and gone, Mrs. Dashwood continued. "Alas, Colonel, we have no dry clothes for *you* here – only Mr. Edward's things, and they would not do. I daresay they would fall far short of covering the length of your arms and legs!"

"It is no matter, my dear lady. I will be off to the Park directly to change."

"Oh, but do take an umbrella," she said, handing me one, "and return to us later. This is to be our last evening together, is it not?"

"For now, yes, and of course I will come. I would not think of losing your company any sooner than necessary."

Mrs. Dashwood gave me a sly look. "Very pretty words, Colonel, but I know whose company you really crave more of! No use to deny it. Now, off you go. The sooner you leave us the sooner you will return, dry and comfortable again."

We were all together that last evening at Barton Cottage – Mrs. Dashwood, her three daughters, Edward Ferrars, and myself – in a very companionable and merry group. Mrs. Dashwood sounded the only cheerless notes, frequently lamenting the imminent loss of all her company, for Edward was departing on the morrow as well, following me to Delaford for his first look at his future home.

A letter from Mr. John Dashwood to his step-mother, newly arrived and read out by her, provided one lively topic for discussion that evening. In it, he suggested a course he thought most eligible to heal the breach between Edward and his mother, saying, *a letter of proper submission from him, addressed perhaps to Fanny, and by her shown to her mother, might not be taken amiss; for we all know the tenderness of Mrs. Ferrars's heart, and that she wishes for nothing so much as to be on good terms with her children.*

I was not the only one amazed by this characterization of the lady, wondering if Mr. John Dashwood could possibly be speaking of the same woman who had been so quick to disown and disinherit her eldest son.

"A letter of proper submission!" Edward retorted. "What? Would they have me beg my mother's pardon for Robert's ingratetude to *her* and breach of honor to *me*? I can make no honest apology, for I am grown neither humble nor penitent by what has passed. I am grown very *happy*, but that would not interest her. No, I cannot in good conscience do as he suggests – I will not! – for I know of no submission that is proper for me to make."

He had risen during this impassioned speech and now stood immovable with arms stubbornly crossed.

Elinor reached up and gently drew him by the arm back into his seat beside her. Then, with the utmost tact, she suggested, "You may certainly ask to be forgiven for having grieved and offended her, for so you did. That much is true. And I should think you might *now* venture so far as to profess some regret for having ever formed the engagement which drew on you your mother's anger."

Edward, looking a little ashamed, said more meekly, "I suppose I might. I have deeply regretted that act of foolishness for a very long time." Holding Elinor's eye, he brought her hand to his lips and kissed it.

"And when she has forgiven you," his ladylove continued, "perhaps a little humility may be convenient when you acknowledge a second engagement, one almost as imprudent in *her* eyes as the first."

This raised in my mind a question. "Does not Mrs. Ferrars yet know your good news, which the rest of us celebrate?"

"No, my mother is still in blissful ignorance of the joyful event soon to overtake her," Edward answered with heavy sarcasm. "The same is true of John and Fanny, else I daresay they should not be nearly so optimistic about my chances of securing her forgiveness."

"But perhaps in this case they are correct," Marianne contributed, in her new character of candor. "Fanny must know her mother well enough to think a reconciliation possible. And if they really do interest themselves in bringing it about, I shall think that even John and Fanny are not entirely without merit."

"That is very generous of you," said Edward. "As for myself, I have nothing to urge against making a try." He turned to Elinor again. "Any relenting on my mother's side, especially if accompanied by a loosening of the purse strings, would be very welcome in making our situation more comfortable. But I still cannot think this 'letter of submission' John suggests is the best way to go about it. No, I had much rather *speak* these wretched concessions than put them on paper."

"Then what do you mean to do?" asked Elinor.

"Instead of writing to Fanny, I shall go directly from Delaford to London and personally entreat her good offices in my favor – in *our* favor."

After a late supper, Marianne took her accustomed place at the piano-forte to entertain us. Mrs. Dashwood sat with Margaret, Edward with Elinor again, and I sat by myself. Some quiet conversation carried on between the others, despite the music, but I could not attend. My focus was all on Marianne. From my position a little removed from the rest, I could listen without distraction and openly gaze at the fair musician without concern that my motives would be questioned. Although I suppose I was only fooling myself to think that there was anybody in the room that night – with the exception of Margaret and possibly Marianne herself – who was unaware of my feelings in the case.

After half an hour, Marianne finished and made as if to leave the instrument. Mrs. Dashwood spoke up, however. "Dearest, do play one more for us. You know the one that I like so much. There's a love."

"The Haydn sonata?"

"Yes, I suppose that is it. I only recall that it does not have a proper name, just a number or something. Do humor me, Marianne, and play it, won't you?"

"Of course, Mama," she said. "I know the one you mean, but you must come and turn the pages when I tell you, like you have done before. Parts of it move along much too quickly for me to turn them myself without stopping and spoiling the music."

"Oh, no; I am a little tired this evening. Let Colonel Brandon stand in my place this time, since he is by. He will assist you much better because he understands music. You will not mind, will you, Colonel?"

"On the contrary," I replied, trying not to appear too eager. "It would be my pleasure."

"There. You see, Marianne. It is all settled."

Marianne gave a nod of assent to her mother and then looked at me. "Colonel, if you please?" I rose and came to her side as she was finding the piece she wanted.

Examining the music she propped up before her, I recognized it as the F-major portion of the six-sonata opus Haydn had composed for Prince Nicholas. "Ah," I said. "I am familiar with this. In fact, I have played it myself. A wonderful but challenging piece."

She looked up smartly, a light in her eye. "That being the case, Colonel, I would like to issue you a challenge. You may turn the pages for me in the first and third movements, and I will turn the pages for *you* in the second."

"A competition? If so, I shall cede the victory to you at once, for it must be at least six months since I played this particular sonata."

"How do you know it has been less for me?"

"Because it is your mother's favorite."

"Ah, yes, but I was away from home from January until April, as you know. At all events, it is *not* a competition I propose, but a collaboration between us."

"In that case, I accept."

~26~

I woke early the next morning at Barton Park, packed my things together, breakfasted, and made ready to depart. The visit to Barton had gone so well as to make it a tempting prospect to extend my stay, which Mrs. Dashwood had kindly begged me to do as I was leaving the cottage the night before. Even Marianne had said she wished I would stay on, so that she "might hear more of Colonel Dunston's story."

My heart soared for what appeared to be a good deal of progress in my slow and steady campaign to win Marianne's favor. I was firmly persuaded that she no longer disdained me, as once she had done. She respected me, I think, and perhaps she even liked me well enough to call me a friend. But more than that I dared not depend on. In any case, it was time to draw back again and be patient, to allow her to think and become comfortable with this much before I asked her for more.

So I kept to my plan, and as soon as Mr. Ferrars joined me, we set off for Delaford.

My positive opinion of Edward Ferrars was steadily growing. The more time I spent in his company, the more convinced I became that I had done right to give him the Delaford living. He was a man of upright principles and good sense, despite at least one youthful misjudgment. In disposition and manner of thinking, we seemed much alike. If these traits alone were not a solid basis for friendship, then our being in love with two sisters – two sisters much attached to each other – must have made our mutual regard inevitable and even more swiftly established.

That Mr. Ferrars was aware of this relationship, I was not long in discovering. As we rode together in my carriage, Ferrars himself soon raised the subject, laying out for me what he had learnt from Elinor on the topic, which had then been confirmed by his own recent observations.

"I heartily wish you swift success with Marianne, Colonel," he said in conclusion. "I know that nothing would make Elinor happier than to see her sister contentedly settled at Delaford just as soon as may be. And what makes her happy is my highest desire as well. You see, now that I know you have no designs on Elinor yourself, I can be magnanimous."

"Designs on Elinor?" I repeated, mystified. "What can you mean?"

"Just that," he said in a tone I could not quite interpret. "I had it on good authority, you see, that that was what you had in mind."

"On whose authority, if you please?"

"Mrs. Jennings assured me it was so. She spoke of her sanguine expectations of visiting Delaford in the not too distant future, dividing her time between Lucy at the parsonage with me and Elinor at the manor house with you. Of course, when I considered that picture of the future, I could not like you as well as you deserved!"

"I should imagine not! Mrs. Jennings's imagination is very rapid," I said, "eagerly jumping from one wrong conclusion to another. I suppose I should not wonder at her assumption in this case, though, as much time as Elinor and I spent together in her house and under her eye. She could not have known our true situations – that we were only, in our mutual misery, providing some friendship and consolation to each other. The truth is, I like and respect your future wife exceedingly well, Mr. Ferrars, and I will be delighted to love her as my *sister*, if the best should occur. But I assure you, neither of us ever had any thoughts of matrimony!"

Edward laughed. "Be easy, my good fellow. I believe you. Even if you had, however, I am so happy at this moment – for the exchange of Elinor for Lucy – as to forgive you and to be in charity with all the rest of the world, including Mrs. Jennings." He shook his head ruefully. "A lucky escape I have made. I still cannot quite fathom how I managed to get myself into such a tangle, though."

"Youthful folly?" I suggested.

"Yes. Many mistakes can be laid at that door. I am only very grateful I shall not need to live with mine – quite literally – for the rest of my life. Now that I am a bit older, and hopefully a bit wiser, it astounds me that such important decisions are ever left to the very young. Does any boy of seventeen or eighteen ever truly know his own mind, do you suppose? – or know his own good? No wonder it led to disaster!"

I thought of Eliza. Yes, at seventeen, I had known my own mind very well. And so had she. It was the will and the decisions of others that brought on disaster... that and my own powerlessness. "One rule will not serve for all," I said. "It is my belief that in some instances the choices of youth may be wise. It might be only their ability to carry them out that is lacking."

"Well, in my case, I am grateful that I *did* lack the means to act on my first foolish inclination, or there would have been no escape. I was unexpectedly given a second chance, and I flatter myself that I have not wasted it. I have chosen much better this time. Where would any of us be without the chance at a second attachment?"

"Indeed," I agreed. Then we both fell silent.

Second attachments, I mused, remembering Marianne's sentiments on that subject, that under no circumstances could such a thing be acceptable. Did she still hold to that maxim? Or had her broader experience of the world now broadened her views as well? With Willoughby gone for good, she must now, for her own sake, accept the possibility of being happy with someone else. Not to mention for mine.

I was still thinking about these things when Edward burst forth, as if he could no longer hold something back. "Dash it all! Brandon, you must think me a pretty fool for how I have behaved. A perfect cad, a bounder."

"On the contrary, Mr. Ferrars. I certainly never would have offered you the Delaford living if I had."

"Thank you, but I still feel I owe you some explanation – owe it to myself to tell you – if we are to be friends and you my patron."

"I disagree, but if it would make you more comfortable..."

"Yes, it would. It is not so much my behavior towards Lucy that I feel needs explanation, for I really do think we can put that down to youth and idleness – that plus the influence of her feminine wiles. My head was turned, and I fell. Then having once entered into an understanding, I could never go back on my word."

"Good man."

"No, it is my behavior toward Elinor that must seem strange to you. What had I been playing at when I was at Norland, to be recommending myself to one young woman while still engaged to another?" He paused briefly, shaking his head with an air of perplexity. "Believe me, I have asked myself that question a hundred times. I have examined my motives as well, and I have not much to say in my own defense, except this. We were thrown together for an extended period. Six months! Seeing Elinor nearly every day, how could I help but fall in love with her, excellent creature that she is? I did not plan it. I did not deliberately single her out for attention. I exerted no effort to make myself particularly agreeable to her. Though I enjoyed her company – as I did the rest of her family – I told myself there was no danger; nothing could come of it because I was an engaged man."

"But Elinor did not know that."

"Precisely! And therein lies the chief problem with my reasoning. She did not know of my prior engagement, nor could I tell her, although once I did try. So we went on – in friendship alone, or so I told myself. When I could no longer deny the truth that I was in love with her, and when I would have offered for her if I could have… Pity me, Colonel Brandon, for I knew she could never be mine. Even then I did not withdraw as I should have. Elinor's reserve, I think, convinced me that her heart was at no risk. And I told myself, 'If you must spend the rest of your life with a woman you do not love and can no longer admire, then at least first enjoy these few bittersweet weeks in the company of this model of superior womanhood. Store up the memories, man, for they must last you a very long time.' Can you understand that, Colonel?"

I could well understand the torture of craving time with the woman one loves, even knowing one can never possess her. So I had felt about Marianne for the months she was attached to Willoughby… and beyond. So I had felt for Eliza after she was married to my brother and memories were all that remained to me. That is why I had joined the army and gone away. "There is great danger in such a situation, Mr. Ferrars, to yourself and possibly the lady as well."

"Yes! Oh, that I had a friend like you alongside to advise me at the time, to save me from myself and from causing heartache to the one I loved above every other creature on the planet! But Elinor has forgiven me, and so I suppose I must learn to subdue my mind to my good fortune, to accept being much happier than I deserve."

~~*~~

When we had come within the environs of Delaford, it was still early enough in the day that a brief stop at the parsonage seemed eligible. Edward had already been cautioned by myself to not expect anything grand, and yet I still inwardly cringed as the house came into view. "There," I said, pointing. Seen through the eyes of a gentleman brought up in some style, it must look very humble and impossibly small.

I signaled for the driver to stop. "I'm sorry the house is not a good deal better, Mr. Ferrars," I said as we exited the carriage, "but I am prepared to undertake whatever improvements are needed to make it a comfortable habitation."

Edward said nothing at first. I knew he would be too polite to complain in any case, and so I watched for clues to his true sentiments in his countenance as he stood looking at the humble parsonage, taking his first impression of the place. Instead of horror or even disappointment, however, I saw a kind of wistful excitement.

"This will soon be our home together," he said, "mine and Elinor's. I still cannot quite believe it."

"The garden needs some trimming and tidying," I suggested, "and the brickwork could use attention."

"No doubt. But it has a friendly charm about it, as if the place is... smiling." He laughed. "I know it sounds daft, but that is the feeling. It gives the impression that families have found happiness within its walls before. And will again, I trust." He turned to me eagerly. "May we go in?"

"Of course, but you should not expect too much." The warning was lost on him, however, as he was already hurrying towards the front door.

Once inside, it became impossible to maintain the pleasant illusion about the place that Mr. Ferrars had apparently adopted. A more practical side of him emerged as we got to work evaluating the condition of the rooms, one by one, and cataloging the improvements to be made.

The size of the house was not so deficient as I had been picturing in my mind. The bedrooms were satisfactory in number and dimensions, at least for now. The parlor and dining room were adequate as well. But the kitchen was undeniably small (not that Mr. Stinson, a bachelor, had ever complained of it), and there were a long list of repairs needed throughout. To begin with, the weather was coming in through a hole in the roof and a broken window in the kitchen. Both had thus far been addressed with makeshift measures rather than permanent solutions. Two of the fireplaces smoked, as evidenced by the discoloration of the near walls and ceiling. And some of the furniture was shabby and worn.

"The whole roof must be inspected, possibly replaced, and all the chimneys swept," I said after we had come about to the kitchen again. "I will need to get my gardener started down here at once. And I've just had an idea. Instead of simply replacing that kitchen window, what would you say to breaking through the wall to add more work space and room for a proper pantry? Do you think Elinor would like that?"

"Undoubtedly!"

"Good. These things will require the longest to accomplish and can be undertaken at once. I think it best to wait on Miss Dashwood's pleasure before choosing furniture and papers for the walls, and so forth. Would you agree?"

"By all means. I would not entrust such important matters to *my* taste."

"Nor mine. When do you expect the marriage to take place?"

"I cannot see that it will happen before late August at the soonest," said Edward, "but perhaps we will need to delay a bit beyond for the expedient of having a house ready to live in afterward. A few repairs are one thing; breaking down walls, quite another."

"Whatever you choose, of course, but you needn't wait for this house. I should be very pleased to have you both to stay with me at the mansion-house until this one is ready for you."

"That is extremely generous, sir!"

"Nonsense. It would be a great pleasure to me. And perhaps then your wife's mother and sisters will come to stay as well on occasion. It is high time that my house should be full of company."

When such thoughts as this occurred, it was difficult not to be carried away too far by my imaginings – carried away to a day when

Marianne might come to my house but not return with her mother to Barton afterwards.

27

That evening and most of the next day, Mr. Ferrars and I continued planning the improvements to be made at the parsonage house. I also acquainted him with my house, the rest of the estate, the village, and with the surrounding parish, soon to be under his spiritual care. Then I did my best to fortify him for his next mission: traveling to London to attempt a reconciliation with his contentious mother and, if that went well, to press for her consent to his marriage to Elinor. Having met Mrs. Ferrars myself, I did not envy him that daunting task.

After Edward departed, I was on my own again and soon learnt to lament the quiet seclusion that I used to enjoy.

When I had first come to Delaford as master after my brother's early death – more than five years past – I expected to thrive in my improved circumstances. Since returning from India, I had been drifting from place to place with no settled home. I lived within my means and cultivated no vices, and yet, other than looking after Beth, I had no real purpose in life either.

Now, at last, I had meaningful work to do. Now it was *my* responsibility to care for Delaford and all those who depended on the estate. I was no longer a child, ignored and disregarded by my father. I was no longer the younger son and younger brother, who had no say. I could now manage things as *I* saw fit for a change. When I recognized a problem or deficiency, I finally had the means and the power to do something about it.

Not that the place was crumbling into disrepair when I inherited it. No, Eliza's money had been put to good use by my predecessors. So much so that it took some time before I could look at the recent improvements without continuously thinking, *That roof was pur-*

chased with Eliza's purloined fortune, or, *Eliza paid for that addition, which she never had a proper chance to enjoy.* How could I live in a house saved by ill-gotten gain without feeling it weighing on my conscience? Although I was not personally responsible for the crime, I now personally benefitted by it.

Everywhere I looked I saw Eliza: the stairs we had raced up together as children, sliding down the banister when we could get away with it, and then running up to do it again; the gardens where we had happily played for so many hours, and where we had exchanged stolen kisses when we were older; the place where her portrait used to hang before I left for India.

That was one of the first things I tried to address when I became master: locating Eliza's missing portrait. I interrogated the servants – any that had been in the house long enough – to see what they might know of the picture's whereabouts. To no avail, though. So I searched high and low myself, every attic and closet, finding nothing. The portrait seemed to have vanished without a trace. Ever since my corresponding miniature had been destroyed (a sad casualty of battle), and especially since Eliza's death, I had hoped her likeness would one day be restored to me in the form of that beautiful portrait. Now it was gone as well, lost forever, presumably. I was left with only my fading memories of her dear face.

Living in that big house all alone, I was easy prey for melancholy reflections. I knew it was not Eliza who haunted me, though; it was my own thoughts, my borrowed guilt for how she had been treated by my family, and her tragic end. The assurance that my sweet friend had indeed forgiven me before she died allowed me to eventually make peace with her lingering presence. Only then could I begin to feel more comfortable in my own home, to feel that I truly belonged and even had some right to be happy there if I could.

If not actually happy, I had at least been content spending most of my time on my own at Delaford during those five years. I enjoyed the estate work – directing the timber and agricultural enterprises and seeing to the needs of the tenant farmers – which so often took me out of doors on horseback. I saw my nearest neighbors at church and occasionally otherwise. Business took me to London three or four times every year, where I had ready access to as much or as little of society as I had a taste for at the time.

My equally frequent visits to Barton Park were one of the things I looked forward to most. John Middleton and I had remained close after our military service together, despite some unfortunate things that had occurred there. He soon inherited, married, and began raising up a clutch of children about him. Lady Middleton did not become a great female friend and confidante to me – not like Elinor later did – but neither was she in any way inhospitable. On the contrary, she always seemed mildly pleased to see me and never gave me reason to suppose that my presence or my demands on her husband's time were unwelcome. The Middleton children were to me much the same as other noisy society: a pleasure when partaken of in small doses.

This was my style of life for five years. I did not mind my solitude; I desired no more company than I had readily within my reach. Despite some voices, especially Sir John's, saying I needed to look about myself for a wife (and despite some indication from a variety of ladies that I might be successful if I did), I made no effort toward that end. None of the women of my acquaintance interested me in that way, and as irrational as it seems, I still felt myself on some level plighted to my first love, though she had married another and had now been dead for years.

All this changed, of course, when the Dashwood ladies came to Barton Cottage.

At first, my admiration had fixed only on Marianne. That had quickly changed, however, expanding to encompass her entire family as well. The love evident between them all, along with the generous hand of friendship they had extended to me, had given a glimpse into what comforts a true home – be it mansion or cottage – might contain. Other than the early fellowship I had shared with Eliza, my own family life had borne no resemblance to it.

After every sampling of the domestic pleasures at Barton Cottage, I came home less able than before to abide the solitude of Delaford cheerfully.

Edward's presence had at first softened the transition, but his influence was now at an end. Only the servants remained in the great house with me, and although their presence preserved me from absolute isolation, I could find no true companionship there. I thought again of the story of Adam in Genesis. God brought every living creature of Eden before him, and although each one was *good* in its own way, Adam found no suitable counterpart among them, not until God created for him the woman Eve. *This is now bone of my bones, and flesh of my flesh,* Adam said. *Therefore shall a man leave his father and his mother and shall cleave unto his wife, and they shall become one flesh.*

Once again, it was probably unwise to dwell long on that particular picture.

The evenings were the worst. I could always find things to occupy myself with during the day. But in the waning light, there was little to do but read. Although I loved books, there were times when I wanted another person with whom to pass those long hours. Constant conversation and revelry were not necessary or even desirable; just a companion to sit by my side before the fire, to share my home and my thoughts. And perhaps music. After being alone so long, that did not seem too much to ask.

I lasted at Delaford little more than a fortnight – just long enough to be sure the work at the parsonage was well started and could go on without me. Then I made ready to leave once more.

It was far too soon to think of imposing on my friends at Barton again, and so London must be my destination, I decided. There, I need never be alone if I did not wish it. There, one could find people and entertainment at whatever hour of the day or night it was required. There, I had other good friends who would be glad to see me: Sir John, his family, and Mrs. Jennings. Perhaps Edward as well, if he had not already beaten a path back to Elinor's side. On my way to town, though, I would visit Beth and her young son again.

~~*~~

After three weeks away, I returned to Delaford, resolved on settling to my work and my quiet life once more. That is not what occurred, however, because awaiting me upon my homecoming was a brief letter from Mrs. Dashwood:

Dear Colonel Brandon,
    Be assured that we are all well here at Barton Cottage and hope you are the same. I write to ask a great favor of you (although I trust you will not think it a hardship at all!).

I know it has not been long since your last, but would you consider paying us another visit, if it is not too inconvenient? Marianne's eighteenth birthday is the last day of June, and I have an idea that she would like nothing so much for a present as to hear the rest of the story you have been telling her by installments. If, however, you cannot come, perhaps you might write it out for her and put it in the post. Either way, I daresay it will be a delightful surprise to her.

Your devoted friend, etc.
Mrs. Dashwood

Marianne would be eighteen at last – a more respectable age at which to be married. Welcome news. But then I had to sigh, remembering that I was also another year older than when we first met. Nevertheless, I had charted a course for myself and was not prepared to give up the campaign just yet.

A quick reminder of the date informed me that I had little time to lose if I was to get myself to Barton Cottage by the end of the month. Two days at home to rest the horses and take care of necessary business, and I would be off again.

Visiting in person was naturally my choice. I could not resist the invitation to see them all once more. And the chance to please Marianne with a gift for her birthday... That was irresistible. A letter would not be the same at all, at least not for me.

I wondered what Marianne would think of the conclusion of Major Dunston's story. I had taken care to warn her from the outset that he was no great hero, but did she remember? Or was she unconsciously expecting a fairytale ending for him and Rashmi? If so, she might feel cheated, and that would not be the *delightful surprise* her mother wanted for her. It was a chance I would have to take, however.

28

There was no time to alert Mrs. Dashwood by post to my coming, so my arrival would be nearly as much of a surprise for her as for Marianne. Or perhaps not. The lady probably knew me well enough to predict what I would do in this case. I daresay she knew she could depend on my devotion to her daughter to bring me to heel at the first whisper of invitation.

When I arrived, I was shown into the parlor, where the Dashwood ladies awaited me. Marianne, to whom my eyes were immediately drawn, looked genuinely pleased to see me. Although, before I could take too much hope from that, I quickly reminded myself that no doubt it was mostly for the prospect of collecting the rest of the story I had promised her.

But first, I bowed and presented her with a bouquet of flowers I had brought with me from Delaford. "A very happy birthday, Miss Marianne," I said, extending my small offering towards her.

She took the flowers with a little flush of pleasure, and she lifted them to her nose. "These are lovely, Colonel. Thank you. I did not know we were to expect you, though."

"Your mother was good enough to suggest it... by way of a surprise, I think."

"Of course," she said, turning to that lady. "How kind you are, Mama."

"Indeed," I agreed. "Mrs. Dashwood, you are the soul of generosity. I am grateful to enjoy the favor of your hospitality again so soon."

"Last time, Colonel, you could hardly have called it true hospitality, for we welcomed you into our home by day but sent you away again each night. We will do better this time."

"No Mr. Ferrars has come in ahead of me, then?" I asked, looking to Elinor. "I saw him lately in town and thought he intended to return to Barton by now."

"We did expect him," said Elinor, "but we received his letter instead, informing us of a delay. Apparently, a little more time is needed to accomplish his goal."

"Ah," I said. "I understand." When I had seen Edward in town, he had been accepted back into his mother's good graces, but he had not yet worked up courage enough to tell her of his new engagement to Elinor.

"When Edward comes with good news, our joy shall be complete," said Mrs. Dashwood. "But in the meantime, we still have much to celebrate: Marianne's birthday and the arrival of our special guest. Colonel Brandon, do consider our home your own for however long you care to remain."

I thanked her for this handsome sentiment. Then Marianne asked me, "Shall I have the rest of my story while you are here, Colonel?"

"If you wish it."

"Of course, I do! I have been on pins and needles of anticipation since you left off, and imagining all sorts of possible ways it might finish."

"Your imagination may have already supplied an ending more to your taste than the one I will give you, Miss Marianne. Imaginations can travel anywhere and accomplish everything. They can fulfill all our darling wishes, whereas I am bound by the truth of what actually happened. That is what I promised you from the beginning, if you recall – no improvements or embellishments."

"I do remember, and yet I cannot help hoping that the real ending is not too terribly grim."

"You will soon learn the truth and judge for yourself. Tomorrow, I think. Would that suit you?"

"Oh, yes! In the same place on the hill, if the weather is fine and Mama does not object," she said eagerly, turning to her mother.

"You shall have no objection from me," answered Mrs. Dashwood. "It is exactly what I could have wished for you, my darling."

The next morning, as we made our way up the hill together, I told Marianne, "Your mother did more than wish for this. She invited me on purpose, so that you might have the rest of your story for your birthday."

"She understands me very well and knows what will please me," she said, keeping her eyes on the path in front of her.

My furtive glance at her face revealed a gentle smile and the hint of another blush. Once again, I had to remind myself to interpret these encouraging signs for what they really were: the result of the wind on her cheeks and her eagerness to hear my story.

"It was a thoughtful suggestion on her part," I agreed. "I only hope you will not be too disappointed with what I have to tell."

Our elevated destination achieved at last, we settled into the places we had occupied on the previous occasion. My fair companion then folded her hands in her lap and looked to me expectantly.

I basked in her open gaze for a moment before drawing myself back to the matter at hand. "Yes, well, where exactly did I leave off, Miss Marianne?"

"Major Dunston had met that rough-looking man, come to be his guide. Oh, what was his name?"

"Mr. Baldwin, I suppose you mean."

"Yes, that was it. Major Dunston hired Mr. Baldwin and paid him what he demanded. I remember that the major was uneasy about the arrangement and the man, which makes me uneasy as well."

"I can understand your apprehension; it is not wholly unjustified," I said, thinking to better prepare her for what she was to hear. "But if you remember, Dunston had no other option if he wanted to save Rashmi. He knew so little of the country himself that he could never have successfully escorted her to her friends in the north on his own. Plus, his own friend, the lieutenant colonel, assured him that he could trust Mr. Baldwin to get the job done. And so Major Dunston was compelled to place his own fate and Rashmi's into that man's hands…"

~~*~~

In truth, I was nearer the end of the story than Marianne probably suspected, for I could tell her of no grand adventure of travelling overland through tiger-infested jungles, such as one composing a tale designed to fascinate and delight might devise. I did not in fact face mile after arduous mile under threat of nature and hostile enemy forces, as I myself had anticipated on my noble quest to save Rashmi. I was neither fated to be hailed a hero nor decried as a disgrace to my regiment for desertion. Little could I have guessed it at the time, but there remained only a very short journey before me, one with an ignominious conclusion.

After I swung my pack onto my back, Baldwin and I went out into the night to collect Rashmi, with John Middleton along to see us off.

Rashmi was where I had left her, and with a little coaxing, she came forth from her hiding place. "This is Mr. Baldwin," I told her with a calmness meant to reassure her. "He is an experienced man who knows his way about this country, and he has agreed to be our guide and protector on the journey, to help us safely to your friends in the north."

Her wide eyes darted from me to Mr. Baldwin to John and back again, looking very much like a frightened rabbit. She finally nodded her hesitant agreement.

"Come along now," said Baldwin, gruffly. "I have my supplies and my man waiting at the road. We had best be off while the darkness holds."

"Of course," I agreed, extending my arm to Rashmi. Baldwin beat me to it, though, taking her by the wrist and pulling her forward as he began to stride away.

A brief skirmish ensued. Rashmi cried out – in fear or pain, I did not know which. I protested at the same time – "Here, now, unhand her!" – as I moved to interfere with Baldwin's calloused treatment of the lady. Then I heard the trample of approaching feet and somebody shouting, "Hold him!"

Only when I felt myself being towed backwards by the arms and shoulders did I realize they were referring to me. "It's for your own good, Brandon!" That was John's voice, I knew. I ignored it, though, struggling to free myself.

Then my skull cracked with pain, and I fell immediately to my knees. The last I saw before losing all sense was Rashmi's horrified expression as she was being dragged away by Mr. Baldwin.

I awoke sometime later – approximately two hours, I pieced together after the fact – with a splitting headache and no clear idea at first as to what had happened. Then the sickening truth came back to me in a flash: the planned night escape, Mr. Baldwin's harsh behavior, Rashmi's cry, my attackers laying hold of me, and… And then John Middleton's words. *It's for your own good, Brandon.*

That is what had occurred, but it made little sense.

I cautiously raised myself from the uncomfortable cot upon which I had been placed, swinging my feet to the floor and looking about. To add insult to injury, I found that I was in what had to be the camp guardhouse, with nobody in sight to help or answer the questions that teemed in my mind.

"Anybody there?" I called out, immediately regretting having done so for the terrible paroxysms the action provoked. I moaned and clutched my head with both hands, waiting in absolute stillness for the pounding to subside.

A soldier – a young lieutenant I did not know – eventually appeared. "Is there a problem, sir?" he asked with an air of disinterest.

I wanted to shout, *Yes, by god, there is a problem! Somebody has perpetrated a great crime against me, and yet I am the one confined to jail!* But I did not do it; I had already learnt that lesson the hard way and now knew better. All my outrage must be saved for a time when my head no longer felt as if it might break in two at any moment.

Instead, I spoke in little more than a whisper. "Send for Lieutenant Colonel John Middleton. It is imperative that I see him at once."

"I'll see if he is available," the soldier answered in a tone that gave me no confidence at all in his doing so. Perhaps he enjoyed keeping an officer who outranked him waiting on *his* pleasure for a change, for it seemed an age before John finally appeared.

He then told the guard to leave us and pulled up a chair on the other side of the bars which confined me. "Glad to see you are back among the living, old friend," he said, cheerfully. "I was a little worried, what with how hard McClintock struck you."

"McClintock? John, what is this about?" I asked with barely constrained rage. "Why have you done this to me? I thought you were my friend."

"I *am* your friend, which is why I could not allow you to make such a fatal error as you were set on doing. Someday you will thank me for taking the decision into my own hands."

"It was not your decision to make, John, as you know very well. Now let me out of here at once. You have no cause to hold me."

"I most certainly do! You were quite drunk and disorderly last night. In fact, you had to be carried in here. Best if you sleep it off a while longer."

"You know that charge is false; I was as sober as you were last night."

He lowered his voice. "True, but your punishment for drunkenness will be a good deal more lenient than the penalty for desertion would have been."

That subdued me for a moment. "Nevertheless, I am sober now, and I insist you have me released." I tried not to let show what I was thinking, that if I could only be at liberty again, perhaps I could still catch up with Baldwin and carry on as I had intended.

"What?" said John, with a slightly devious smile, "and see you undo my good efforts by charging after Baldwin and your Indian princess? What kind of a fool do you take me for? No, my good man, you shall cool your heels here for another day or two. By then, they will be long gone. By then, I hope you will also recover your sense and see how futile it would be to carry this noble quest of yours any further. Depend on it; Baldwin will get the job done very well without you. Spend your money as you please; I will not interfere. But there was never any need for you to risk your life and ruin your career by accompanying him on the venture."

I closed my eyes and rested my head in my hands. I was beaten and I knew it, deceived and outwitted by my life-long friend, whom I had unconsciously considered my intellectual inferior. It was another humiliating defeat. Once again, I had failed to protect a woman who had depended on me in her hour of need. Once again, my good intentions had come to nothing. As with my proposed elopement with Eliza, this plan to save Rashmi had been undone by my own incompetence. I had been proved a very poor kind of hero.

My silent mortification was of little consequence, however; Rashmi's safety was all that mattered, and of that I could know nothing at present. John might think Baldwin would follow through on our bargain, but I doubted it severely. He had the money and the woman now, fully within his own control. What incentive was there for him to go to all the trouble of keeping our bargain? None. He might simply pocket the silver and dispose of Rashmi in a way that would leave her as miserable as before... or more so. My mind effortlessly conjured up half a dozen likely scenarios, none of them good.

Rashmi was gone, and I might never know where. All I could do was pray for her safety and that the man who had taken her away was more honorable than I had given him credit for.

29

"So, what happened to Rashmi, Colonel?" Marianne demanded impatiently when I had reached this point. "Was she taken to safety or not? Do not keep me in suspense."

"I am sorry to tell you, Miss Marianne, that I do not precisely know," I admitted. "Dunston was nearly frantic, as you may imagine. He made dozens of inquiries after her, but he never could discover any definitive information on her whereabouts. And Baldwin never returned to Madras, so there was no opportunity to interrogate him or know if he had done what he had been paid to do or not. Now you see why I warned you that my friend was no great hero. All Dunston's good intentions came to nothing in the end. He tried to rescue the lady in distress, but ultimately, he failed."

We sat without speaking for a full five minutes while I anxiously awaited Marianne's reaction. She looked… Was she pensive or stunned? She stared straight ahead at nothing at all, it seemed, a frown creasing her lovely brow. I could not blame her if she were unhappy with me. To have been served up such a disappointing ending after investing so much of her time and heart… And on her birthday too!

"Forgive me, Miss Marianne," I said at last, breaking the silence between us. "It was a poor trick that I have played on you. You did ask for a happy ending, and I failed to deliver it."

Instead of responding to this, she spoke as if she had not heard. "What became of Major Dunston?"

"Well," I said, stalling for time. "Nothing much, really. Instead of the heroic adventure he had intended, he stayed with his regiment. He served honorably for another three years, I suppose you might say. Ironically, instead of facing court martial for desertion, as he probably merited, he was promoted... twice, before eventually returning to England. I never saw or heard from him again after that, but I doubt he ever amounted to anything much. As I have told you, he was a very ordinary man with no particular talent or genius."

After another contemplative silence, she said, "It strikes me that he must have done something very fine with the rest of his military career, to be twice promoted. He was *your* friend, Colonel. I am surprised you cannot be more charitable in your assessment of him," she added, almost teasingly. "In any case, I thank you for telling me his story."

"So... So you are not too disappointed for it ending unfavorably, or at least inconclusively?"

She considered a moment. "Because it was a true story and not a fairy tale – as you warned me in advance – I could not have reasonably expected a happily-ever-after. Of course I would have wished to know Rashmi was indeed got away to safety, but in the end I am quite relieved that Major Dunston himself came to no harm through the misadventure. I would not have seen him ruined. He was a good and honorable man placed in an impossible situation. And since we cannot know Rashmi's outcome for certain, I shall choose to believe that what happened was the best ending achievable."

I breathed a sigh of genuine relief. "That is very generous of you, Miss Marianne."

"Not at all, Colonel. You are the generous one, doing so much for my entertainment. I hope I should know better than to be ungrateful."

We said no more on the subject as we returned down the hill. Indeed, we barely spoke at all along the way. It was not an uncomfortable silence but one of mutual consent, I believe, both of us having things to think about. I certainly did. Marianne's gracious reception of the final chapter of my story – what I had worried over for so long – had indeed surprised me. I could not help but feel that her reaction would have been different a year earlier. It was a more mature and reasonable response than I had expected from the lady.

Before going into the house, Marianne paused, asking, "Do you have more stories of India, Colonel? Perhaps you will tell me another sometime."

~~*~~

Mindful of the danger of presuming too much from my time with Marianne on the hillside, I very deliberately devoted the majority of my attentions to the other ladies of the household during the remainder of my stay at Barton Cottage. I did not ignore Marianne, but neither did I repeatedly seek her out. I did not contrive to be always by her side, suffocating her like a heavy blanket.

Proceed slowly. Be gentle. Do not frighten and overwhelm her with too much too soon. Allow her to come to you when she is ready ...or not at all.

This is what I repeatedly counseled myself. So I went along when Margaret impetuously took me by the hand, tugging me out of doors for an explore of her favorite place – the path along the stream. I lent Mrs. Dashwood my ear and full attention when she spoke of her ideas for improvements to the cottage, then volunteered my assistance when she settled for a new arrangement of the parlor furniture instead. And I spent plenty of time conversing with Elinor, whom I knew and enjoyed so well.

She, quite naturally, was very curious about her future home, and she peppered me with questions on that subject every chance she got. How many bedchambers were there? Was the parlor smaller or larger than the one in which we currently sat? Which direction did the best windows face and what was the view? Was there a sunny spot for a good-sized kitchen garden and a place for a hen house?

"You cannot imagine how envious of Edward I am!" Elinor exclaimed during one of our discussions, "that he has seen Delaford parsonage house and I have not!"

"A situation that will soon be remedied, I trust."

"Forgive my impatience, Colonel, but it cannot be soon enough for me."

"Quite understandable, Miss Dashwood, and so this is what I propose. When Edward returns to Barton, you must convince him to bring you – and your mother and sisters as well, of course – to Delaford. Stay as long as you like. There is plenty of room, and I would be glad of the company. Then you may see the work under-way at the parsonage and help with the details men have no business deciding – furniture styles, papers for the walls, and so forth. I know you are of a practical turn of mind and will be able to look past the current disorder to what it can and will become under your care."

A warm smile spread across her face, and she turned to her mother. "Did you hear that, Mama? Colonel Brandon has invited all of us to Delaford as soon as Edward arrives. Is not that kind?"

My proposal was received with great excitement, and further discussion of the scheme followed until it was quite a settled thing. The Dashwood ladies would indeed come to Delaford as soon as could be arranged. When Edward at last arrived, he would find he had no say in the matter at all, although I could hardly imagine he would object.

~~*~~

I only stayed three nights, although I was repeatedly assured that was not long enough.

"I had promised myself that you should stay a full week complete, this time, Colonel," said Mrs. Dashwood. "My dinners are planned and everything! Can you really have such pressing business at home as to justify depriving us of your company again so soon?"

Making my excuses as graciously as possible, I held firm. My early departure was consistent with my working theory, that to avoid making my company irksome to Marianne, I must not force too much of it upon her. Besides, now that the promise of the Dashwood ladies returning my visit had taken up residence in my imagination, I found I was eager to be at home again. I was keen to check on the progress at the parsonage, that Elinor's first impression of her future home should be a good one. But it was much more than that. The idea that Marianne would also be of the party set my mind spooling with anticipation. I could not help thinking – fervently hoping – that it might occur to her while there, that Delaford could, if she wished it, be *her* future home as well. That whilst her dear sister dwelt at the parsonage, she might reside close by as mistress of the mansion house, and perhaps that would not be entirely unpleasant.

When I arrived, I tried to view the estate as if for the first time. I succeeded, if it can be counted a success to see afresh all the untidy details long overlooked and forgotten: the way the front gate hung unevenly, the clutter that had gradually collected alongside the stable block, and so much more. These things would not be invisible to a newcomer as they had become to me.

Proceeding inside, a dozen more deficiencies immediately met my eye. Things that had never bothered me before, living alone as a bachelor, now took on new significance. How would a potential mistress view the mismatched furnishings in the drawing room? Could she abide the oppressively dark draperies in the library, even temporarily? What of the piles of books strewn everywhere?

All these things could be changed, of course, and yet a bad first impression was difficult to overcome. With the master not being everything she could hope for, I did not wish to heap other obstacles in Marianne's path as well.

No doubt the servants thought I had gone completely mad when I suddenly insisted that the chandelier in the front hall should be lowered and thoroughly cleaned again, much ahead of schedule, and that every guest bedchamber in the house be inspected and aired at once. And so on. It was quite out of character for me.

I gave my own, most particular attention to the music room, however. I wanted Marianne to be able to envision herself, as I already had, spending many happy hours there. I hoped she would do more than imagine it, though; I hoped she would not be able to resist seating herself at the gleaming Broadwood grand, which dominated the room, and running her fingers expertly over its keys. Oh, how my heart would thrill to hear her pulling forth the sweet music I knew she and the instrument would be capable of together. Would she think it something special, the perfect conduit for the rich songs brimming in her soul?

I sat down at the beloved but recently neglected piano-forte and played several bars of the first thing that came to mind – a Handel sonata – before answering my own question. "No, she will not think it special!" I said aloud in dismay. "Not in its current state."

I pulled the bell cord to summon help, and the housekeeper was soon with me. "Mrs. Albright," I said. "Please be good enough to send for Mr. Andiron at once. This instrument is sadly out of tune."

"Yes, sir. At once."

"And be sure it is well polished afterwards. Not a single finger-print must remain."

"Of course, sir."

Then I took stock of my library of sheet music in the nearby cabinet, doing a quick inventory. It was an extensive collection. Nevertheless, it would be a treat – for myself and hopefully for Marianne as well – to have something new added. Mrs. Dashwood was partial to Haydn, I knew, and Marianne to Bach. I went to my study and quickly dashed off a note to the proprietor of the shop in London I had dealt with many times before, asking him to send some of each immediately.

Afterwards, I proceeded upstairs with a sense of definite purpose, my intent being to survey the guest bedchambers. Mr. Ferrars would have the one he had used the last time, but I would consider which one should be assigned to each of the Dashwood ladies. There were plenty and so no need of sharing, I knew, though I had not looked into any of them in ages.

Although it was tempting to give it to Marianne, I reminded myself that Mrs. Dashwood should by rights have the largest and best available. Margaret must be placed in the room next to hers, with a door connecting. That did not admit a doubt. Those decisions made, I looked into the two directly across the corridor, which were very pleasant rooms as well, nearly identical to each other except for color: one done in blues and the other in golden yellow tones.

The one furnished in gold would be Marianne's, I decided, and I walked to the windows to consider the view. It was not equal to that enjoyed from the family bedchambers in the other wing, but I could imagine that Marianne would be pleased with it, for, elevated as it was, it had a similar aspect to the place on the hill above Barton Cottage that she liked so well. Everywhere there was light and texture and life to see – green hills and rocky outcrops, sheep and cows in the pastures bordered by hedgerows, a blue sky streaked with calling birds, and even a glimpse of the river. The picture was filled with God's creation, which was always a visual feast.

My dear friends, I suddenly realized, were not the sort of petty people to criticize the minor imperfections I had been obsessively fretting over on their behalf. No, indeed. And to carry on as I was would be an insult to them and do me no credit either.

I raised the window, planted my hands on the sill, and leant out, filling my lungs with the fresh country air – once... twice... and three times. *This* is what I had to offer: myself and a life in this beautiful place. That would either be enough or it would not. A few inconsequential details would make no difference.

30

I did my best to put aside my striving and simply go about my business until whenever my guests should arrive. When they did come, I received them with friendliness and calm – outward calm, at least.

Mr. Ferrars had seen Delaford before, of course, and so no exclamations of surprise or delight were to be expected of him. But the ladies were much more animated, Mrs. Dashwood especially. Her smiling eyes darted about when she entered the house – from me to the height and breadth of the hall, lighting first upon one object and then another.

"My, my," she said excitedly, clasping her hands together in front of her bosom. "Is not this grand? It reminds me somewhat of the entry hall at Norland. Do not you think so, Elinor? It is perhaps a *little* smaller but those high windows give such lovely light. Colonel Brandon, you have a very fine house here!"

"Indeed, you have," agreed Elinor.

Marianne only nodded and faintly smiled.

I bowed my thanks and said, "I hope you will all be very comfortable here."

"There can be no doubt as to that!" cried Mrs. Dashwood.

"The footmen will have already taken your things to your bedchambers," I continued. "If you ladies are tired from your journey, you may wish to be shown up at once. You can always see more of the house later."

"But I am not the least bit tired, Colonel," said the mother. "Are you girls?"

"I am not!" exclaimed Margaret, who seemed to have grown another inch since I had so recently seen her.

"Nor I, Colonel," Elinor answered. "I would love to see more of your house. Marianne?"

We all turned to her expectantly, and what could she do? Looking conscious, she said, "I have no objection."

Not a rousing endorsement, but it seemed to satisfy.

"Oh, good," said Mrs. Dashwood. "Do lead on, Colonel!"

"With your permission, Brandon," said Mr. Ferrars, "I will await you all in the drawing room. I have already had the tour."

I nodded, saying, "Make yourself comfortable."

We left him there, and over the next half of an hour, I showed the ladies through the primary rooms of the main floor, receiving their compliments and answering all of their questions.

I could not help surreptitiously watching Marianne as we went along, for signs of approval or otherwise. She *looked* with great interest but *said* very little, mostly nodding or agreeing in monosyllables to the comments of the others. But I did have the satisfaction of hearing a sharp uptake of her breath when she caught sight of the newly tuned and freshly polished Broadwood grand in the music room, which I had deliberately reserved for the last.

"Magnificent," she whispered.

Exceedingly pleased, but not wishing to make too much of her reaction, I simply said, "You may of course play it whenever you wish." Then, after a minute's more appreciation, we proceeded up the grand staircase so that I might escort them to their bedchambers. There I left them and returned to Mr. Ferrars below.

He looked up when I entered the room. "I have left the ladies to themselves upstairs," I told him. "Ah, I see you have remembered the location of the brandy. Good." I went to pour myself a glass of the same.

"Yes, you did say to make myself comfortable."

"And I meant it. I suppose you will be eager to view how the work at the parsonage is coming along?"

"Very much so, and to hear Miss Dashwood's opinion of the place. I hope the house is in a condition to appear to advantage."

I had to laugh at the irony. "Hardly," I said. "The work is coming along satisfactorily, but it will be a few months yet. In truth, the place is in a terrible state at present. I'm afraid we must trust to Miss Dashwood's ability to see beyond the dirt and disarray, to use her keen mind and imagination. The first, I know she has; the second, I dearly hope she does. Otherwise, this premature viewing may prove a sad mistake."

"Ha! I have every confidence in Elinor; she will prove equal to the challenge. She is not afraid of a project, you know. Remember, she has agreed to take *me* on!"

Edward's confidence was put to a severe test the next morning when we all convened to walk the short distance to the parsonage. First, it began to rain, necessitating the deployment of umbrellas we had brought with us just in case. Then we found that the workers, constantly hauling materials in and out, had stirred up the dirt path leading to the front door, making it impossible for the ladies to traverse it without soiling their shoes. The gloomy weather cast a pall over the whole place, inside and out, leaving us truly challenged to find anything positive to say about the situation.

"Oh, dear," was all Mrs. Dashwood could manage upon stepping inside.

Elinor, venturing a little farther, gave a gesture and a questioning look towards the gaping hole in the kitchen wall, which was letting in more light but also the rain.

I quickly explained. "They've taken down the wall to make an addition to the kitchen. If you had seen it before, Miss Dashwood, I am sure you would agree it was necessary."

Elinor nodded again. "Of course."

"May we see upstairs, Colonel?" Margaret asked, craning her head in that direction.

Mrs. Dashwood, no doubt observing the crumbling ruin about her, held her daughter back and asked with some alarm, "Is it safe?"

"Quite safe," I reassured her. "The structure has not been compromised in the least, and no major renovations were required there."

Edward took his intended bride by the arm and said encouragingly, "Let us go up."

After they had done so and returned, Margaret in their wake, and when everybody's curiosity was fully satisfied, we all made our way back down the muddy track and towards the mansion house again. No one smiled. No one spoke. It was as mournful a procession as I had ever seen on the way to a cemetery.

Finally, Edward ended the miserable silence. "Well, I believe we can all agree *that* was a resounding success!"

Instantly, the tension was broken and everybody laughed.

"I like the way the house opens itself up to the outdoors," joked Elinor.

"True," Marianne agreed. "It is so much better for taking in the scenery than the solid walls and tight little windows most houses possess."

"And what a convenience that great hole will be for laying in provisions to the kitchen!" added Edward, jovially.

"The slippery pathway is sure to foil intruders," Mrs. Dashwood remarked.

"An ingenious innovation," I agreed.

Margaret glanced from one to another, looking like she was enjoying the game but not quite sure how to get into it herself.

Later, we were able to discuss the situation at the parsonage with more clarity, dismissing both the overly gloomy thoughts and the contrived hilarity. Then, when the sun came out and we returned the following day for a second look, everything appeared much brighter. It no longer seemed to Mrs. Dashwood that her daughter would be always doomed to have the rain coming in and the heat going out.

~~*~~

Marianne declined her mother's urging to play for us the first night of their visit, pleading tiredness. But the second afternoon, I found her exploring the music room on her own. Once again, I did not wish to react too strongly, although inside I was delighted to discover her there.

"You will find that tall cabinet filled with sheet music," I said casually before continuing on my way. I had left the new Bach right on top, and soon I heard the first tentative notes of it drifting through the great hall to the drawing room, where the rest of us had collected.

"I knew she could not stay away from that instrument for long," Mrs. Dashwood, sitting beside me, said with a nod and a significant look. She added for my ears only, "To catch a rabbit, one must simply use the proper bait."

I only smiled politely.

Although I was glad for Mrs. Dashwood's support, I did not like that anybody should think I was setting a trap, even a benevolent one, for her daughter. Although it was common enough for a man – especially an older man, I supposed – to use a display of wealth and position to entice a young lady into marriage, I was just prideful enough to wish that she would eventually choose me for something more – that she should agree to marry me at least partly for myself, not solely for what I possessed. But could one ever know for sure? Perhaps not.

That evening, Marianne, of her own free will, sat down in the chair next to my own.

"I'm sorry to have no more stories to tell you," I said, considering that had normally been the only reason she sought out my company.

"I cannot believe that is true. Someday I should like to listen to somewhat of your *own* experiences, Colonel, but I must say that I have not yet stopped thinking about Major Dunston's."

"I am surprised to hear it. As you now know, he was a very ordinary man – more of a failure than a hero."

"So you have said more than once, and I know that must be what you believe. But I disagree," she announced resolutely. "In fact, that is the part I cannot stop thinking about: your poor opinion of him. If you will not stand up and call your friend a hero, I must!"

I was quite stunned by this outburst. It took me a moment to respond. "I should never wish to contradict you, Miss Marianne, but I must indeed ask for clarification. On what grounds can you possibly call Major Dunston a hero?"

"Ah, so you are prepared to listen?"

"Of course." She had my full attention.

"I have my case well prepared. You shall hear my evidence and then we shall see if I have not convinced you."

"Agreed."

She leant forward and held up one finger to start, adding to it as she went along. "First, Major Dunston proved self-sacrificing by giving all his money for a cause that could not benefit himself. Second, you must admit he was brave in being willing to risk his future and possibly his life, all to help a person he barely knew. He saw a woman in danger, and he acted without hesitation to protect her, ready to go to great lengths to do so. Not one in a dozen men would have done as much. No! Not one in a hundred! Furthermore – and here is my third and most important point, Colonel – I must dispute one of your assumptions, which I consider faulty. Contrary to what you apparently believe, one does not need to be successful to be considered heroic, otherwise valiant soldiers who die in battle for a great but losing cause would be known as failures. And they are not." With this, she sat back and folded her hands, looking confident of her victory.

I quickly came up with an objection. "That is hardly the same thing, Miss Marianne. Fallen soldiers may be called heroes, but I… As I told you, Major Dunston did not die. In fact, he suffered no harm at all."

"Come now, Colonel, do you mean to tell me that you think it is by their deaths these fighting men I spoke of were made heroes? That sounds more like something *I* once might have said. No, dying does not make a man heroic; it is how he lives. It was while the soldier *lived* that he chose to serve his country and brave the perils of battle. While he *lived*, he declared himself willing to make the ultimate sacrifice for the noble cause. By my definition at least, he would be a hero whether he returned home safely or died on the field of honor."

I looked at her, somewhat awed by this line of reasoning, which was new to me.

"Well, Colonel, what do you say? Are you persuaded? I do have one more point, if necessary."

"By all means, do finish making your case."

She smiled, seeing success within her grasp. "I dispute something else you said – that Major Dunston failed to save Rashmi. I say, he may very well have succeeded. He certainly saved the lady from the horrible fate she would have faced at home, had he not intervened. And it is entirely possible she reached safety in the end, despite the fact it could never be verified."

I could answer nothing to this; I could not immediately find any fault with her logic.

"And so, have I convinced you that your friend Major Dunston is a hero after all?"

"You have certainly made him an excellent defense, Miss Marianne. I am quite impressed. I suppose if you wish to think him a hero, I shall raise no further objection. As for me, you must grant me some little time to consider your arguments and adjust my thinking."

It was true. Her impassioned defense of Major Dunston, her innovative interpretation of his actions, had astounded me. That, in spite of everything, she should consider him a hero, not a pitiful failure... That she should consider what *I* had done heroic... It was a revolutionary perspective deserving study, but it would not easily supplant all I had been used to believing for so long.

~31~

It seemed that by each subsequent encounter with Marianne, there was at least a small bit of progress made in my favor. At the current pace, however, I could not help wondering something. If I *should* be so fortunate as to eventually succeed in winning her affection, would I live long enough beyond to enjoy it? Or would I be a doddering old man by then, more in need of a nurse than a wife? I wavered constantly between hope and discouragement, and had to continually remind myself to be patient. Still, when I considered the larger picture – how far we had come – I had to be pleased.

My houseguests stayed five nights before saying their farewells and returning to Barton. After delivering the ladies home, Mr. Ferrars intended to try his mother one more time for an improvement in his income before taking possession of the Delaford living. Meanwhile, I had promised to speed the work at the parsonage, for Elinor had declared that she would not marry her Edward until their home was ready to inhabit.

Eager as I was to accommodate the wishes of these dear friends, a thousand little delays cropped up to thwart me at every turn. Bad weather, workmen's bad health, and unaccountably bad luck were given by the foreman in excuse, but I put most of the trouble down to mistakes and dilatoriness. The materials procured were either incorrect, insufficient, or wasted, and replacements could not easily be acquired. The only men who seemed to know their business absented themselves for long periods for undisclosed reasons, and substitute workers either did not exist or were untrained. When it appeared progress was being made on the addition at last, I was told that, due to a catastrophic miscalculation, the whole thing must be torn down to the ground and started over again.

I kept Edward and Elinor apprised of this string of setbacks, one after another, until finally Elinor resigned herself to doing what was expedient instead of what was ideal. She gave up the notion that she and her new husband would be moving directly into the parsonage after the wedding, and consented to accept my invitation for them to stay in the mansion-house instead, for as long as it should be necessary. Consequently, the ceremony was postponed no more; it was scheduled to take place at Barton church in the middle of September.

Naturally, I travelled down to Barton in order to be present for the happy day. Sir John and Lady Middleton were in residence at the Park by this time, and so I stayed with them. Mrs. Jennings came from London especially. Indeed, I doubt if anything could have kept her away when she heard the news of a wedding, for she seemed to take a great deal of personal satisfaction in any such occasion.

"I knew how it would be, Colonel!" she told me, all aflutter when I arrived. "You may remember how swift I was to discover that Miss Dashwood had a beau in her pocket – the mysterious 'Mr. F' – and that is when I knew we should have a wedding at Barton before long if only I could help things along a bit. And now, so we shall!"

She seemed to have completely forgotten the time when she had been equally certain that *I* was the one Miss Dashwood would marry. Sometimes a little amnesia was a kind convenience, and it would have been cruel without purpose to remind her of her mistake.

"Quite right, Mrs. Jennings," I said. "You have an uncanny wisdom in these matters, and what you say always comes to pass."

She looked delighted. "And you must not think that I have overlooked you in all the excitement, Colonel, for I shall not be satisfied until you are married as well, both you and Miss Marianne. Once this wedding is over, I will make it my highest priority to look about for somebody for each of you, although I have not completely given up on the idea of making a match of you both together. Really, Colonel Brandon, I think you should consider it – as a kindness to yourself as well as to me, cutting my work in half, if you see what I mean. There was a time, I think, when you did look on her with considerable admiration. And although some say Miss Marianne has lost her bloom, there can be nothing in that. Why, I saw her not two days ago and I could observe no difference from before. If anything, she is grown into a more mature beauty. Do you not agree with me?"

"I do, Mrs. Jennings."

"There, now, that is the first step already taken."

"I promise to do as you say, Mrs. Jennings, to consider Miss Marianne, if in turn you will do something for me."

"This *is* good news, Colonel! Name your condition, and I will be only too happy to comply."

"You must promise to leave the rest to me. No hints to Miss Marianne. None at all. Do you understand?"

"But, sir, you cannot be serious. All lovers need a little encouragement."

"Encourage *me* all you wish, my good woman, but leave the lady alone. I am convinced that if she is pushed, she will only run, and that is not what we want, is it?"

"Ah! You have given this much thought, I see."

"I have."

"Perhaps more than thought, too. And are things moving along? Can we set the date?"

Unfortunately, Sir John happened into the room in time to hear this last. "Set a date? What's this, Brandon? You old fox! Has that pretty little filly agreed to marry you at last?"

"She has not, and she may never do so if she is prodded and teased about it. Now you must *both* promise to resist the temptation to do so. Leave the poor girl alone, and allow me to handle things as I think best."

Mrs. Jennings looked as if somebody had just given her a new toy and then told her she must put it up on a shelf and not touch it again. But Sir John proved his friendship by taking my part. "What do you say, Mother?" he asked, putting his arm about her shoulders. "Shall we give Brandon his own way in this, at least for a while? He is no fool, and I am inclined to think he may be right about Miss Marianne. She can be a skittish little thing."

I was exceedingly grateful when Mrs. Jennings finally agreed. It might not last, but at least for now Marianne might be safe from counterproductive raillery.

~~*~~

The simple ceremony uniting Mr. Edward Ferrars to Miss Elinor Dashwood came off without a hitch, and it was not long before the couple returned back down the aisle, arm in arm and jubilant. The whole party moved to Barton Park for the wedding breakfast afterwards, which gave Lady Middleton a chance to shine. Her elegant table was spread with even more bounty than on ordinary occasions, and her only regret seemed to be that her guests were unequal to the task of consuming it all at one sitting.

When the newlyweds had done their part, and when they had received the well wishes of everybody present three or four times apiece, they departed on their wedding trip to Bath. Since they would not be arriving back at Delaford for a fortnight, I stayed on at Barton for a week, where a party was formed nearly every day between the residents of the Park and those at the cottage. Once again, I tried to strike the right balance between giving Marianne too much and too little of my attention, neither neglecting her nor making a nuisance of myself by being always in her way.

A few days after the wedding, however, Mrs. Jennings took me aside to scold me for my restraint. "Tsk, tsk, Colonel," she said wagging her finger at me, "what kind of way is this to be making love to a beautiful young lady? You have almost ignored Miss Marianne tonight, barely speaking to her. Why, you have spent more time with her mother than herself! If it were me, I should think you did not care for me one fig."

"My dear lady, is not an attention to her mother an attention to herself? Besides, there is more than one way to woo a lady."

"I suppose so, but I cannot say that I have ever seen a successful courtship carried on so calmly. You must show a little more passion, Colonel! Think of what captured the lady's fancy before. Mr. Willoughby certainly left her in no doubt of his affection!"

I stiffened. "Do you suggest that I pattern myself after that libertine?"

"I do not! A more unworthy young man I have never met with in my life, and yet that does not mean *everything* he did was wrong. You might do well to take some lessons from him."

"I cannot agree, Mrs. Jennings, and I intend to make quite certain that Miss Marianne sees no resemblance whatsoever between Mr. Willoughby and myself."

"Well, I daresay there is no danger of that happening. As things stand at the moment, the contrast between the two of you could not be more pronounced! You know that I hold you in the very highest esteem, Colonel. I am sure there is no better man in all the world, and so I tell everybody who will listen. But I have yet to see any signs that you know how to win the devotion of a lively young lady such as Miss Marianne Dashwood."

Although I hardly credited Mrs. Jennings with having the very best of sense, I could not hear her view of my chances without feeling a little disheartened. I had to hope she was incorrect, even if I could not convince her of it. Then an idea came to me. I said, "Think of the parable of the sower and the four soils in Matthew. Mr. Willoughby's affection was like the seed falling on the stony ground."

"Oh, dear, now you have taken me beyond my depth, I fear!"

"You remember. The plants sprang up quickly, looking very prosperous, but they withered and died just as quickly when the sun became too harsh, because the roots were shallow. But the seed that fell on the good soil grew and thrived. It takes good soil, care, and patience to grow healthy plants, Mrs. Jennings, plants with roots deep enough to survive trials and yield fruit. I will trust to time and gentle attentions."

"Well, well, Colonel. You are become quite the philosopher! I only hope you know what you are doing, but I must say that I have never yet heard of a young lady being won over by logic or high-minded theories. A girl like Miss Marianne wants to be flattered and adored! She wants to be swept off her feet with dancing and romance!"

"We shall see." That was all I could say.

I had spoken to Mrs. Jennings with conviction, but I was far from confident that my words were true, at least as it pertained to Marianne. It really made no difference, however, for I was not willing or able to make a change. If Marianne still required the more overt romancing that had won her heart before, she would never respond to me, for I would not – could not – behave to her as Willoughby had. My love and adoration must be shown in more subtle ways. I could only hope the superior steadfastness of my affection would make up for the possible inferiority of my style in expressing it.

32

A few days after I returned to Delaford, Mr. and Mrs. Edward Ferrars arrived, looking well-rested and happy. They soon settled themselves into the suite of rooms I had set aside for their use – arrangements that granted the newlyweds as much privacy as could be provided them in somebody else's house. For meals, they had no other choice but to join me, which they were very welcome to do of course, for I enjoyed their company. Otherwise, they could keep to themselves as much as they liked.

Renovations to the parsonage had by this time advanced enough that it required a good deal less imagination than before to picture it as a fit place to inhabit in the not too distant future.

"Perhaps by Christmas," I told them as we inspected the progress the day after their arrival.

"Oh, that would be lovely!" said Elinor. "Just imagine: a cup of negus, a cheerful fire in the hearth, and the smell of a fine dinner cooking in the new-furnished kitchen."

"I *am* imagining it," answered Edward. "The only thing I cannot quite see in my mind is who will be cooking that fine dinner. Certainly not you, dearest!"

Elinor's hands flew to her hips. "I *can* cook, I would have you know!" she told him in no uncertain terms. "A little, at least. And what I have not yet mastered, I will learn. We shall not starve."

Though it felt awkward to interrupt this exchange between husband and wife, I did so anyway, starting by clearing my throat. "Pardon me, but if I might make a suggestion, I believe I have a reasonable answer to your problem." They both turned to me and waited. "A girl of fifteen from my household. Her name is Alice Campbell, and she is the daughter of my cook, from whom she has learnt the trade. Since I am told that the girl is desirous of securing a position of her own, I believe you might engage her – as a maid of all work, perhaps, her cooking skills included – for a very reasonable amount. You are welcome to speak to her about the possibility, if you are interested."

"We are," they said in unison. "Thank you, Colonel," Elinor added, a sentiment echoed by her husband.

Although Mr. and Mrs. Ferrars were not yet installed in the parsonage, *he* took up his new responsibilities as rector of the parish at once. Having received his ordination, he began reading the prayers and giving his first sermon on the second Sunday of October. It was not a great success, I suppose, as to the quality of the performance. But the parishioners seemed to like his self-effacing manner and his sensible, pretty wife. With these two assets in his favor, I believe Edward completely won them over within the month, procuring him a great deal of grace until his sermon-making should improve, and a number of dinner invitations as well.

I found our living arrangements quite comfortable for those three months, and it was a treat for me to have a regular source of companionship and intelligent conversation in the Ferrarses. Yet I looked forward to the change ahead. My friends would still be close at hand at the parsonage when I wanted them, but now I anticipated the addition of more and different guests in my house to add to the general merriment. Before I left Barton, I had procured the promise of the Middletons and that of the Dashwood ladies that they should all be my guests at Christmas.

An exchange of letters had passed between her mother and myself in the meantime, but this would be my first opportunity of seeing Miss Marianne in person since the wedding, and a plan had begun to form in my mind for how I should behave towards her. It was time, I believed, not to expect an answer, but to at least make my intentions clear, so that she might begin to think of the possibility in earnest.

A second resolution, just as daunting, had taken shape as well. For weeks, I had been suffering pangs over the falsehoods I had told Marianne regarding Major Dunston. Although it had seemed a harmless ruse at first – just a more comfortable way of telling the story – the longer it went uncorrected, the more my conscience smote me. A lie was a lie, no matter how I might try to excuse it, and I could not hope to move forward with something like that between us. I would need to confess it as soon as possible, come what may.

Confessing the truth had been made all the more awkward, however, by how Marianne now viewed Major Dunston. I could more easily have owned to being the failure I considered him than the hero *she* believed him to be. Telling her now that I was the one who had done those things... well, it might appear that I was desirous of drawing her praise unto myself. Perhaps she might even disbelieve that I now spoke the truth. Or if she did believe me, she might be angry that I had deceived her before. It was far too late to wish I never had, though. The damage, if any, was already been done; it only remained for me to face the consequences, whatever they might be.

I ran these resolutions through my mind again and again, trying to envision how the conversation with Marianne might develop – which disclosure I should make to her first and what words to use. Should I give some time in between or make a clean breast of it, telling her all at once? These questions figured prominently in my thoughts and prayers right up until the day the Ferrarses moved out and my other company moved in, with no clear answer emerging.

It was the fifteenth of December, and in the morning I had seen Edward and Elinor installed in their less grand but more private quarters, with an eager Alice ready to organize and serve them. Then the Middletons – Sir John, Lady Middleton, their children, baggage, and necessary attendants – made a very noisy arrival a few hours later, with the carriage I had sent for the Dashwood ladies following in their wake. I stepped forward to welcome them all and hand the ladies out: Lady Middleton from the first carriage, Mrs. Dashwood from the second, Miss Margaret, and then finally Miss Marianne.

I greeted her in the same manner as I had the others, saying, "Welcome back to Delaford, Miss Marianne." Then I took her gloved hand as she stepped down, holding it a bit longer than strictly necessary before releasing her. It was nothing I had not done before, and yet this time I felt a particular charge of excitement in the small personal task. This time, I had been thinking, "I will propose marriage to this woman ere she departs."

We all hurried into the house, for the air was very cold, and a light snow had begun to fall.

"How kind you are, Colonel Brandon," Mrs. Dashwood began to effuse as coats were removed and parcels handed off to servants. "Sending your very comfortable carriage all the way to Barton to collect us! And then it must go there and back again at the end of our stay. What a bother we are to everybody, not having a carriage of our own."

"Nonsense, my dear lady. I was only too happy to do it, as you must know."

Sir John joined us in the hall. "They would have been welcome to use my second best carriage, Brandon, saving a full trip in both directions. But you would insist on having your own way!"

"I would, indeed," I agreed. "Why should the ladies ride in a second-best carriage when they can have the best?"

Sir John laughed. "Right you are, Brandon!"

"Have Elinor and Edward removed to their own house now, Colonel?" Marianne asked looking about as if hoping to see them.

"Yes, just. This morning, in fact, Miss Marianne." A thought occurred to me. "Forgive me. I should by rights call you 'Miss Dashwood,' now that your sister has surrendered that title."

"You may call me what you like, Colonel. Established friends need not stand on ceremony."

I bowed. "As you say."

Marianne continued to me. "So no doubt there is still much for Edward and Elinor to do?"

"No doubt. They have a servant to help them, though. And they are to dine here every night until they are properly settled, of course. While you remain with us, in any case."

"Colonel Brandon," said Margaret, in a teasing way. "Is there still a great hole in their kitchen wall, letting in the rain and this snow?"

"Not anymore. It may be snowing out of doors but not in. The hole is gone and a new kitchen in its place. You will see it for yourself very soon. Should you like that, Miss Margaret?"

"Oh, ever so much!"

The party was made complete when the newlyweds joined us an hour later. Conversation and laughter swelled, and when added to the exuberance of the Middleton children, the house seemed filled to the rafters with cheerful noise, as it had not been in decades. Marianne's eyes sparkled, I noticed, reminding me what Mrs. Jennings had said – that such a girl needed liveliness and dancing.

When my mother had been alive, she occasionally organized a large house party with feasting and dancing. Although Delaford did not boast a proper ballroom, the great hall in the old style had served the purpose well enough, with the double doors open to the adjacent music room. The drawing room on the opposite side had been set up for cards, and a sumptuous supper laid in the dining room.

I had been too young to participate in the festivities, but I still remembered. Eliza and I would spy from the landing above, watching the couples dancing. In our silliness, we imitated them and would usually end collapsed on the floor in loud and helpless laughter, which then earned us a stern scolding and banishment to the schoolroom for the duration.

The practice of giving such parties ended when my mother died, and it had never been revived.

It now struck me, though, surrounded by my chattering guests, that I had nearly enough people beneath my roof already for a ball. And why not? If I could entice a few more friends to join us, including some young people, and hire a group of musicians...

Once I had struck on the idea, I could not let it go. Marianne had already seen Delaford peaceful and sedate; she should see that it was capable of something else as well – that *I* was capable of something else.

The next morning when the Middletons and the Dashwood ladies walked down to see Edward and Elinor's house for themselves, I remained behind to set my plan into action. Speaking first to my staff – primarily the cook and the housekeeper – and apologizing for the short notice, I inquired how soon sufficient preparations could be made. Could we be ready by December twenty-second, when the moon would be at its fullest, making night travel safer? With reasonable assurances on that score, I sent a footman off to engage the services of a local string quartet who often played for assemblies and private dances. Once these pieces had been put into place, the invitations could go out as well.

A ball at Delaford; what an inspired idea! I did enjoy dancing, when I could procure pleasing partners. In such a group as I proposed, that would be assured, for I was already on friendly terms with everybody who might come. And as an added advantage, I could hope to enjoy at least one dance with Marianne Dashwood. My excitement was building, and I only wished I had thought of the scheme earlier.

33

A few days later and preparations were progressing apace. The musicians were definitely engaged. Mrs. Campbell had her kitchen staff busy grinding almonds for white soup and whatever else could be done in advance. And Alice would be borrowed back from the parsonage for extra help before and during the event.

I was fortunate enough as to secure the acceptance of five other families for our dance, to add to those already staying. So according to my calculations, we would be able to create a set of at least eight couples, even allowing for those who would not participate at all and for some sitting down during any one dance. It would be enough to make a respectable showing and to allow for adequate change of partners. I only hoped it would be a congenial group as well.

Nobody could have been more enthusiastic about the prospect of a ball – even one as small and informal as this one would be – than Miss Margaret Dashwood, for it would be her first.

"Please, Mama!" she began as soon as I announced the plan. "May I dance too? I am nearly sixteen, you know."

It seemed impossible, but as the rest of us had grown a year and a half older since we all met, so had Margaret. She was almost as tall as Marianne now, and even a bit taller than her mother.

"You are still much closer to your fifteenth birthday than your sixteenth," her mother corrected her. "But I see no harm in it, since there will be nobody here but nice friends of Colonel Brandon's."

"Oh, thank you, Mama!" the girl said, jumping out of her chair in her excitement. She ran to her mother and kissed her. "You are so kind!"

"I only wish we had come with proper ball gowns," Mrs. Dashwood continued.

"Forgive me, Mrs. Dashwood," I said. "The fault is mine for giving you no notice. But nothing grand is required. This is not the London season. It is only an impromptu country dance among friends."

"It is as you say, Colonel, and I am sure we shall manage very well. We will combine our resources and see what can be made of them."

Lady Middleton generously offered to lend anything that might be of use to the other ladies from the closetful she had brought with her, and soon all the females had their heads together making plans.

Since nobody could talk of anything else, I quickly gave up the idea of having a serious conversation with Marianne before the great event. Besides, I did not wish to spoil the cheerful atmosphere buoying us all along by introducing heavy topics to her mind. Much better to wait for a time shortly before her departure, I decided, for if Marianne were in any way discomfited by my revelations, she would not wish to remain long in my company afterwards. She would wish to be soon away – away from me. Not a happy thought, this, but I had to recognize it as a possibility.

And so, like the others, I devoted myself to preparations for our little ball, including doing my share to make Miss Margaret ready. Marianne proposed the idea – that she should play the dances likely to be performed whilst Edward and I took turns partnering her younger sister in practicing the steps. Elinor was pressed into service as well to make two couples.

One of us was forever moving wrong, it seemed, and all could not be blamed on Margaret, the least experienced dancer. I had my turn and so did the others, the result being a comedy of errors, which our onlookers apparently found very entertaining.

Laughing the loudest was my oldest friend, until I called him to account in a teasing way. "Well, Middleton, since you find our efforts so ridiculous, I can only conclude that you believe you could do a great deal better. Come now, take your place here across from Miss Margaret, and give her the benefit of your expertise."

"Not at all! Not at all!" he demurred, while laughing still more. "I am much better where I am."

I therefore had no choice but to forcibly usher him ahead into place, saying, "Oh, but I must insist, sir. Indeed I must." All the while, the others standing about supported me, clapping and urging John forward. "It is time I retired to the music room to see if I am needed there," I said. With that, I left him to do as well as he could, whilst I turned aside to consult with Marianne.

"What shall you play for them next, Miss Dashwood? *Do* make it something to challenge Sir John's advanced capabilities. Or would you like me to play instead?"

"I will play if you will turn the pages, Colonel," she said, pulling out and situating a new piece before her. "The Scotch Reel moves along too quickly for me to turn them myself," she added with a smile and a conspiratorial look up at me.

"An excellent choice, Miss Dashwood! And pray, do not dawdle."

"The Scotch Reel," she called out to the dancers, and I heard my old friend groan.

Marianne began, setting a reasonably sedate pace as first, which was only fair to Margaret. After I had turned her page a time or two, however, she started to gain momentum and speed, little by little and then much by much, until her fingers were flying across the keys to the finish.

The hapless dancers, having long since given up their exercises, simply laughed and applauded along with the rest of us.

"Well done, Miss Dashwood," I said. "None of the dancers could keep up, but I am glad my piano-forte did not fail you."

She ran a caressing hand over the keyboard. "It is a beautiful instrument. I thank you for allowing me to play it."

"The pleasure is all mine, I assure you. An excellent instrument deserves a talented performer to play it. I do my best, but you, Miss Dashwood, are a *true* musician."

"You cannot judge by a reel, surely. It may prove alacrity, but it gives little opportunity for expression."

"You forget that this is not the first time I have heard you. I have heard you play not merely with skill, but with great feeling, discernment, and sensitivity. You play as if you would speak what is in your heart through the music you create, as if music is your native tongue, the language in which you are most fluent. Is not that as it should be?"

She looked at me for a long moment before answering. "Yes, Colonel. That is precisely as it should be. I could not have expressed it better myself."

~~*~~

The preparations for the ball had been so enjoyable – giving us something to talk of and work together towards – that I almost feared the actual event would be anticlimactic. Or that something would occur to prevent its taking place. But the day was clear, bringing no new snow to block the roads or clouds to dim the moonlight, and everything was in a state of readiness.

At five, the guests started arriving, and that is when the first irregularity appeared as well.

"Colonel Brandon," cried Mrs. Holderman as she came in the door. "How good of you to invite us! What an age it has been since we have had a ball in the neighborhood!"

I bowed, murmured my welcoming civilities to her husband and to herself. Then I froze. With them were their two sons, whom I expected to make good dance partners for Miss Margaret, but also a beautiful young lady who was definitely *not* their invited daughter. I recognized her as someone I had met before, more than once.

"Ah, I see you remember our niece Francesca," Mrs. Holderman continued. The striking young lady eyed me, and with a coy smile, curtsied. "Our daughter Catherine was not feeling up to dancing tonight, and I did not think you would mind if Francesca came in her place. She just arrived earlier today, and so there was no time to make you aware of the change."

"Of course, Mrs. Holderman. I am delighted," I said, even though I was not. I turned, briefly taking her niece's gloved hand and bowing over it, saying, "How pleasant to see you again, Miss Drury. You are most welcome."

"Thank you, Colonel Brandon. I am delighted to be here… and to see *you* again too. It must be a year ago that I was last at Delaford, when I visited my aunt and uncle at Christmas."

"Exactly so," I agreed. "I remember. I hope you will enjoy the dancing tonight."

"I am sure I will, for I am vastly fond of dancing." She smiled and waited expectantly, until I suddenly knew what was required of me.

"Would you consider reserving the first two dances for me, Miss Drury?"

She rewarded me with a radiant smile. "Thank you, Colonel. I would be glad to. I fear I will know nobody else."

"I would be happy to introduce you to the others. I am certain you will not lack for partners, Miss Drury."

She and the Holdermans moved on, and I turned my attention to the Phillipses, just arriving. And yet, my thoughts lagged behind with Miss Drury. She was a complication I had not reckoned on, although perhaps I should have, for she seemed to visit her relations every Christmas. When we had first been introduced a few years earlier, I had the feeling that I had been marked out as a possible match for her by her aunt and uncle, for they made obvious exertions to forward our acquaintance.

Miss Francesca Drury was a beauty; there was no denying it, with her regular features, bright blue eyes, and hair nearly black as a raven's wing. She was probably eighteen when I first met her, and it was a surprise to me that she remained unmarried still, but perhaps the girl had no dowry. In any case, I was simply not interested. Miss Drury lacked something, although it was difficult to define the missing ingredient – substance, depth of feeling, some spark of animation or ethereal delight? I thought so from the beginning, and of course now there was another reason for my indifference.

Nevertheless, much was due her as a prior acquaintance, as my guest, and as a relation of the Holdermans. And so I would dance with her and pay her all the gentlemanly courtesies required. I was determined, though, that none of it would prevent my bestowing equal attention upon Marianne and my other guests. Accordingly, as soon as everybody had arrived and I had opportunity, I went to speak to Marianne to secure her promise of a pair of dances. Perhaps I had made a strategic error in not doing so beforehand, for I now found her all but surrounded by young men: the Holderman brothers and Mr. Richard Seagrave. It seemed I had invited not only unwanted attention for myself, but some for her as well – unwanted, at least by me.

Here, I must admit that I took unfair advantage of my height and station as host to first attract Miss Dashwood's attention and then draw her away from the others.

"Miss Dashwood, I would speak to you a moment, if I might."

"Certainly, Colonel," she said, coming away with me a little distance. "What may I do for you?"

"Forgive me for interrupting your conversation, but I wished to ask you for a dance, if it is not too late. You seem to have already acquired many admirers tonight."

"You are quite mistaken. They are mere boys, really. Well, except for Mr. Seagrave, I suppose. But they are eager to dance, as am I. We have that much in common. You plan to dance as well, Colonel?"

"Naturally. If I may be so bold, perhaps I might claim the two after the supper break, should you have them free."

"Of course, Colonel. I will be happy to reserve them for you."

"Thank you, Miss Dashwood. I shall look forward to it." Then I bowed and left her to attend to my next duty: signaling the musicians to begin, after which, I looked about for my first partner, Miss Drury.

Strange that when I had contemplated giving this ball, I had only pictured Marianne dancing with *me*, when of course there would be others. Seeing her set off with Mr. Seagrave in the first dance brought back all the misery of months ago, when I had had to watch her glide across the floor with Mr. Willoughby, again and again. At least, *he* was not present this time.

Miss Drury and I got on well enough for our two dances, although I really cannot remember much of what we talked about. I asked after her family, who lived in Derbyshire I recalled, and she carried on from there. And then there were the usual exchange of compliments – mine to her for her "excellent dancing," she to me for the "elegant arrangements" of the ball.

Afterwards, I introduced her to Sir John, who danced the next with her, while I danced with Lady Middleton, then Miss Margaret, Elinor, Mrs. Phillips, and Miss Phillips in succession.

Marianne was never without a partner, I noticed, and she seemed to be enjoying herself. After Mr. Seagrave, she danced with Edward, the younger Mr. Phillips, Sir John, and then the Holderman brothers, one after the other.

It should have been of no importance to me whom she danced with; I had other duties as host. It was my responsibility to be sure that *all* my guests were well cared for and entertained, not only Miss Dashwood. Still, it was not such a crowd that I could lose myself or her in it. She must draw my eye wherever she was. The night sky might be full of stars, but the moon will always outshine them.

Finally, after the supper break, it was my turn to lead her out onto the floor.

"I believe this is my dance, Miss Dashwood," I said as I bowed before her. She only nodded and took my proffered hand. We said nothing until the music had begun and we had moved through the first several figures. There was so much I wanted to say to her, and yet this was not the time. Instead of something novel or witty, I eventually said, "You dance very well."

"So do you, Colonel – surprisingly well."

"Why 'surprisingly'? Did you think me unschooled in the art?"

"No, it was not that. It is just that I never saw you dance more than one or two dances before. I thought perhaps you did not like it or that… But you have been dancing every dance tonight."

She looked conscious, and I suddenly knew what she must have been thinking but would not say. She was surprised that a man of my age could carry on so long without becoming fatigued. Of course she was. No doubt she and Willoughby had used to share jokes on the topic of my age and supposed infirmity, and she had yet to completely get over thinking of me in that way. I was glad to know that the evidence of tonight had apparently made her realize her mistake.

"Anything set to music must be a pleasure to me," I said genially, "and I do not mean to allow a single minute to go to waste."

"Will you dance again with Miss Drury?"

This surprised me. "Perhaps. Why do you ask?"

"Oh, no reason." We carried on, but a minute later she picked up the thought again. "It is only that it seemed a very particular attention that you danced with her first. And she is a very pretty girl."

"She certainly is," I agreed without elaboration.

There was a slight crease between Marianne's brows now, and it suddenly occurred to me that she might be jealous of Miss Drury.

No, that was ridiculous. I discarded the idea at once. Marianne could not possibly care how many pretty girls I danced with. Still…

"I am the host," I said. "It is my job to be sure everybody is well taken care of. And so tonight I will dance with whichever lady needs a partner."

This seemed to satisfy her. Her smile returned, and we carried on until we reached the bottom of the set. There we were stationary for a few moments. "Your sister Margaret seems to be enjoying herself," I remarked looking up the set to where the girl was dancing with William Holderman, the younger of the brothers.

"Yes, she certainly is. You will be her hero forever, Colonel, for arranging this ball."

Hero. There was that word again, although used in a more frivolous context in this case. "It was no very difficult feat, I assure you. One could wish it were always so easy to earn a lady's admiration. Usually much more is required, I believe… or should be."

"Not for a girl just fifteen!" she declared, laughing. "For her, it is sufficient only that you give a ball and procure permission for her to dance at it."

And for a lady of eighteen, what is required? I wondered but did not ask. Marianne was in very high spirits. Tonight, I would simply bask in the extra brightness of her eyes and the particular radiance of her smile, content with the knowledge that I'd had at least a little something to do with putting them there.

34

The ball was an unqualified success. Yes, I'd had to put up with the annoyance of seeing Marianne dancing with other men, and of fending off Miss Drury's flirtations. But these were trifling when compared to the privilege of giving pleasure to my friends and neighbors... and perhaps advancing my own cause as well? That remained to be seen.

The next few days, which included Christmas day itself, passed more quietly. Edward had by this time become more comfortable in the pulpit, developing a diffident style of preaching that seemed to allow him to exhort his parishioners as necessary without giving offense. Of course, Christmas required nothing more than a traditional message of joy and wonder at the miraculous birth of the celestial child.

The party from Barton meant to be off two days later, and so I knew it was time to take Marianne aside for a serious conversation, as I had determined to do.

With other people always about, though, it was difficult to find an opportunity to be alone with her without attracting attention or raising speculation. And that would never do. I wanted no discomfort or officious questions for Marianne to bear afterwards.

At last I saw my chance. Most of the others were at cards, and Marianne herself was just coming out of the music room. "Miss Dashwood," I said, "would you come with me for a moment? I believe you have never seen the conservatory, and I would dearly like to show it to you before you go away again. Even at this time of year, there is much beauty to be seen."

"Very well, Colonel," she said. "But should we not invite the rest?"

"Perhaps a different time. They are all settled to other things, as you see."

She glanced into the drawing room to confirm my words, then smiled and walked on with me.

The stated purpose for our errand was not a complete falsehood; I did wish Marianne to see the conservatory's beauty. There were a few roses blooming and some fine orchids as well. I thought she might also be interested in the ambitious fig tree, which needed constant pruning to keep it from breaking through the glass ceiling above. Every year it bore a generous crop of fruit as sweet as honey. Then there were several varieties of palm populating the corners, and a small pool resting in the midst of it all.

I led Marianne through on the circular pathway, explaining, "My mother was very fond of a garden, inside and out. Do you see these orchids?" I asked when we reached the display. "She tended and propagated them herself. In fact, many of these plants are either survivors from that time or their descendants."

"What a lovely legacy she has left you."

"Yes, other than her portrait in the gallery upstairs, I have little enough to remember her by. That is one reason I like coming here. I feel a connection with her in this place as nowhere else, for I am fond of a garden, too." When we had completed our circuit and reached the pair of wicker chairs (where Eliza had posed for *her* portrait years before), I said, "Won't you please sit down for a few minutes, Miss Dashwood? I have a confession to make to you."

She hesitated but then did as I asked. "What can you possibly mean, Colonel? A confession?"

"Just that," I said, taking the other chair, my heart quaking for what my disclosure might do to our fragile friendship. "I have been false with you about something. And though I meant no harm by it, my conscience will let me keep silent no longer." I paused. "It is about Major Dunston's story," I said gravely.

Her countenance at once evinced her surprise... then concern or even anger. "The story was false! None of it true, then?"

"Oh, no! You misunderstand me," I said in alarm. "It was *all* true, every word of it, except..." I took a deep breath and then hurried on, needing to get the words out before I could change my mind. "The story is true except there is no Major Dunston. The story I told is my own, but I took a notion in the beginning that you would find it more interesting if it were about somebody else instead. It was wrong of me to deceive you, though, and I most sincerely beg your pardon."

There was a long silence, during which I vainly tried to read Marianne's reaction, to determine what my fate might be. Would she hate me now? Would she lose all respect? Perhaps she would never speak to me again.

Finally, after what seemed an age, she laid a hand on my sleeve and said, almost solicitously, "Oh, Colonel!" Then, unaccountably, she began to laugh.

I should have been relieved, I suppose, that she did not seem angry, but I was bewildered instead. "Miss Dashwood, what is the meaning of this?"

"Oh, Colonel," she began again. "Now *you* must forgive *me*! You looked so terribly serious, confessing your sins like a true penitent, and I have laughed in your face. But you see, I thought it was understood between us. I have known all along."

"All along? How can that be?"

"Well, I suppose I did not know for sure from the beginning, only suspected. Whenever somebody says, 'Oh, let me tell you what happened to my friend,' or what their 'friend' did or thought or said, it makes me feel sure they are really speaking of themselves. Plus the thoughts and emotions attributed to Major Dunston seemed so real as to be all your own – felt and remembered more deeply than if they had belonged to another person. If I had still harbored any doubts about the matter, though, your slips of tongue would have convinced me. So immersed in the story were you at times that you said 'I' instead of 'he.'"

Did I? Well, of course I must have done. "Then why did you not say?"

"I think perhaps…" she began tentatively, stopped, and began again in a gentle way. "I think perhaps you are a very private man, Colonel Brandon – private and modest, not comfortable or accustomed to going on and on about yourself. So I could see that it was easier for you to tell the tale as if it belonged to somebody else. I was enjoying the story, and I thought if I questioned you about your little deception, you might have become too embarrassed to finish. It was better to let you go on as you had been."

"So I am embarrassed *now* instead."

"You needn't be," she said, moving her delicate hand to rest atop my own much larger one. "It was a worthy story about a worthy hero... one whom I am proud to know and call my friend."

I looked down at her hand on mine, wanting so badly to cover it with my other, drop to my knee, and tell her the rest, to confess all that was in my heart. But did I dare? No, I must not, I reminded myself. I must not risk undoing the progress I had so painstakingly made over the past weeks and months. I must stay the course, adhere to my original plan, which had served me well thus far. So I remained where I was. I stilled my nerves. Then I chose my words carefully.

"Miss Dashwood, Marianne," I said softly, raising my eyes to hers. "There is something else I would speak to you about..." She withdrew her hand and opened her mouth to protest. "No, wait," I said quickly. "Have no fear; it is not what you think... not precisely at least. As discerning as you obviously are, it would be vain to deny what you doubtless know already. You understand my wishes, but I will not discomfit you by asking you something that must be unwelcome. At best, it is too soon for that question. At worst... Well, never mind. I only wished to make my intentions clear. I assure you they are honorable and steadfast, but I expect nothing from you in return. I will not even mention it again, I promise. It will be entirely up to you whether or not we ever speak on this subject again. You may open it, if and when you wish, but I never will. Do you understand me?"

After a pause, she drew breath and spoke in a low tone, almost shyly. "Yes, I believe so. You do me great honor, Colonel. Thank you, for your compliments and for your... kindness."

I allowed myself a moment to absorb her words, and then I stood abruptly. Shaking off the remains of my amorous thoughts, I held out my hand to Marianne. "Come, Miss Dashwood. It is time we rejoined the others before we are missed. I would not have you exposed to any importunate questions."

She rose with the help of my hand, then self-consciously dropped it again.

Seeing this, I said as we walked, "I have made you uncomfortable, I think."

"Perhaps. Yes, a little."

"Please forgive me, and do not trouble yourself about what I have said. It does not signify. We shall go on just as we were before – as friends. I hope I may always count you my friend, Miss Marianne."

"Of course, Colonel."

Despite these mutual assurances, Marianne took obvious care to avoid me for the rest of the day. Her mother did not, however. Mrs. Dashwood cornered me scarcely an hour after her daughter and I returned from the conservatory.

"Well?" she asked in an expectant whisper.

My time away with Marianne had clearly not escaped *her* notice. "I have nothing to tell you, Mrs. Dashwood," I said in equally hushed tones.

"But you were gone together for half of an hour, and Marianne looked so flushed when she returned. I thought perhaps…"

"I showed her the conservatory. Perhaps it was overly warm there."

"Surely not!"

"Mrs. Dashwood, do calm yourself, and I will tell you this much. Marianne can no longer remain in any doubt as to my wishes. That is enough for now. I shall bring no pressure to bear, and I would sincerely beg that you will not either. If made uncomfortable, I believe she may very well refuse to ever see me again. That will not answer your hopes or mine."

"Heavens, no!"

"Then you must trust your daughter to know her own mind and choose what is best for herself in her own time. Can you do that?"

"You ask a hard thing of me, Colonel, for how can I be inactive where the welfare of one of my children is concerned? I can only promise I will try."

"Good, and in the meantime, dear lady, I hope I shall still be welcome to visit Barton now and again, as you are to continue your visits to Delaford as often as you wish."

By the next day, as all my company prepared to depart, Marianne was at least able to look me in the face again. That was encouraging. To make her easy and further convince her that I had meant what I said – promising never to mention the topic of our conservatory conversation again – I made my goodbyes to her without any significant word or meaningful look. I did not even succumb to the temptation to tenderly press her hand or hold it overlong when I helped her into the carriage.

Still, we were both thinking of what had passed between us. How could it be otherwise? And Marianne looked pensively back at me as the carriage drew away.

~35~

After the Christmas party, intercourse between Delaford and Barton Cottage continued at regular intervals, by the post and by travelling one way or the other. I travelled to Barton in early February, but, given the choice, Mrs. Dashwood really preferred to come to Delaford, where she could not only hope to promote her middle daughter's future felicity but also observe her eldest's marital happiness already in progress.

Each time they came, Marianne seemed more and more comfortable with me and with her surroundings. She began choosing my company over the company of others, and we spoke on any number of subjects, sometimes late into the night after the others had retired. Our conversations became as warm and unguarded as those I had been used to sharing with her sister, and then even more so.

Marianne wandered freely throughout the house and grounds, as if they were her own. She daily took her acknowledged place at the Broadwood grand without feeling the slightest need to ask my permission. But when I overheard her instructing Mrs. Albright on the proper way to rotate and store linens, I earnestly rejoiced, for surely only a woman who had begun to imagine herself mistress of the house would undertake to do such a thing.

Then, when Mrs. Dashwood and her daughters were again at Delaford in June, Marianne came early one morning to find me in my study, which she had never done before. I looked up at the sound of the door, my pen suspended above my ledger. Seeing her standing there, I was about to ask if anything were the matter, when the calm, clear look of her countenance convinced me there was no need. "Miss Dashwood." I simply said, laying aside my work and rising.

"I hope I am not disturbing you, Colonel Brandon," she said, still lingering in the doorway.

I could not help wondering what her presence might mean, but I was more than glad for it. "Of course not. Do come in."

She shut the door behind her and walked towards me. That she would choose to be alone with me, especially behind a closed door, was certainly singular. Feeling my hopes surge, and with my heart pounding in my chest, I met her halfway. "Is there something I can do for you?" I asked, reaching out with open palms.

Slowly and deliberately, she placed her small, warm hands in both of mine. My fingers closed automatically about them, and nothing had ever felt so right.

"I believe so," she answered, taking a step nearer and looking up at me through her thick lashes. "That is, I do hope so."

"You only have to name it and the thing is done," I said. "You must know that."

Every word – hers and mine – seemed to take on incredible weight, charged with the looming significance of the moment. We both felt it.

She smiled shyly, dropping her eyes. "Yes, thank you, Colonel. I do know it. And now, if I may, I shall tell you what I have on my mind. You will remember a certain private conversation we had together six months ago… at Christmas… in the conservatory." At this last, she looked up to meet my gaze again.

I nodded and held my breath.

"You said then that there was a certain question you wanted to ask me whenever I was ready to hear it." She paused and swallowed. "I wish very much that you would ask it now."

My heart swelled with equal measures of joy and disbelief. After the many long months I had loved and hoped and prayed and waited, was I now truly to be rewarded with this angel for my wife? I could not trust that it was real. "Can it be true?" I asked in wonder, still holding her hands.

She gave a delightful little laugh. "It can and it is!"

"But… But are you are certain? Quite certain this is what *you* want, I mean. You must not do it for me or for anybody else."

"Thanks to your patience, Colonel, I have had ample time to give the question very careful thought. I have had ample time to consider the difference between my former, naïve ideas of love and happiness, and the more mature and accurate view of them I now possess. I find that my opinions are quite transformed. How differently I feel about everything now! – about what I want, about what will make me happy."

She freed her left hand to lay it against my cheek. I could not help but press into it, savoring the exquisite sensation of her touch.

Steadily meeting my gaze, she said, "A life with *you* is what I want, Colonel, because I am thoroughly convinced *that* is what will make me happy. The fact that it will be giving pleasure to you and to all my dear family and friends is simply a tremendous bonus."

It still seemed impossible. Too good to be believed, but when I looked into the depths of her smiling eyes, I read there that it was so.

My last scruple now done away, I fell swiftly to one knee to ask the important question she had more or less answered already. "Dearest Marianne, will you do me the great honor of becoming my wife? Will you, indeed?"

"Indeed, I will!" she said.

Then Marianne was pulling me to my feet once again, and the next moment we were in each other's arms. I kissed her – gently at first, so that my pent-up ardor would not frighten her. I was then surprised by an answering hunger on her side. Her arms came round my neck and she rose on her toes to press her responsive lips to mine again… and yet again.

I remembered Elinor once saying that her sister could not love by halves. Perhaps this is what she meant. Now that Marianne had committed to me, she would hold nothing back, giving herself freely. That she should at last come into my arms willingly was enough of a miracle; that she should come so enthusiastically was more than I had dared to hope.

Still embracing her tightly with my cheek pressed to hers, my joy overflowed. "My own darling Marianne," I whispered in her ear. "How I have loved you. How I have longed for you! Now, how happy you have made me."

"Have I also shocked you, Colonel?" she asked after another rather passionate kiss.

243

I leant back only enough to look her in the face again. "Do you think you could accustom yourself to calling me Christopher? And as to your question, it is more that you have *very* pleasantly surprised me."

"I have been very pleasantly surprised as well, *Christopher*. Indeed there is nothing I expected less than that I should be overtaken by what I long believed and emphatically declared an impossibility! But my former prejudice against second attachments is completely done away, thanks to you, my wonderful, steadfast, darling friend. My hero. Oh, how glad I am to have been proved wrong!"

So it was that in September, almost exactly two years after we met that day at Barton Park, we were married at Delaford church in front of our friends and family. Edward himself performed the ceremony, Margaret was bridesmaid, and Sir John stood up beside me. Marianne and I heard the counsel on marriage from the *Book of Common Prayer*, and we exchanged the vows furnished therein. Then at last we were declared man and wife and invited to share a kiss, sealing those vows before God and a company of witnesses.

"What God hath joined together," Edward read in conclusion, "let no man put asunder."

And so the blessed bond between Marianne and myself was irrevocably made. I cannot adequately express my feeling of sheer bliss as we strode back down the aisle, our two souls become one. I could not stop smiling.

At the wedding breakfast at Delaford afterwards, Mrs. Jennings exclaimed, "Well, Colonel, I am heartily sorry now for ever having doubted you! You have won your bride and done it in your own way. I can only say that you might have had her six months sooner if you had allowed me to help, but I suppose that is neither here nor there."

That glorious day was nearly a year ago now.

Oh, what I owe John Middleton for inviting the Dashwood ladies to live at the cottage! My life is transformed. I am no longer a hollow shell of a man, still grieving the loss of his first love. I am no longer living under the weight of my family's dishonor and my own failures. I am reborn a man who is a hero in the eyes of the woman he loves. I am a husband and, God willing, soon to be a father as well. I am richly, richly blessed.

I can now see hope for the future, and I imagine growing old with my wife and children about me. Perhaps Beth's son may grow up among us as well. Marianne knows the whole story, and we have already had Beth and little Henry here for a fortnight's visit. It went so agreeably that we both concur; when we have completed our honeymoon year, we mean to ask them to stay at Delaford again, this time permanently if they like. Now that I finally have a proper home to offer, it is the least I can do for them and for the memory of Beth's dear mother – to restore a little of what was taken from Eliza.

One other effort I have made on Eliza's behalf: I have at last returned her portrait to this house. My sister Evelyn finally confessed to me that she has had it all these years, in safekeeping at Whitwell. It seems she happened to come on a visit to Delaford at an opportune time. While she was staying, Maximus went into a storm of rage over Eliza's leaving, vowing he would rid the place of every trace of his unfaithful wife, and nearly making good on that promise. To save it from the burn pile, Evelyn secretly spirited the portrait away. It hangs in the family gallery once more, as is only right.

Now that I have seen the picture again, I wonder that I ever fancied such a strong resemblance between Eliza and Marianne. I am inclined to think it only struck me so at first because it was what I somehow wanted to see. Or perhaps because I did not yet properly know Marianne. Now that I do, I look at her very differently. Now it is impossible for me to see only the mere superficial – the color of hair and eye, the shape of her nose, the line of her jaw. Now when I look at my wife, I see the whole person – the woman I love with my entire heart and soul, all her depths and shades, all the splendidly unique traits that set her apart from every other woman on earth.

Moreover, with Marianne's help, I have at last laid my ghosts to rest. Eliza's sad fate no longer haunts me, for she is in heaven where nothing can harm her again. As the sweet friend of my youth, her memory will always be with me, but her presence has receded into the past, where it belongs. Rashmi has also been consigned to a place in distant history. Marianne has convinced me that there was nothing more I could have done for her. I have taken to thinking, as she does, that Rashmi did reach safety and a new life. Imagining the best for her gives me far more peace than thinking the worst.

Marianne had but one ghost to banish herself, which she was well on her way to doing long before our marriage. "I could wish Mr. Willoughby was a more principled man – for Beth's sake not my own." This she told me during one of the candid conversations of our long courtship. "Other than that, I desire no change. My mind is at peace knowing that his regard for me was sincere; I had not imagined it or been tricked by him into thinking it so. But otherwise he was very false – a man playing a part. In fact, the Willoughby I thought I was in love with never truly existed."

That was the last time his name was mentioned between us.

And so now there is only Marianne and myself, with no one to come between... except the child growing in her belly, who will further unite, not divide, us.

Ours was a gentle courtship – no urgency or eruptions of violent passion – but no less beautiful for it. The passion was not absent, only primed and ready to spring to life at the proper time.

The most exquisite garden does not bloom suddenly, with a loud clash of cymbals and an explosion of light. No, it happens in a gradual unfurling. The tender kiss of the sun for warmth, a light caressing breeze, a thirst-quenching shower, and the mystic influence of time: these things have their way with the garden until one day you notice that, without fanfare, the flowers have quietly opened to reveal their full glory.

It is an eternal mystery, a sublime miracle. And the same must be said of love, for otherwise who could explain how a young, vibrant beauty, such as Marianne Dashwood, came to feel any particular regard for a staid, timeworn fellow like me?

I do not deceive myself into thinking Marianne loves me as deeply as I do her – not yet, in any case – but she has confidence that the seed embedded in good soil will grow. She believes in what it will become. After all, the gardener plants, not based on what he can see today but on what he can envision for the months to come, when what he has planted reaches its promised potential. It is an act of faith.

God has numbered my days, and He has blessed me beyond measure. Therefore, I have faith in the future as well.

I am seated at the small writing desk in my bedchamber as I set down these final thoughts on paper. In the next room, I can hear the little, now-familiar noises of Marianne's nighttime ritual – muffled voices as her maid assists her to undress and take down her hair, the creak of a wardrobe being opened and closed, the click of the outer door as the maid leaves, her work completed. Then all is silent.

Marianne and I said our formal good-nights before we parted company in the passageway. Nevertheless, I wait expectantly, my pen still poised in my hand. Then I hear what I knew I would – another door, this the distinctive sound of the one which connects our two suites, and then quiet footsteps approaching. As if completely unaware, I do not move. I just wait, anticipating the touch that I know will come – *her* touch, which never fails to enliven all my senses. I trust it never will.

My skin excites when, from behind, her hands slip over my shoulders and down, crossing over my chest and pulling her body tightly against mine. Her softness envelops me, and I feel her warm breath and tempting kisses on the side of my neck. Then she whispers in my ear, "Time to put down your pen, husband, and come to bed."

The End

About the Author

S hannon Winslow specializes in writing for the fans of Jane Austen. Her best-selling debut novel, *The Darcys of Pemberley* (2011), immediately established her place in the genre, being particularly praised for the author's authentic Austenesque style and faithfulness to the original characters. Since that auspicious beginning, Winslow has steadily added to her body of work – several more novels and one nonfiction piece – to make a total of twelve books published so far:

- *The Darcys of Pemberley*
- *Return to Longbourn*
- *Miss Georgiana Darcy of Pemberley*
- *The Ladies of Rosings Park*
- *Fitzwilliam Darcy in His Own Words*
- *Colonel Brandon in His Own Words*
- *For Myself Alone*
- *The Persuasion of Miss Jane Austen*
- *Murder at Northanger Abbey*
- *Leap of Faith: Second Chance at the Dream*
- *Leap of Hope: Chance at an Austen Kind of Life*
- *Prayer & Praise: a Jane Austen Devotional*

Her two sons grown, Ms. Winslow lives with her husband in the log home they built in the countryside south of Seattle, where she writes and paints in her studio facing Mt. Rainier.

Learn more about the author and her work at her website/blog: www.shannonwinslow.com.

Bonus Preview Excerpt

Thank you for reading *Colonel Brandon in His Own Words*! Now consider continuing in the same vein with Jane Austen's most iconic hero. Ms. Winslow has also given *Fitzwilliam Darcy* the chance to tell his complete story *in his own words*. Below, you'll find the description and the complimentary Prologue for your perusal. Happy reading!

Fitzwilliam Darcy in His Own Words

What was Mr. Darcy's life like before he met Elizabeth Bennet? – before he stepped onto the *Pride and Prejudice* stage at the Meryton assembly? More importantly, where is he and what is he doing all the time he's absent from the page thereafter? And what is his relationship to a woman named Amelia?

With ***Fitzwilliam Darcy, in His Own Words***, the iconic literary hero finally tells his own story, from the traumas of his early life to the consummation of his love for Elizabeth and everything in between.

This is not a variation but a supplement to the original story, chronicled in Darcy's point of view – a behind-the-scenes look at the things Jane Austen didn't tell us. As it happens, Darcy's journey was more tortuous than she let on, his happy ending with Elizabeth in jeopardy at every turn in his struggle between duty and his heart's desire, between the suitable lady he has promised to marry and the woman he can't stop thinking about.

Fitzwilliam Darcy in His Own Words

Prologue

I still occasionally suffer that recurrent dream – a nightmare, really. I awake at Darcy House in London. Morning light is filtering through the diaphanous draperies at the windows, painting ghostly shadow patterns across the opposite wall. I feel a great sense of wellbeing at the start of a new day. All is right with the world, or at least my portion of it.

Then I turn toward the other side of the bed and see... not Elizabeth, as I expect, but the Honorable Miss Amelia Lambright. Only of course she is no longer an honorable miss, not when she has spent the night in a man's bed. Then I suddenly remember why she is there. Her name is Miss Lambright no more; she is Mrs. Darcy now. My heart lurches and I break into a cold sweat, not because the former Miss Lambright is so horridly unappealing, but because she is not Elizabeth.

I tell myself it surely must be a hallucination or some trick of the light. So I shake my head to clear any cobwebs, rub my eyes, and blink. Still, the wrong woman is before me. *Please, God, let it be a dream!*

I fight to awaken, to claw my way back to the world where I belong, the world where Mrs. Darcy has not blonde but dark, satiny hair and sparkling eyes. My throat constricts; I cannot breathe. I cannot find my voice to call out. *Elizabeth, where are you?* I must find her! My life depends on it.

When on these disturbing occasions I at last come to myself, it is many minutes before my heart and breathing return to normal, and longer still until my mind can quiet itself. Even after I have verified that Elizabeth is indeed beside me where she belongs; beheld her face, a peaceful portrait of repose in whatever meager light offers; pulled her warm, familiar form to fit close against mine;

and heard her sleepy but unmistakable voice murmuring my name with affection...

Even then my soul quakes within me for how close the vision from which I have just awakened came to being true, how close I came to missing Elizabeth altogether. Then she and I would have been only two ships sailing the same stretch of sea, perhaps even passing within sight of each other occasionally but never happening to come into a common port together, at least not until it had been too late.

My happier outcome depended on the slimmest thread of unlikely circumstances being precariously strung together without error. At any one of a dozen junctures, the course of my life could have carried me in a completely different direction.

When I consider this, I shudder. Then I thank God for His providential care in guiding me safely through. I thank Bingley for Netherfield. And Wickham. Strangely enough, now, years later, I can think back with some philosophy, enough to acknowledge the part he unwittingly played. Were it not for Wickham and his nefarious but timely interventions, I would likely be married to Amelia Lambright today.

Fitzwilliam Darcy in His Own Words is available in
paperback, e-book, and audio formats.

Printed in Great Britain
by Amazon

83502625R00150